REALM OF ASH

Thea Atkinson

CHAPTER 1

The place was lousy with the undead.

The Rot Gut wasn't just a bar. It was a trap for the unsuspecting humans who foolishly wandered inside and ordered its signature drink laced with crystallized absinthe. Those who found themselves in the seediest corner of Soul's Harbor and stumbled upon the tavern felt the energy leaking out from beneath the door the same way a woman sensed something off about a man who means to do her harm.

The smart ones listened to that instinct and turned away at the first sight of its shadowed facade. The others—those who ignored the warning and stumbled in, chasing a final nightcap—didn't come back out.

So yeah, I knew what waited behind that thick wooden door and beneath the seizing neon sign, the sights I'd see within shadowed booths built of scorched oak and tables framed by sturdy teak. Vampires, mostly. The odd revenant.

The stink of hunters' sweat and old blood would hang in the air like a noose.

But I wasn't some oblivious human ignoring every nuanced warning. I knew one more thing about the tavern. If hunters left the place unmolested, they'd leave unmolested.

The owner was an abstinent vampire who'd built a kind of Switzerland for monsters and hunters alike of his bar. And while my female intuition crackled behind my ears as I pulled my motorcycle up to the curb, it wasn't half as loud as my hunter instinct.

Something was off. More off than usual. And Gideon was in there. I needed to get him out...alive.

I revved my motorcycle engine one last time, letting it purr before shutting it off. The smothering silence that fell over the night air felt wrong, like the magic Fayed cast was thick around the perimeter. It took a moment to adjust, to catch the faint thrum of music—a lacquer of normalcy laid over something wicked.

I gave the neon sign a short glance as it phased in and out in ways that mimicked a racing heartbeat, then trained my gaze on the alley splitting the tavern from its run-down vacant partner. A flash of red cut the darkness there, caught by the light of a passing set of headlights the way a predator's eyes reflected light.

Male. Powerful. Not vampire. Something *else*.

I kept my eyes on that spot as I dismounted, pulling my jacket tight. Whatever he was, he didn't move into the light of the sidewalk, which meant he either knew I was a hunter or was waiting to ambush me, thinking me a naive human woman looking for a last drink.

I wasn't taking chances. I slid a short ironwood stake from my saddlebag and tucked it into my boot. There were several species of vampires, and while I knew none but the most sentient of them would frequent the Rot Gut Tavern, I wasn't taking chances on Fayed's commitment to etiquette. Without being obvious, I skimmed the darkness again. The stranger had edged further out from the shadows, his silhouette sharp against the flickering light of the neon sign.

The gaze he traced over my frame was a predator's tongue testing the size and shape of me. The faint aroma of smoke tangled with that of cinnamon before dissipating, leaving my palate tingling.

I brushed off the unnerving sensation that prickled the hairs on the back of my neck and gave him a bold nod to let him know I'd seen him and wasn't afraid, The stake in my boot tapped rhythmically against my calf as I headed for the entrance. Even though it offered a sense of protection, that gaze stayed on me, and by the time I was close enough to the door to hear the quiet hum of the sign, I knew he was going to speak to me.

"Can't sneak up on monsters making that sort of noise," he drawled in a voice smooth and warm enough to be a pat of melted butter. "But I must admit, I do like a woman who knows how to make her ride purr. You trying to tempt the monsters of the world, Ponytail?"

He pushed off the wall, peeling away from the shadows in a movement so fluid and deliberate, I felt like I was watching a panther uncurling from a tree branch at the sight of prey. My peripheral vision was filled with him. Alarm bells started clanging away in my mind.

I dropped him a bland glance to show how I felt about that comment. "Dude," I said. "The only temptation you need to worry about right now is my urge to cut your throat."

A dark chuckle thrummed in the air. "Careful, Ponytail. Talk like that won't scare off monsters like me. For us, that's just foreplay."

I shivered at the huskiness of his voice despite myself. This was a creature used to having control. An ancient thing, I knew. But even though pre-fight adrenaline flooded my veins, begging me to engage, I ignored his comment. Because, tempting as it would be to take test myself against a monster as powerful as this one no doubt was, I had to remember: I was there for Gideon.

My ex-lover was the sole reason I stood in front of the door in the first place, and only then because a certain protégée had come ringing around my apartment with a frantic request for me to check in on him. She was worried, she said. Gideon wasn't himself. He'd closed off, walling himself outside her reach. I wanted to tell her the emotionally available Gideon she knew was a mask anyway and she best get used to it, except the genuine fear in her voice roused me from my sluggish night of binge television.

Well, that and if Gideon was balls deep in trouble, it might be interesting to see how far up that trouble could go.

I'd check on him, I told her, suspecting that if he wasn't in his bunker of a garage, and hadn't taken her out on the hunt, then the only other place he could be was tossing a few back in a place she didn't know about. She quickly decided, in light of the look that no doubt was rampaging over my face, that going home instead of accompanying me would be in her best interest.

I watched her sprint down the steps without looking back from my window as I pulled on a sports bra and tank top to replace the oversized t-shirt I'd been lounging in. By the time she'd slid behind the wheel of her lemon yellow Mini Coop and was driving off, I had my riding jacket on and was heading for my motorcycle.

I rarely visited the tavern. I didn't agree with the no-touch, no-attack rule, but Gideon loved the place. He said it was a perfect spot to gather intel on our targets.

He lied about that, and we both knew it. In truth, he spent time there because it was the only place in the city he hadn't already been bounced and banned from. Had a habit of brawling, did Gideon. Not always with the monsters of the world the way a good hunter should.

So I wasn't surprised to find him hip-hugging the bar from a tattered stool, a shot of mezcal in one hand and three empty shot glasses sitting in pools of water in front of him. My heart squeezed looking at his hunched shoulders. A pang of hurt knifed my heart, not unlike the one I'd felt when I'd opened my door to see his new girlfriend on my porch step, except this one whispered of something more than jealousy. I realized in that instant she'd been right to be worried.

Fayed, gave me a long look as I entered the tavern. As a man, he was gorgeous. As a vampire, devastating. All mocha skin with silken black hair and flashing emerald eyes that changed somehow as he took me in with a pointed gaze.

Don't make trouble, his look said before he inclined his head toward Gideon and the rather large looking fellow sitting beside him. A bloke who cast an eye toward me the moment I opened the door, as though he'd sensed me long before the latch disengaged to swing open.

The way the hairs on the back of my neck tingled as that ocean-hued gaze landed on me was all I needed to tell me the man sitting next to Gideon, talking to him in hushed voices, was *other*.

He was too perfect, the way other-kin tended to be, as though when they put on a human mask, they picked out the most perfect one they could find, hoping to blend in as human without realizing that even the most beautiful of our species tended to have some sort of wabi sabi to their features that made them that way.

I didn't think he was vampire, although I could just make out small indentations in each side of his lips that might indicate lengthy canine teeth. What he was, exactly, I still wasn't sure, but when his eyes went to half-mast as they fell on me, I figured he was working out whether I was friend or foe the same as I was doing for him.

For the second time in one night, a shiver ran up my spine at an *other's* gaze. Not completely unpleasant. Rather, the anticipation of perfectly chilled ice cream on a heated afternoon.

No. That wasn't an apt metaphor at all, I decided as I watched the two of them huddle together at the bar. His gaze, greener than Fayed's, was full of heat. I wrestled for a moment over a better analogy and couldn't come up with anything less cliché than settling into a chair beside a cozy fire after getting dunked in a freezing river. I had to make a mental effort not to rub my arms in anticipation of warmth.

Because that sort of thought would get me nowhere but one more bad decision, and I'd had made enough of those in my days to feel reasonably gun-shy, I dragged my gaze from his and nodded my agreement to Fayed. A quick nod acknowledged the silent pact between us that I wouldn't 'cause trouble, and he lifted his chin toward the shadows of the bar. Nothing much, just a subtle gesture that might have been no more than his natural movement.

Within seconds, figures from all over the darkness, huddled around tables and lurking in corners, stood and moved stealthily toward the nearest exit. Within moments, there was only one vampire in the room, two hunters, and that someone next to Gideon—that some*thing*—else.

It seemed Fayed wasn't taking chances that I wouldn't wreak havoc in his tavern no matter how sincere I tried to look.

I flashed him a half-smile filled with chagrin. I knew full well he'd done the right thing for his patrons. Havoc and chaos did seem to follow me like the tattered corner of a security blanket, and while most hunters kept the place neutral, I wasn't most hunters. How Gideon was able to frequent the bar without Fayed silently warning his patrons to hit the dusty trail, said more about me than it did him. Gideon was badass as they came. Or least he had been in his day.

Apparently, he wasn't worried he could be in danger as he sat, back to the door, because if he heard me approach, he didn't even bother looking over his shoulder. Some small part of me ached over that. The other, more competitive part—the one that had spent hours trying and failing to best him in training sessions—gave myself a mental fist-bump, all the while trying to ignore the fact that I was clomping toward him with the grace of a hippo. The hunter I knew would have noticed the sound of a pin scoring fabric.

As if to prove my mentor was slipping, it was that gorgeous stone-faced man sitting beside my cheating ex, talking to him in low tones out of the corner of his mouth, who turned his eye on me first.

"You have company," he said to Gideon, leaning close enough to make the conversation between the two of them seem conspiratorial and secret. His gaze dropped to my chest then back up to my throat where I knew—just knew—he'd caught sight of the scar roping my neck and was wondering if I had a penchant for the darker side of sex.

Everything about the way he grazed the raised skin with his eyes made me feel naked. And angry on top of it. So, I lifted two fingers in the air toward Fayed, grateful to have an opportunity to shift focus and reclaim my composure. The vampire turned with a short nod of understanding to pull a bottle of tequila down from his stores. It was half empty and I wondered if the three shot glasses in front of Gideon were just the latest round.

I shook my head and pointed to an unopened one because the Gideon I'd known forever would not accept a drink from an opened bottle on a vampire's territory. And with him sitting there right next to me, I wasn't about to give him reason to judge me.

I shot him a glance, taking in the small hole in the collar of his t-shirt. "You're taking chances getting drunk in a vampire bar, Gideon."

Gideon swiveled on his stool, making it hiss on the hydraulics. My gaze trailed to his rugged, battle-worn face, so familiar I would know every line of it in the dark. His eyes weren't bloodshot, but they were circled with blue-black smudges. The gray slouch hat he wore hung down further than it should and touched the back of his earlobes. A generous sprinkling of salt seasoned the equally generous pepper-colored stubble that grew in uneven patches along his jawline. Cleary he hadn't shaved in days. My heart squeezed like someone had wrapped a winch around it.

My nostrils flared as I slid onto the stool on his other side, out of reach and touch of the other sitting to his right. The bar stank of something more than booze and sweat. A hint of copper clung to the air and made my nose twitch. Dozens of signs wall-papered every spare inch of free space: *See the green fairy. Order Rot Gut.* I knew the come-on wasn't mere propaganda. The fairy was real, a mix of absinthe and magic and something that would leave unwary humans hallucinating and vulnerable.

It should have made me upset to see the outright manipulation, but I was too bothered by Gideon's unwashed smell to feel anything but concern for the man hunched over his drink.

"What are you doing here, Ava?" he demanded in a tone that would have startled anyone else. Except I was used to the bark in his voice. It was one of the things that made my knees weak back when I'd been a devoted, foolish teenager. I hadn't been that girl for almost ten years. And the weakness in the knees had turned to cement over the last six months.

"Maybe I should be asking you the same thing," I countered. "Wanna tell me what you're doing?"

He waved me off with a hand clutching a shot glass in pinched fingers. "None of your business anymore, is it?" Dropping his head back, he bolted down the shot. He didn't so much as grimace, which meant he'd no doubt shot back plenty already.

But his tone, that was something else. The bitterness in it was enough to make my eyebrows climb half an inch. I reminded myself—again—what I was there for, and it wasn't to grace any comment bitter or not, with gentle reminders of all the reasons we'd broken up.

"I'm here under duress, believe me," I said, feeling unexpectantly stung at his bitter response.

His harsh crack of laughter was enough to set my teeth on edge. "Coal-hearted Ava," he said. "Not a hint of softness or romance in that soul of yours."

It wasn't the words so much, but the hateful tone that made my stomach feel like a trampoline for a very large anvil. And damn him for acting as though I didn't care. I was here, wasn't I? It was so hard not to take the bait. After all this time, after all we'd been to each other.

"You never complained about my black heart whenever I saved your ass from a rabid vamp," I countered as I ran my palm over the bar, testing for evidence of multiple shot glasses wetting its surface. Gideon wasn't the sort to drown his sorrows in booze. That was more my style than his.

"Did you know your precious Shea came to see me?"

At that, his head snapped around to face me full on. His gray eyes narrowed.

"Why would she do that?" A flicker over my face, my throat. Testing me for truth with a carefully guarded expression. I pretended not to notice, feeling through the puddles of melted ice to the stickiness beneath. So. Definitely more than three shots. He was not in a good head space.

"Beats the hell out of me," I said with a shrug that I hoped he'd see as a truce as I injected as much tease into the words as I could. "Lord knows, I'd let your ass soak in enough booze to pickle it if I were your lover."

"Well, you're not anymore, are you?" he snapped back, and that somehow managed to take my breath away, finally.

My eyes darted toward Fayed as he placed the bottle of unopened tequila in front of me and held my gaze with a silent intensity. He didn't have to say anything to suggest he knew as well as I did that Gideon was fibbing. If my mentor's heartbeat was dancing a tango in three inch stilettos, a vampire would know it. The flare of the blood-drainer's nostrils gave away the truth.

"A shot glass too," I said to him before pulling my hand over my ponytail and smoothing it over my shoulder to draw out the moment. I needed to stay focused because this was already going five ways sideways and I had a hair's trigger on my temper as it was.

I did not want to be doing this. This was Shea's business now. Not mine. The man had cheated on me, for Pete's sake. Going fair and voluptuous from my dark and lean when he'd replaced me with the chesty blonde who, but for her golden mane, reminded me of Lara Croft with her tight pants and white tank tops. A chick who smiled with all of her teeth showing far too frequently to be authentic.

She was even wearing a white tank beneath her chic jacket when I'd opened my door to see her standing on my step, breaking all the boundaries between 'ex' and 'other woman'. Just seeing her made me want to puke. And that made me want to throat-punch her because feeling that sensation made me want to curl into a ball because I hated the thought that the both of them could hurt me so badly without raising a finger.

All that pain and exhaustion leaked through my voice when I faced him and held his gaze. "Go home, Gideon," I said in a voice as tired as I felt.

Gideon hunched down lower on the bar. "You go home, Ava." He shoved the bottle along the bar, pushing it hard enough that it moved almost a foot. "I've got things to do here." He slammed the bar top with his palm. "And you're getting in the way."

I hooted, injecting a false note of bravado into the noise. "You think I want to be here?"

When he looked at me, his eyes glinted with what I decided was icy mania. "Then why *are* you here? You made it clear you wanted nothing to do with me."

I barely smothered the gasp as my jaw ticked to the side. "Shea sashayed up to my door tonight right in the middle of my *Outlander* binge," I told him. "Said she's worried about you. Now what do you suppose would have her risking her ass on a visit to my apartment, begging me to come looking for you when I could be drooling over Jamie Fraser?"

"Shea wouldn't do that. She knows better than to interfere."

I brought to mind Shea's full lips and imagined them pouting and saying, yes, yes, Gideon. Of course, Gideon, right away, Gideon. Then I laid it over an image of myself. The lips didn't match one bit. And not just because my mouth was smaller, with a pronounced cupid's bow and larger top lip. I wasn't sure how long it had been since I'd agreed with my mentor without arguing. Maybe that was what he liked about Shea. That gushing sense of adoration and compliance.

"Right," I said, barely able to keep the bitterness of my own voice in check. "Obedient little Shea would never go against a direct order."

Before Gideon could argue once more that things weren't like that, before he could repeat the hateful words that I was to blame, that he'd had to train someone who wouldn't get him killed, I poured another shot. Because I was losing control here. This was Gideon. My lover. My mentor. The reason I wasn't dead in an alley somewhere already. And he was hurting. Something was wrong. Something perhaps big enough to make him do something drastic. And I would do what I could to help him despite his being a prick right then.

I would not retaliate just to feel better over the whole awful ordeal.

So, I swallowed down those pain-filled emotions along with the tequila. A battle, no matter how big or small could turn on a sigh. I wasn't about to concede this battle. Not when he needed me. And I couldn't let him goad me into doing something foolish like leaving him there in a state that might get him killed.

I leaned back to get a better look at the bloke over his shoulder. He was powerfully built, I realized. Not just big and broad, but muscled. Like a big beautiful dog. Strength laid down cord after cord in his neck and shoulders. The hand lying on the bar was massive and calloused. A fighter of some sort. Some small part of me yawned and stretched, waking from a warm sleep to an eagerness to see those muscles in action. And I tossed that rude chick back into the icy cold room she'd stepped out from. I was here because the woman Gideon was screwing was worried enough about his welfare to walk right up to my door. And now, dammit, so was I.

I stared down my ex one more time, desperate to get through to him by using the only thing I knew he would react to.

"Does your buddy here know the kind of danger he's in just by sitting here with you? Or is he the danger?"

It was a phishing expedition, a clumsy attempt to find out what sort of creature the man was, and Gideon should have caught on to it, but he didn't. He just blazed me again with that manic gaze.

"That's not why I'm here, Ava," Gideon growled. "You think I'm here to commit some sort of hari-kari? I'm here on business. Now shove off. You're going to queer the deal."

I had thought that, yes. For Shea to enlist my help in wrangling my ex had to mean the worst. That he'd finally tired of all the killing. The trauma he witnessed in normal, everyday people suffering the horror of being in the wrong place at the right time had finally got to be too much. That he'd decided he'd done enough to halt the spread of evil and violence and wanted out. He was more tender hearted than me. I'd learned to compartmentalize the violence. My moral compass was skewed but I knew the difference between a monster and a victim. I didn't have to question what was right and what was wrong when it came to saving another human's life.

But Gideon...he'd been doing it much longer than me. The line blurred and the killing scored a piece of a hunter's soul if they weren't carefully guarding each pinprick entrance to it. It happened sometimes with the more inveterate hunters. *Out through the back door*, we called it for those who couldn't sit on the sidelines of retirement because they knew too much and couldn't go on killing day in and day out.

But this wasn't that. This wasn't a considered mulling over of suicide. The signals were all around me if I paid attention. The stolid, angry drinking. The strange partner. He'd had news. Bad news that meant he'd enlisted supernatural help.

My gaze dropped to the floor and the duffel bag sitting at his feet. It was half-zippered. A gauzy piece of material hung from between broken teeth like a lolling tongue.

This was a hunt. A dangerous one.

I shouldn't ask. It was none of my business, but I couldn't help myself.

"What deal?" I asked, spinning on the stool to face sideways. All the better to take in all of Mr. Brooding Silence beside my surly mentor.

Gideon sighed, even as the guy fiddled too intently with the coaster in front of him. "A Witch. Nasty one."

I narrowed my gaze at him. That was entirely too easy. The man on the other side of Gideon clenched his fingers around the shot glass, which I noted was still full. So he was nervous of accepting drinks from a vampire too. Was he a supernatural hunter of some sort? I'd heard of them.

"What about you?" I said, loud enough that he should realize I was talking to him. "What sort of man are you to be idly chatting about removing a nasty witch from the world?"

Everything screamed inside of me that he possessed magic. Lots of it. And I wanted to know what kind.

He swiveled his head in my direction and the first thought that streaked through my mind was that he was *way other*. Head-on those aqua-marine eyes were too bright to be real as they moved from green to turquoise. Not fake enough to be contacts. Just straight up impossibly gorgeous. I felt like I should be wearing a bikini and jumping off a diving board into that gaze.

A sudden, charming uplift of one corner of his lip set my heart racing. "Not a witch, if that's what you're thinking," he said in a pleasant, almost placating voice. "Something else." His left eyebrow twitched toward his lush hairline. "And I think you already know that."

No coyness there. Just shameless ego. I could only nod. The thing moving in my chest reached up and grabbed hold of my voice box.

"What he is shouldn't matter to you, Ava," Gideon said. He swallowed hard, and the cords in his neck moved, the muscle beneath his ear fluttering.

I toed the duffel bag with my boot. "What's this? Part of the deal?"

Gideon glanced down. At sight of the bag, his face lit up. "That's a fucking miracle, is what that is."

"I've never known a miracle to send a man off the deep end of drink."

He swiveled around on the stool to face me, legs splayed open so that the duffel bag was centered between them. "Took it from a goblin. He swears that shirt will glamor any human who wears it. Change their face, their body. Hell, it's even supposed to change your species."

He let go an exhalation that indicated he was most thoroughly impressed.

The man on his other side didn't seem so enthralled. He actually huffed, then flicked his gaze over the back of Gideon's head and pushed off his stool, gathering the still undrunk tequila along with him. I watched his back as he prowled toward an empty table, the way the shoulders moved, the muscles knotted and unknotted in his back.

"Forget it," Gideon said in a tight voice, forcing me to eyeball him. "He's not into mortal women."

I crossed my legs and leaned on the bar toward my mentor. "And which part of that sentence should I consider key?" I asked. "The mortal or the women?"

"Let it go, Ava."

"So you admit he's not human?"

"You know he's not." Gideon ran a hand over his hat, peeling it off and tossing it onto the bar. Fayed glared at him, unnoticed, and I swept the thing onto my lap, clutching it as I held his gaze.

"Well," I said. "What is he?"

"Wouldn't you rather know about Lilah the witch?" he asked, and my jaw ticked sideways. He knew me too well. He might not distract me with drink or sass, but mention a monster to coal-hearted Ava and dangle it like an apple ripe and ready for plucking...Well, I'd bite. I couldn't help myself.

"A witch?" I said suspiciously. "Not a vampire?"

He nodded, holding my gaze.

A soft hiss of pent up breath escaped me. He didn't need to say the witch practiced the dark arts. If he was teasing me with her at all, it had to be a case of the worst dark magic. A thrill ran up my spine. This was what Shea was worried about, and with good reason. Black arts took special skill and dedication...the sort that would put a whole seethe of vampires to shame.

If Gideon was planning to glamor himself and face that alone, Shea had every right to visit me unannounced with the plea to stop him. What my ex planned to do was on the level of an Ava-type move that Gideon always complained about, the kind that he said would get him killed.

"Just how bad is it?"

He scrubbed his head with both hands. "Bad enough to need an army and maybe a nuke or two."

He grabbed the hat from me and shoved it back on his head. It sat at a jaunty angle that only served to make him look more drunk. "She's at least two hundred years old. Uses cursed objects to power her long-life."

The pinched look that crinkled the corners of his eyes indicated there was more. I waited patiently as he cast a look toward his companion, now seated at a table staring into the still-full shot glass, then turned to me. "She's bad, Ava. Some poor kid found a ring beneath a play set at school, and within the hour, he was trying to slash his way through the class with scissors. He wanted to cut his teacher to ribbons. His words. Not mine."

"Jesus."

He nodded, blinking as though he wanted to sober up in a hurry. "Yeah. I've contacted the Hunter Network. Vicki Graves and her partners are coming. They'll be here within the week. A squad will settle down outside her property on the edge of the park and go in when she least expects it."

I jerked my thumb over my shoulder, in the general direction of the stranger's table. "So he's here to help?" I asked, wondering why Gideon hadn't contacted me if they were sending a squad in.

And then I took one look at the glasses he'd left empty on the table. I knew him well enough to recognize shame drinking when I saw it, even if I hadn't noticed it right away. I blinked at him stupidly for several seconds, trying to work through what might have him feeling so guilty he'd try to drink it away.

"Oh my God," I said. "You're planning to send Shea in. To show the Network what she can do, and you didn't want me anywhere near the place while she takes the witch out."

His averted gaze was proof I was right. It hit me like a sucker punch to the stomach. Bad enough he was screwing her, but to infer that she was good enough to gain him entrance into the powerful organization I could never get him into made me want to curl into a hard little ball.

"She follows orders," he said in a quiet voice. "She doesn't argue. She's just as good as you...except she fucking listens."

The last words almost so painfully heated the words could scald a cat. My throat restricted to the point I wasn't sure I could breathe. Everything in the room seemed to shrink closer, pressing against me. That he'd said it finally. Those words were poison in my hear.

"You mean she's better than me," I said through a tight throat. "Not just to sleep with, but in every way."

God. I didn't know what hurt more: that he planned to introduce Shea to the Network or that he'd thought he could erase his betrayal by drowning it in liquor.

He skimmed me with an assessing look that straightened my spine instead of bowing it. I wanted to break something very badly right then, but I forced myself to raise my hand toward Fayed instead. I wanted the vampire's attention. Because I was going to walk away from this bastard once and for all, and I was going to damn well send him off with a goodbye toast.

"Another shot of mezcal for Mr. Miyagi," I said, but Gideon clamped down on my wrist with his hand, easing it down onto the counter between us.

"Forget it, Ava," he said.

I fought his hold, struggling to break free with all I had, but he'd always been stronger than me—at least physically. My hand flattened against the bar, my fingers wading into the pools of condensation.

"I don't need another drink," he said. "I'm finished for tonight, and so are you."

Finished. Because he'd delivered the killing blow at last. He was done with me. Maybe Shea knew it and sent me here.

He shot a look toward the stranger watching us from his table. Those eyes met mine, and he lifted the glass in my direction. A soft sound, maybe a whimper, escaped my lungs. He'd heard. Oh my God, he'd heard my shame.

"It's for your own good, Ava." Gideon's breath came out in a long exhale. "Now. I'm going to take a leak. It's best for both of us if you're gone when I get back."

That was it. The guilt that dogged his posture, his eyes, was gone. He'd dismissed me. I'd come here to make sure he was okay, and all I'd done was allow him to absolve himself of the guilt that brought him here.

I waited till he'd shoved off the stool, till he'd melted into the shadows of the wall that led out into the back alley, until the man at the table finally gave his attention to the shot glass. And then I swooped down and yanked the glamor shirt from Gideon's duffel bag.

I left the unopened bottle of tequila on the bar and fled the front door with the garment dangling from my hands. I didn't care if Gideon came back to find it gone. Didn't care if it ruined his deal. Didn't care if he hated me for it.

Because I'd loved him once. And tonight, he handed my place to someone else. He could keep the guilt. He could keep the girl. But the kill?

That was mine.

Chapter 2

IF THE WITCH NEEDED to die, I would do the killing. Like Gideon said: a woman two centuries old would be practicing the darkest of magics to earn a life that long. And darkest magic always meant blood and death and agony. The greater the pain, the stronger the magic.

I wasn't going to let another kid get caught up in such horrors, and Gideon should have known that. Which meant either he used that little nugget to distract me from whatever he was doing in that bar that had Shea so worried, or he wanted me to have the information. Maybe it was both. One didn't have to independent of the other.

But what was clear was that hunting was all I had left now. My sister wanted nothing to do with me. My parents were gone. Gideon had been the only thing, the only person, I could count on. Now, he'd abandoned me too. Hunting had never done that to me. It had been the one thing that seamed the cracks of my psyche like molten gold seaming the cracks of ancient pottery.

And maybe that was for the best. A hunter's life should be solitary. It was the best way to keep innocent people from becoming collateral damage. Gideon needed to be around for Shea, much as I hated to consider it. But she was young. She needed him more than I did. And as I strode across the bar to the exit, I told myself it was a relief to finally be free to face each battle knowing there was no one to worry for my safety. I wouldn't be leaving someone heartbroken if I went down against a monster.

I sighed as I dropped my hand onto the door's handle. Indeed, it would be a relief to give up the hope that someone else, some other loving human being, could keep the cheese grater rasp of memory from scoring my psyche every time my mind was idle. With no one left to bring those horrors into the light, I could leave them in the dark rooms and closets I'd crammed them into. I didn't have to ever again stand in front of that door alone and fear the wedge that would crack the seal and let that shit back into the light of day.

The brooding stranger was gone when I exited the bar and stepped into the air and exhaust of the city, but his scent lingered. Residual pheromones piqued my memory. Snippets of memory flashed in my mind of grade-school Valentine's Day parties and candy hearts crunching between my teeth with the heat of spice. I hesitated, my gaze drifting to the side of the building where he'd stood. I knew he was gone, but that crackling energy he'd left behind skimmed down my back like fingertips tracing my spine.

I shook it off by dragging in a breath. I had a job to do. Gideon's mention of Heart-Center Park was enough for me to figure out where Lilah practiced her arts. So, I rode to the outer perimeter for twenty minutes, motoring around until

I discovered grounds big enough to match a witch's needs. Large, wooded, stretching at least a block sideways. About as isolated as a person could get in a city this size.

The trees bordering the property were lush and evergreen, with lacy branches dangling long fronds of fragrant needles. Every bough seemed perfectly placed to just offer a hint of habitation but disguise the abode nestled within it. Too perfect, really.

So that was exactly where I pulled up to the curb and hopped off my cycle.

I peered into the dark woods of the cul-de-sac over the cycle's leather seat, peering into the dense brush of spruce and hemlock. The forested area was large, sweeping out sideways and back a long way before they scored out the smallest glimpse of lace-cut illumination from the shadows.

I strode around the back of my bike to crouch at the edge of the tree line, giving the area a full scan. If I panned the area side to side, I could make out several moss-carpeted paths meandering through as they lead to the source of that faint glow of light. With lips pursed thoughtfully, I scanned the distance, measuring out the width and distance each path cut from the shrubbery.

Several of them crisscrossed each other. Rabbit trails or raccoon paths but big enough for me to shoulder my way through. The karambit sheathed to my thigh and the spelled blade I had stashed in my saddlebags might be all I needed.

To hell with the Hunter Network. To hell with Gideon and his gutsy new, voluptuous protégée, who would be the obedient hunter I never was. They never wanted me anyway.

But even if I was a shitty human being, I could offer this world something. I was a hell of a hunter. And no hunter worth her salt would sit around and wait for the cavalry when kids were in danger.

So I rummaged through my saddlebags for the spelled blade. I always kept a bit of cash and a few weapons handy inside, so I was careful to mind the sharp points of ironwood stakes that, along with scorched in runes, could double as vampire stakes and spelled weapons to the right creature.

Vague touches of cold pewter from holy oil and holy water slid past my touch before I found the spelled blade. I pulled it, leg sheath and all, from the bags and strapped it to my left thigh.

After a bit of consideration, I peeled off my jacket then my t-shirt before stuffing it all into the bag. I hoped to hell the garment I'd grabbed from Gideon's duffle worked like he said it would, because if I got caught in there murdering what to all eyes would look like a regular human being, then I could claim to be saving the world till the cows came home and I'd still end up in jail.

A tail of the fabric peeked out like a wayward rag as I shoved my hands back inside the bags. I tugged it free and shook it out above the cycle and it settled into a perfect shape, as though it expected to be unveiled like an heirloom. I gave it another quick snap. A faint waft of cinnamon bloomed from its folds along with a trace of something electric. Like the smell of the air before lightning strikes.

I Chewed the corner of my mouth as I skimmed it with a scrutinous glance. Just how much skin did it need to contact to work? Or did it just need to be pulled on?

I decided it wasn't worth taking the chance. Off went the bra as well. With the cold air licking my skin into goose bumps, I hastened to pull the thing over my arms and smooth it down over my stomach. By the time I was going for the buttons, they'd turned to hooks and eyes. My fingers paused as I blinked stupidly at the garment. Not a button-up shirt at all, I realized, but an itchy lace corset.

Great. Just what a hunter needed when she was planning to creep into a witch's lair and slash her way through to the witch's death. Itchy boobs. The sigh that fled my lungs was one of frustration and indecision.

But after one long, unsatisfying scratch of my ribs and a quick check to make sure my knives would slide easily from their sheaths on my thighs, I picked my way through the woods until the sight of the witch's lair broke through the protective veil of trees.

In the dark, the house had all the appearances of a little old lady's retirement home. I had my doubts that the quaint stucco bungalow I saw nestled in the midst of an herb and flower garden was its true form. A witch worth her crackers would want to repel would-be thieves, intruders, or hunters from poking about, and thus would have glamored it into a cottage that begged for chickens to run amuck about the yard. Innocent. Old-world charm. Nothing to see here.

But no one lived on an elite piece of property like this on the outskirts of the city, where gardens and wooded areas provided distance from one another. Just the size of the lot was a clue to the building's true size.

Expansive and grand, the grounds sprawled across an entire city block, adorned with the charm of vintage street-lamps that exuded an old-world aura. The scent of hollyhock and lavender came to my nose as I crept along the property line. My eyes scanned the surroundings, searching for the perfect patch of darkness, a shadow that would envelop me, granting me the cloak of invisibility.

I had prepared myself for a full-on onslaught against castle-level fortifications, all the while hoping for a small interior. All the better to rampage in, slash the witch's throat, and saunter away while Gideon was still waiting for reinforcements.

Running my hands over my thighs to be sure my blades were still right where I'd put them in their sheaths, I took a long, slow breath. I shot Gideon a mental fuck you, then pulled out my karambit. The weight of the weapon nestled comfortably in my grasp, a testament to the countless hours dedicated to honing my skills. Out of habit, I instinctively tested the sharpness of the blade against the delicate skin of my wrist, verifying its readiness.

Each knife I owned got sharpened and stropped to a hair popping sharpness after each use, but an obsessive check of the edge never hurt anyone. Not if they lived a hunter's life.

I felt a few fine hairs pop free of my skin and, reassured, tightened my grip on the handle as I roamed the building with my gaze. The few stars visible in the city skyscape conveniently disappeared behind a cloud mass, cloaking the entire yard in one big shadow. Perfect. This was my chance.

I kept low, loping over the grass with blades in hand.

With every step I took, the bungalow seemed to flicker and dance as if caught in the throes of a weak technical signal. Its foundations appeared to waver, testing the limits of solidity. As I approached, an overpowering odor of sulfur assaulted my senses with such intensity that I involuntarily recoiled.

Definitely witch country.

The back door was right there, but I didn't intend to go in blades a-slashing. Witches like Lilah didn't live this long by leaving themselves unprotected. She'd have spells set to trigger at any sign of intrusion. She probably already knew I was outside.

No, I'd go through the front door. She'd not expect that. It just meant I had to swing around the corner and—

A solid blast of energy hit me like a board of greased wet lumber. I staggered back, rocking on my heels. Pain ricocheted down my spine as every vertebrae knocked against the other, reminding them to stay in place.

My knees buckled, dropping me to the grass as neatly as a stalk of corn being shorn by a scythe. My karambit thudded to the turf. I found myself heaving over my hands, my chest working in spasms that had my stomach doing its level best to dance with my heart somewhere in the middle of my throat.

Good God, I was going to puke. Right there on the witch's lawn, I was going to bring up the greasy French fries and gravy I'd had for supper, and it would take the last of my energy to do so. The witch would find me still heaving up threads of bile like some rookie, and she'd have her magical way with me. I imagined her bleeding me empty and using my pain to gain another year of life.

Or worse, I'd just lay here retching up my stomach lining until Gideon came poking about with Shea and found me in a pile of my own vomit.

That was the image that got me moving again.

I bit back the nausea. Forced the water back down. Dragged myself forward on all fours just to find the energy to get back up, and even then, I only managed to cover a mere three paces before the lingering remnants of the magic sliced through me like a high-pressured blast. All that supernatural energy came at me like a fire hose. It cascaded over me, leaving no inch of my body untouched. My feet knocked into each other, and I collapsed again, beaten down by the force of it.

Arms splayed out at my sides, lying there prone, I would make an easy target, and I knew it. I just couldn't do more for a few moments than gasp at the air. The taste of honeysuckle and sulfur mingled on my palette, trying to trick me into thinking this was all just a walk in a park on a Sunday morning. Go home, Ava, the breeze whispered. Don't risk it.

No way that was going to happen, either. Someone had to do something about the witch and do it now. I didn't need another flash image of one more kid finding some gum wrapper somewhere and deciding to slit his own throat. It didn't matter how strong the stink was, how forceful the pressure of the magic. I was not going home.

So, I waited it out, and slowly, the magical surge receded, lingering longest on my scalp as if bidding a reluctant farewell. Maybe the magic itself had a sentience, was testing the area for movement. Maybe the witch just expected the magic to repel the threat, a test shot in the dark to warn trespassers not to come too close.

Or maybe she was waiting for me to make my move and was just giving me a taste of her power. Whatever the case, whatever had happened to trespassers in the past, I was going forward.

I shifted my weight, rolling onto my back, my gaze fixed upon the fading moon above. A deep inhale and exhale brought my breathing back to normal while I allowed the remnants of power to dissipate into the night sky.

I dragged in the will to move along with a good dose of oxygen and finally managed to flip over onto my side, facing the bungalow. With any luck at all, she wasn't in there right now, watching me, powering up for another blast behind the lace curtains that danced on the breeze. But just in case, if I was going, I'd best get going.

My hand scrabbled for the blade I'd dropped until my fingers found it resting on a thatch of turf. I closed my fist over the handle just in time to hear the door squeak open. A shadow moved with the fluidity of ink, out from the interior to stream over the front of the building like a black tide climbing a beach.

I stood, dumbstruck and yes, a lot terrified as my eyes took in that blob of darkness and warped it into the very shape that kept me awake at night as a kid, trembling beneath my blankets. A remnant of a stupid B movie I'd snuck down to watch at midnight while everyone else was sleeping. Memories flashed at me in black and white and fuzzy, silver-fished static. The back of my neck went cold as the mottled, cold grey of the bungalow's façade disappeared beneath the inky black of a kraken.

The long-gone child in me whimpered.

"Oh, hell no, now," I whispered to the hulking shadow that streamed over the doorjamb from inside to swallow up the entire front of the house. Because it was indeed a kraken. And it stunk like the sulfur of a low-tide.

It was just a shade, a familiar of sorts, meant to trip upon movement on the property. That was all. The monster didn't have to have a nasty beak and black ink and...shudder of all shudders...slimy flesh. I told myself it wasn't real.

So, with my heart in my throat, I pushed off from a racer's lunge and hurtled toward the leviathan. Each step I took just made the slideshow of images flash at me all the faster, all the more terrifying. My breath came uneven and ragged as I pushed on, determined to force my muscles to keep moving, keep pounding forward no matter what I saw. Water sluiced around me, gathering height as I ran. As impossible as it was, with the ocean being miles away, the tide came in like it was gushing through a gaping hole in a massive ship.

The enormous creature stretched over the top of the thatched roof, its tentacles ranging far and wide, trying to block the door. The mouth of the thing cloaked the maw of the entryway, and its beak snapped open and closed as it slid down the front of the bungalow.

A spray of thick mucus hissed out at me before I could temper the momentum of my charge. The viscous liquid struck me full in the face, knocking me three steps back. My feet splashed in water that had somehow, in those seconds, risen past my ankles. My combat boots squelched.

The kraken inched further down the façade, its revolting suction of tentacles moving over the stones and stucco. When one of them reached for me, my long-ingrained primitive reaction was so abrupt, I pivoted sharply and stumbled against the weight of water. I almost fell backward into the lake that now surrounded the house. An icy clutch of dread gripped my throat.

Horrible images of me thrashing about in water too high over my head flashed through my mind. I gasped automatically, and had to steel my nerves, remind myself I wasn't a four-year-old at the community pool with some bully tossing me in and telling me an octopus would get me if I didn't swim.

I was on land. This was just a ruse to show me Lilah had no plans to just let me take her out without a fight. That I'd have to kill her to get out again.

"No problem," I said aloud to the rising waters that by now had made my calves tight from the cold. Muscles trained by hours of calf raises and box jumps cramped and I flexed and released, hoping to refuel the oxygen to keep them firing. "I'm not leaving until you're dead, anyway."

The kraken chortled her response. Its beak opened, showing an eerily lit stomach beyond a slug of tongue. I thought I heard moans of pain eddying up from the depths of its belly as though some poor soul had been ingested whole and was crying for help. Like every time I faced a foe, some part of my mind skimmed the phrase Gideon had used before my first hunt, one inked on the inside of my forearm. *Fight like you're already dead.*

I breathed those words as I gripped the karambit tight and launched myself at the kraken's beak. Slicing as I went, I dove for its innards. Globs of goo and rubbery flesh spread over my hands as I dug deep and sliced hard.

The stink of rotten fish grew so strong I gagged and had to hold my breath.

But no matter how I hacked and slashed, how the kraken grumbled and vibrated with fury, I couldn't find the thing's end. Rather than moving into a throat and gullet and on into a belly as I expected when I forged on, my feet trod into a sinister cavern, its darkness swallowing all light. The air hung heavy with an unmistakable metallic scent of blood.

Amidst the ominous stillness, someone called out in pain, the sound of anguish a dull razor's edge on the weight of darkness. The telltale smack of flesh-on-flesh violence, of fists thudding into yielding skin and deeper into harder, unyielding bone. Laughter bubbled up at me, brutal. Not my own.

I felt terror, but I felt something else too: Rage. Impotence. And a gut-wrenching sensation of prescience that made my veins turn to ice water.

A shiver of unease danced down my spine. Amidst the cacophony, I could have sworn I heard my own voice, distorted by torment, pleading for mercy. I tasted blood as though I'd been struck in the jaw. A cracking sound snapped into the joint as I moved it, testing for injury.

Nothing. Parlor Tricks. Illusion. Nothing more. A bloom of hope in my chest. If this was all the witch had, a bit of hallucination and conjured shadows, I'd be home catching up on *Outlander* by midnight.

I couldn't help laughing at the pathetic scare tactic.

"You think a bit of blood scares me?" I asked, my voice echoing through the chasm of the kraken's belly.

"Not your blood, hunter," came a throaty voice that could easily have been a seductress on the other end of a 911 line. "Your death."

CHAPTER 3

THE AIR SEEMED TO thicken with malevolence. For a moment, my breath caught in my throat at Lilah's words. The images reeled at me in full cyan, magenta, and yellow. The whispers, murmurs, and shrieks of sudden pain were almost sentient, very nearly corporeal. I swayed on my feet against the brush of them.

The karambit handle dug into my palm as I clenched it. Grounded me. Reminded me that if this cacophony was meant to show my future, the voice was all off. It wasn't me yelling into the darkness, pleading for the beating to stop. I didn't sob like that.

So it was clear. My head was not in the game the way it should be. I had no business feeling fear when that witch was out there hoping to trap still more victims with her rancid magic.

I swallowed down on the primitive flight response. Swallowed it down and turned it into a ball of loathing I could lob back at her.

"You've got the wrong hunter if you think death scares me," I said.

She chuckled again. "Then you're a fool, hunter. He never comes with so much warning as I'm giving you now. "

The sides of the kraken ballooned in on me, pressing its slimy flesh against mine where the corset didn't cover. A blob of something landed in my hair, plastering a chunk to my cheek. Revolting, shuddering disgust rolled through me, but I pushed on, forging through the smothering stink of the kraken's belly, forcing my feet through murk and muck.

As I went, that voice grew louder, and I knew I was drawing nearer to the real power. I had her. I just had to push on. Push through. Push back the noxious stench that had pervaded the air. When it started to fade, finally replaced by a rhythmic thud of a heartbeat, a beacon guiding me on, I slashed out with the karambit once more, sideways and down in an arc that should have flayed the beast's side right open.

In that moment, when a flood of rancid liquid, viscous and thick, splashed over my shoulders and cascaded down to my boots, the air grew thick, the oxygen devoured by an eerie hush that suggested I wasn't just *there* in the belly of the kraken, swallowed by the witch's lair. I knew I was somewhere *other*.

Impossible as it might seem, I'd traveled to another realm. My boots got left behind in the monster's belly as I landed barefoot in a dark cave. My wrists mated together in bonds that chaffed my skin. Wood? Vines? Certainly not iron or steel.

Guilt rose hard and heavy to my chest, the sensation that I wasn't enough. I was never enough. Killer, that's what the shadows whispered at me. And killers didn't deserve to live. They didn't deserve to enjoy a life of peace and happiness.

A chatter of feet shuffling on earth caught my ear, and then...

For a moment—just one—my entire body felt as though it was being torn apart inch by inch. I staggered beneath the intensity of pain. Punched out blindly, instinctively, and met nothing.

A growl sounded in the darkness, echoing my agony. It was fierce, that growl, low and primal, and predatory. It wasn't mine, but I knew the timbre of it the way my bones knew my marrow. Like a déjà vu that's impossible to grasp, the threads of recognition dangled before me. I reached for them, sensing the weighty importance of grabbing hold.

In a heartbeat, they were gone, frayed and disintegrated, leaving me feeling abandoned and desperate. The pain lifted. The suffocating heat of the illusion receded. I was slammed back into the kraken's belly. The vomit-inducing stench clawed at the back of my palate once more.

"Bitch," I rasped out through the tightness of my throat as I hunched against the nausea. "Is that all you've got? A bit of parlor tricks and illusion."

"It was worth a try, hunter," she whispered. "There is still time to turn back. Leave me now and you'll never know the danger that lurks in the shadows of your future."

"Fuck that," I ground out, inching forward, pushing at the fleshy gelatin that kept pressing in on me. "It doesn't take a witch to know danger lurks in a hunter's future. Save your tricks for someone who cares."

The chuckle that moved over my head was dusky and dark. "Save them for someone other than you, then?" she rasped out. "An admission of your true nature or a Freudian slip?"

"Why don't you show yourself?" I asked. "And find out?"

"Spoken like a true killer, Ava Ashe."

"I'm a hunter," I said, the rasp in my voice barely audible at the sound of my name on her tongue. "Hunters kill, yes. But we kill the evil things that plague the innocent. Nasty, deviant things like you."

"A killer is a killer," she said, and I could hear the shrug in her voice. "No matter the intention. Pretend to feel mighty and arrogant, if you like. I know the guilt that haunts you. The razor-sharp edge of it glints at me like a fine gem. I'd like to taste that. Come closer. Let me bleed it from you."

"Oh, don't worry, bitch," I spat out. "I'm coming."

With an effort that forced a grunt from me, I sliced through the gloom once more. And again. Again. The kraken's flesh flayed open for me, but still the darkness persisted. My karambit took another razoring slice through the shadows, met resistance once more, and I heaved all my muscles into the motion.

That strike gave me what I needed, finally. A glimmer of light piercing the dark. Without hesitation, I hacked and stabbed until the darkness bled light. And then I pushed through, ignoring the suction of skin as I forced my feet forward. Into the belly of the witch's lair. Into the heart of real danger and threat. A place where illusion and magic would have to meet me head-on in reality.

While I expected the interior to be as black as the witch's heart, I was momentarily surprised to see it possessed a warm glow that washed the entire room in an ambience of home and hearth.

For a second, an ache of longing corded into my throat. Panning the space, I marked each nuance, orienting myself so automatically, I barely registered what I was doing until I replayed the picture back in my mind, one large panoramic vision I could call to me when needed.

The dimly lit room was adorned with an eclectic mix of mystical artifacts and potions. Shelves lined the walls, displaying jars filled with various powders, dried herbs, and shimmering liquids. The air was thick with the scent of peppermint and cinnamon. Such homey, inviting scents and sounds. Such a welcoming space.

Deceit. That's what it was. I knew it even through the splinters of moonlight that filtered through the small, grimy windows, casting eerie shadows that danced across the worn wooden floor. The flickering glow of candles cast a soft light that reflected off ancient tomes and crystal spheres.

Whispers moved through the shadows in the places where the walls joined. The sound of crackling flames rose from a hearth in the corner like fingers of toasted bread charring the air. It was such a warm contrast to the chill that hung in the air that for a second, I sagged in relief. The occasional creak of the old cottage and the distant hoot of an owl outside possessed a haunting allure of old world peace and calm.

And there, amidst the bracken and ephemera, stood Lilah.

Tall, with hair blacker than my own, and a willowy figure that sported swaying full hips, she stood in front of a wooden pantry shelf. Back to me, I could see she was no old crone. She was as young and nubile as a yearling fawn. My body measured hers in that instant, sizing her up, comparing her to my own athletic build. Where her curves were sultry and come-hither, mine were rounded with muscle.

Ties of a crimson apron hung down the length of her legs to mid-thigh and etched out tiny circles in the air with her every swaying movement as she stuffed items from the shelf into a velvet bag with gold lacing.

I wasn't sure if I was angry because she was so beautiful or because she'd found that beauty in the blackest magic a witch could practice, born from pain and suffering and more than a little death. I'd feel no regret taking her breath from her lungs or stopping her heart. Hatred as black as her essence threatened to consume me, hot and potent, as I watched her filling that bag.

Knowing she'd gained every supple inch of skin from life-energy that wasn't her own, that would keep me going. Past the innocent-looking eyes she'd eventually turn on me; the pleading in her face when I delivered the killing blow. Because they always showed that one second of regret, of horrified surprise that they were about to die, and that one instant was the one I had to steel myself against. Not the initial strike. Not the battle I might face to get there.

No. It would be the last flicker of their lost humanity that could get me killed.

I had to prepare for the instant when pity reared its ugly head. A moment when I might pull back, hesitate, the deepest core of humanity poking through the shroud of darkness to search for mercy. A moment I needed to storm past like Caesar crossing the Rubicon because monsters like her showed no mercy to their victims.

So I pressed on because that heart would stop today. Later, in my bed, I might feel one more ounce of my own humanity slip away. I'd mourn it for a moment, and then I'd stuff it into the place I put all those moments, into a drawer over-stuffed with pieces of my psyche, and I'd slam it shut like an eager bride jumping on an over-stuffed suitcase.

Holding onto that determination, I trod into the room, extracting myself from the kraken's hide and shaking off the feel of its skin as it retracted back into the ether she'd drawn it from. A popping sound released the pressure in my eardrums. A wave of oily liquid, warm and fragrant with sulfur and rosemary, cascaded over my hair and down the back of my neck at the same moment. Beneath the lace corset shirt, the grease trickled down my spine, making my skin creep and crawl.

The room wavered into focus as I slid on the viscosity beneath my boots. I slid and slipped and nearly took a dive face-first into the chest of a large, fleshy woman who'd not been there a second earlier. She wore an old-fashioned boudoir peignoir over her breasts. Her head bobbed on a thready neck webbed with crepey flesh.

In one hand, she held a fat pottery urn that dribbled the last of its cargo of oil. She swept a lace cape over my face, veiling my vision and giving her a gauzy, ethereal appearance through the material.

"You've got to be kidding me," I barked out from beneath the fabric, addressing the comment toward the witch and not the ugly creature in front of me. "A boggart? You've got nothing stronger than that?"

I swatted at the creature's robe with the karambit, slicing through in a fit of annoyance with a swish that sounded very much like a zipper opening panels wide.

I elbowed through the hole, aiming for the boggart's jugular. It shrieked in rage and grabbed me by the throat before I had a chance to bring the blade back around to dig into hers.

I coughed on the air that got stuck mid-breath. Several feet away, the witch ignored me as though I was no more important to her than a bug crawling on the sill of her window. Just kept filling that damned bag.

"Face me on your own, witch," I squeezed out around the boggart's grip. "I want to see your face when I cut your throat."

She tossed a glance over her shoulder and smiled, a serpentine movement of those ruby lips. "You *are* facing me, hunter." A chuckle. Dark and throaty. Seductive, even.

As if her smile had turned on a switch, every inch of my body where the oil touched burned worse than a swarm of fire ants burrowing beneath my skin. I could have cut myself and run lemon juice over the wound and not felt such a sting. I lobbed a few choice curses at the witch on a wheeze of air that found its way past the boggart's grip.

"Bitch. You spelled the oil."

"I spell everything," she said, turning back to her work. Despite being all the way across the room, her voice came as clear as if she were standing next to me. "It's kind of my thing."

Prickles of burning itch spread over my face. I struggled in the boggart's clutch as I watched the witch stuff a dozen more objects into the bag. A watch. A ring. A few coins. The pouch didn't bulge out any more than if it stored a few slips of paper. All while I choked and gagged around the fingers clenching off my air.

Suspended in the air, I fought to reach for the spelled blade still sheathed on my thigh. Its ability to absorb and store magic was the reason I'd brought it. If I could get close enough to use the damn blade, I could take her own dark magic and turn her magic against her.

I just had to get to it. But I was losing the last of whatever air was still languishing in my lungs. The boggart's face was bloated with rage as she shook me. I flailed for the blade, missed, and grabbed again as the creature rattled me in the air as though I were a soiled washcloth. My spine snapped, vertebrae clacking into place and out again. I bit down on the pain.

By the time I willed my hands to stop tearing at the boggart's fingers and drop to my legs, the witch was already reaching for a huge tattered tome from the shelf above her.

Her grimoire. She really was aiming to bail. She opened the bag wide, the mouth of it stretching to accommodate the book.

My fingers scrabbled for the sheaths strapped to my thighs. I fought to get just one of them in my clutches, but just as I touched the blade's handle, the boggart shook me once more, wailing about her beautiful nightgown being destroyed. this time, my hand breezed past the handle of the knife.

The witch had dropped the book into the bag and was already gathering the laces together the way the darkness was gathering at the edges of my vision.

Maybe Gideon was right to replace me. Maybe I was losing my edge and coming here was a mistake. I'd been rash, angry, cocky. My own damn insecurities would be responsible for her disappearance, only to resurface later, unaccosted and free to commit her atrocities on more unsuspecting kids. The Hunter Network would have to start all over again.

She cast a glance my way, and in that second, I saw all the hollow blackness of her gaze. Like the inside of her kraken, it was cavernous and ugly.

Jet-colored hair whipped around her face and spun out around her as though electricity had hold of the ends and was manipulating them like marionette strings.

She figured the boggart had me. Figured she'd won already.

She turned back to her work, confident her magic had me taken care of, that she could take flight to some other sanctuary without worry because, in seconds, I'd be dead.

Chapter 4

As the boggart's suffocating hold constricted around my throat, a surge of terror electrified my spine. A flash of full-body memory barreled through me like a high-speed train, dragging from the depths of memory the sensation of a hemp rope, the sound of a gritty, smoke-rasped voice. I was sixteen again, hanging from a rope in a gymnasium, struggling to breathe.

Panic clawed its way through my veins as that echo from a lifetime ago rose like a spectre to taunt me.

I kicked out, a replay of that long-buried moment, and just like then, I struck nothing. Every gasp for air became a struggle. My vision wavered, darkening at the edges. Back then, it was a man, with man-level strength, trying to strangle me. This time, the monster was supernatural, with supernatural strength.

This time, I wouldn't survive the strangling. This time, there would be no one to save me.

Survival depended on my resolve this time and not happenstance. And I could do this. While I'd been a foolish girl before without a hunter's training. Now, I had what it took. I just had to calm down, bury the terror, the blind panic. I had to...

Kick hard and high. This time with purpose instead of mad, instinctive flailing. Once more. Raising them with a snap of energy. Aim the thrust with intention. Destabilize the boggart's stance. Strike in the chest, then the throat before gravity pulled my legs back down. Seconds. I had seconds.

The impact shuddered through her chest. I felt it in her grasp for an instant before she redoubled her grip. Merely kicking up and out wouldn't be enough to dislodge that iron grip. My core needed to be engaged. Move each muscle with intention, engaging it, channeling what strength lay in my deep core. Engage, twist, buck back. Kick out in a strike that met her nose—

I gasped for air as her hold broke.

Stumbling at the unexpected release, a mix of surprise and fury coursed through me. I landed on my feet and almost twisted my ankle at the sudden impact of heel to floorboards.

A growl of sheer anger tore through the air as the boggart narrowed its beady eyes on me. I acted fast, afraid if I hesitated, there wouldn't be enough fight in me to resist another chokehold. I snatched the enchanted from its sheath. Raised it to chest level.

Silent as the swoop of a hawk, I lunged forward, my blade slashing through the air with precision. The boggart, caught off guard, swung her meaty arm at me with fingers splayed wide open. A jiggle of triceps skin, and those fingers climbed the base of my throat, seeking a death grip.

But this time, I was ready.

"Fuck that," I ground out. "Not again."

Blade up. I stabbed forward and yanked sideways.

A screech of pain blasted my ears at a decibel loud enough to make me wince. For an instant, I thought my eardrums might pierce, but then the boggart's form wavered, and a popping sound freed the vacuum in my hearing. With a shudder, she vanished. Gone like the kraken.

I stood in the wake of disappearing shadow, breathless, heart pounding. A prickle of energy ran up my spine. A gentle reminder that I wasn't alone. That the real fight was yet to come.

I spun to face the witch. Her delicately arched eyebrow climbed to her hairline. She hadn't expected me to win, it seemed.

"You put on a good show, I'll give you that," I said through the raspy ache of my throat. "But, bitch, your time is up."

The almost lazy smirk she shot my way urged my boots forward, footsteps thundering against the worn floorboards. I didn't bother with stealth; there was no point now. My blade, crackling with the magic it had gathered from the boggart, glinted in my grip, poised high above my head, ready to strike with all the force I could bring to bear, using gravity and thrust to my advantage.

My muscles burned. Laced with a flood of lactic acid that would hurt like hell tomorrow if I lived through tonight. I lunged forward just as she spread her arms, the pouch filled with a jumble of shapes dangling inches from her torso on one side, a hand clenched into a fist on the other. By the time I was within a half-dozen steps, she had sucked in a long breath that ballooned out that ample breast of hers.

She winked at me, those black eyes flashing, then she breathed the air out in a long exhale.

A furious wind pushed at me, screaming in my ear like a banshee. My ponytail sailed out behind me, tugging at my scalp as I fought to keep my balance. Where it touched bare skin, the air felt thick with glass shards, stinging, gnawing at me like gnats. Hunching forward, I plodded on, determined to meet her, resolve biting into my cheeks as I grit my teeth.

She watched for several long moments as I struggled against the wind. It seemed to amuse her. For a second, the air pressure lessened. I gained another foot. Keep laughing, bitch, I thought. Just you keep laughing. I thrust my full weight into the breeze, hunching low, karambit at the ready, the spelled blade held aloft.

She canted her head at me, curious. The wind picked up once more. Pushed me back half a foot. I fought to regain the distance I'd lost, grunting with the effort. As if it satisfied her I'd failed the test, she shrugged one shoulder and turned back to filling her sack with objects on the shelf.

Humiliation and rage blazed a trail through my throat.

"Fuck you, bitch," I said, curling inward to make myself smaller, lessening the surface area fighting against the current that seemed only to be affecting me. "Is that all you got? A little gas?"

"What I have is fuel," she said without turning around. She hadn't raised her voice to cut through the whistling of the wind that sailed past me, but I heard her clear enough. "Plenty to burn the skin from your bones and char the marrow before you take another step."

"Then why don't you?" I demanded, throwing my foot out in front of me once more, my legs feeling like they were wading in thigh-high freezing water. "Show me what you got."

Her deflection of the insult gave me the answer. She didn't want to use that sort of energy. That kind of energy would cost her, and she no doubt thought she could beat me without it. But just what was she saving that energy for, I wondered.

Didn't matter. She was as good as dead. If she didn't want to use most of her power, all the better for me. I'd made it to within a yard of her and I knew I needed to change tactics or lose her altogether. I imagined Gideon sending Shea out to find me still battling an invisible wind, and I redoubled my efforts. I was going about it all wrong. I'd never cut into the force of air by trying to punch through it. I had to shift my thinking, change the attack.

With a lurch, I flung myself sideways, the way a swimmer fights against a rip tide. The sudden movement freed me from the unrelenting gusts. Shoddy as the maneuver was, it was enough to give me a head draft toward Lilah, and by the time I was in range, I'd long forsaken the effort to be graceful and quick. The attack was noisy as hell as my boots clomped over the floorboards. My breath was a ragged thing that would have given me away to a deaf man.

She spun on her heel to slide a lazy gaze up and down my height as I stood before her. Totally unimpressed, even though the karambit dripped with the kraken's flesh and streams of gauzy peignoir waved in the current with each step I took. Rage that she could think me so inconsequential worked the lines of my mouth.

A little smirk lifted one corner of her full mouth. "Still here, hunter?"

Black eyes crinkled at the corners. Despite the evil glint in her eyes, and her reputed age, she was stunning. I thought of that boy on the playground, the image of his teacher fending off brutal stabs from a pair of scissors, and I ground my teeth together. Blackest magic. Evil through and through.

The witch must have seen the resolve settle into my face and neck, because an arrogant dimple revealed itself in the creaminess of her left cheek.

Her fingers slipped into the mouth of the pouch she held at her side. "Bring it, hunter," she said.

She didn't have to tell me twice.

Her fingers were still in the bag when I crossed the blades over my chest and scissored them in a slashing motion. The boning in the corset pinched into my ribs at the effort. I thought I ripped the seams open at the sides as I exerted all the muscles in my core to slash those blades back together. I slipped in close, like a lover. I slashed. Stepped out again.

I hadn't expected to meet flesh. It had been a testing move, hoping to catch something, to measure the distance, but as red lines of fluid opened up in her throat, a thunderous rumble crawled through the floor beneath my feet. It shook the foundation. A din of tinkling, tearing sounds ricocheted through the space as windows shattered.

The enchanted knife hissed as the magic gathered from her blood and coated the blade. Blood sprayed back at me, catching me in the left eye. I raked my fingers over the fluid, scraping it away.

The handle grew warm in my palm, pulsing from the magic being absorbed. Still shocked at hitting the target, I rooted my feet against the shifting movement, calling upon my core for balance. Holding my ground as the floor tore open in seams was a struggle. Every ripping strip of wood punctuated the roll of thunder as she collapsed onto her ass and slumped to the side against the cabinets.

Those magnificent black eyes rolled up to stare at me. Unseeing. Dazed but not dead.

I'd done it. I could scarce believe it. A last-second swoop for the final strike, bearing down with that hot blade, the magic stinging my nose and burning my sinuses, and I'd finish her. But before I deliver that final blow, a vial of something wretched smelling toppled from a shelf above us. Black smoke hissed from the fissures and uncoiled on the floor like a snake stretching its scales in the sun.

With every inch it moved, it ate up feet of wooden boards and left behind a crack in the floor so wide an entire body could disappear within it. I had to think fast or get swallowed up. I started to run for the door, then remembered the glamor on her cottage. The boggart. The kraken. This was just another parlor trick. If she had any real power left, she'd bring it to bear on me to save herself. But she wasn't.

This was just a dying echo of her magic.

I let the magic slither along the boards, let the thunder roll and the floor shake as it devoured the kitchen piece by piece, waiting for it to dissipate, just to be sure it was all illusion and not a trap laid for me to break my neck before I could break hers. I kept my eye on her black gaze as I stepped neatly back and out of the reach of her hands, watching for the moment when that dullness of death should creep into her irises.

"Are you finished?" I asked. "Had enough of delivering death to a reckless hunter?"

She sagged sideways as her hands went to her throat to staunch the blood flow. It was useless, and she had to know that. I felt no pity. She'd chosen her death the moment she'd planted that ring beneath the playground swing set. I advanced on her, staring into her face, waiting to feel some sort of emotion beyond the numbness. Nothing. Not even the bloom of victory. Hands at my side, I watched as a gargling noise slid free of her lips. I blinked. Swallowed. I should feel something. Where was that damnable pinch of humanity that should be rising by now, whispering beneath my skull that I was a killer. That she'd been human once. That irritating voice that liked to plague me at three AM until I shoved out of bed and jammed on running shoes so I could race the pity from my mind.

Where was all that? Why wasn't it dogging me now?

It took the stealthy movement of her fingers spidering toward the bag to make me realize she wasn't as weak as I'd thought. Her magic had cocooned me, holding me rapt while she marshaled enough to cast one last spell.

"Oh hell no," I said and jumped to clamp my hand over her mouth. "No way you're pulling a spell out of your ass now."

The karambit dropped from my grip onto the floor so I could palm her into silence. She rolled onto her shoulder, that dying gaze narrowing in surprised fury.

Only then, carefully, did I pick my blade back up and sheath it as I eyed her, pressing my palm tighter against her mouth. I held her there. My chest rising and falling hard and fast as she tried to suck in air and pulled in the flesh of my palm instead. Pinioned, her back sagged against the cupboard doors. Another thrust of the knife and I might kill her, but I wanted to be sure. I wanted to know she was dead.

So I held my hand over her mouth and I watched her eyes, my body attuned to each flutter of muscle in her body. I felt it when she started to lose her grip on life. I measured the tension in her neck.

It seemed to take forever before her long, lean legs splayed out on either side of me. I snicked in close, listening with more than just my hearing, watching her face with more than a mere gaze.

The smoke started to clear, but the gunnels in the flooring remained. Beneath the trenches of it, I could swear I saw glistening movement. A sort of hissing came back at me. So, not just an illusion. The tearing of the floor had been real, each chasm a land mine ready to claim me. I'd have broken more than one bone if I'd fallen through.

Even so, it had been too easy.

"What happened to all that fuel?" I asked her because there was no final ghost peering back at me. Not yet. "Saving it for a rainy day? Because I would think this day might have rained a bit more than you expected" "

It wasn't just a desire to taunt her that prodded me. It wasn't arrogance. I needed to see if she had more. Because they always did. And I wasn't going to let go till that ounce of blood that tipped the scales into death had dribbled free of her.

I tightened my grip, gave it more pressure. Enough that I could feel her teeth biting into the backs of her lips. She watched me with deadpan eyes as I waited, crouched over her in an awkward posture. I'd wait forever if it took that, no matter how much my back ached. Even if the residual adrenaline made my chest heave until I broke a rib. Muscles in my spine ached to be stretched out and rolled free of the tension bundled into them. But I didn't take my palm away.

Instead, I leaned closer still, near enough to see the fineness of her pores. I wondered how many victims she'd bled and pained to get such flawless skin.

"Death is too good for you," I said. "You've tortured and killed your last kid."

Black eyes narrowed at me.

"Yeah," I said with a curl of revulsion lifting the corners of my mouth. "I know about the kids. I know about the dark objects too."

I jerked my chin toward the pouch as it lay against her chest, growing wetter and blacker with her blood. "It was very thoughtful of you to pack them in such a tidy carrying case for me."

A long blink. Black fluid bubbled up through her tear ducts. She tried to cough beneath my hand, choking on the fluid that was backing up into her throat. And that was when the pity rose as it usually did when the kills took this sort of intimate violence. I averted my gaze from hers. The inevitable panic I'd see, the fear, all of that might spark an emotion in me that those poor kids couldn't pay the price for. I had to remember that. Emotions, any emotions other than rage and hatred were a liability.

So even though part of me wanted to feel bad for her, wanted to just feel the way a normal person might as they looked into the face of death, I forced myself to remember instead, the kid in his class razoring his way through his classmates until they bundled him up and took him to Bedlam.

Then whatever pity wanted to rise in my chest burned out there instead. I felt it burst and go out like a flare. And in the moment the embers died, I finally allowed myself to look at her because I knew any inclination I might feel for sympathy was gone. My vision shuttered as I considered her. Every inch of my neck cried out for a harsh touch to relieve a terrible itch. My eyes burned.

It was taking too long. She should be gone by now.

One single moment where something moved in the depths of those black eyes. Just one, and I knew. There was at least one more awful relic. Something holding her power, keeping her alive, maybe.

The realization struck me like a firebrand. I pulled my hand away. It dripped with greasy black fluid, what passed for blood in a witch so full of dark magic.

"Where is it?" I asked, my voice sharp.

Her gaze darted over my shoulder and flicked back to me. A greasy grin slid over her face.

The power in the handle of the spelled blade was already raising pepper-sized blisters on my fingers. It would have to be purged, and soon. I couldn't hold on to it for much longer, but I'd be damned if I'd drop it now.

"Well," I said. "Where is it?"

"My guess is she swallowed it," said a voice from behind me.

My heart stuttered at the unexpected intrusion. The witch dropped her head back against the wood of the cupboards and lifted an eyebrow a fraction of an inch. Surprise? Relief? I couldn't tell because her delicate eyebrow fell again, and her eyes closed. Gone. Finally.

My chest hiccupped once, and then, with a stutter, my heart hammered away again. Adrenaline gushed in from all corners. Every muscle in my body went rigid.

Lilah's hand struck the floor, her fingers open. In its palm sat a fat, black gemstone. I snatched it from her and slipped it into my pocket. Then I swallowed. Slowly. Noiselessly.

There was no hurry to turn to see who intruded on this sacred duty. No hurry at all, despite the waving, straining hairs on the back of my neck screaming at me to pay attention. To whip around. Defend myself.

The sound of scuffling boots whispered over the floor. Lots of boots. Enough that I knew when I looked over my shoulder, I wouldn't like what I saw. Some part of my mind suggested I should have heard them coming, and another part, the wiser, quieter portion, told me I wouldn't have heard them even if I had been listening for them. I wasn't slipping or too occupied to notice.

The truth was, they weren't human. And they'd made no sound.

I steeled myself to face whatever was behind me.

"If she swallowed it," I said before turning around, "then I guess you'll find yourself rifling through her unmentionables in a few minutes."

The spelled blade burned hotter than a few seconds earlier, but I resisted the urge to drop it. Only after I'd brought it close to my chest and out of sight did I turn. When I did, the soles of my boots squeaked on the tiles, the rubber protesting the sudden movement.

One very tall man stood at the entrance to the cottage. Shadowy figures loomed behind him, barring any escape from the door. No evidence of the boggart or the kraken proved they'd ever existed.

I didn't need to pull my gaze away from the intruders in the doorway to recognize the seething mass of shadow indicated at least a dozen more men surrounding the building. A blur of movement in my peripheral vision indicated there was enough to guard each window. I remembered they'd shattered, each of them, when the witch brought her magic to bear. They might be even now clambering through broken panes all over the first floor.

My heartbeat ratcheted up as another surge of adrenaline soaked my muscles. A sort of joy bubbled up into my throat. The witch had been a disappointing experience at the end of it all. Her death hadn't given me an ounce of satisfaction.

But here...here was a battle a hunter with a death wish could fully engage.

The man in front of me was striking enough, tall. Skinny enough to remind me of a length of copper wire. Black swathed him top to bottom, from the heavy boots he wore to the black cap nestled so close to his eyebrows that his deep-set eyes should have been black holes of shadow except for the way they shifted from a bright blue to purple. Light played over his fingers in jagged shards that resembled a Van de Graaff generator.

But it was the enormous dog bristling quietly behind him that took most of my attention. The head on the thing had to be the size of a Newfoundland's, but the body was that of a bulldog. Black as pitch, the only part of it that didn't look like it would disappear into shadow were its eyes. They glowed orange and red like a bed of coals in a fire that had once burned hot enough to melt iron. Something about them shot warning signals like flares up behind my eyelids. The faint scent of cinnamon and smoke drifted over the room.

"Fae," I said as I pushed up from the crouch that had me at a disadvantage. With a subtle movement, I slipped the spelled blade behind my back as I stood. I didn't know much about the Fae folk, but I did know they possessed magic the way witches could only dream.

"You have a good eye," the man said, and I eyed him, careful not to make a sudden movement.

I let my gaze skate from the uncomfortable way his eyes changed to the immaculate styling of his hunting attire. Because he was a hunter, too. Even if he looked like he belonged in a suit, he was a predator through and through. His skin was almost ghostly white, and the bits of hair that showed beneath his toque held the same purple tinge as his eyes.

"Not hard to recognize a Fae with eyes like that," I said and let my gaze roam, almost casually, to the big dog at his side that had already lowered its head as if it was deciding just how long it would take to eat me.

"Does your dog bite?" I asked, thinking I could throw him off balance for a second. Any amount of time might prove the instant that I needed to either escape or attack.

That grin came quick and easy. "I believe the response you're hoping for with that ridiculous joke is that it's not my dog."

The grin's unexpected appearance didn't fool me. I lifted one shoulder in a shrug that only served to darken the man's gaze. The bristling hound beside him, holding my gaze so intently that I could barely breathe only served to put me on even higher alert. I lifted my chin. My back went rigid. Defense, I told myself. Get ready to rumble.

"Most humans would be quaking by now," he said. "Are you feeble-minded, human?"

From behind him, the shadows moved. The telltale sounds of windows being breached as the last shards of glass crashed inward indicated the rest of the ambush was intent on crawling into the building.

"What I am," I said, "is in a hurry."

He strolled closer, almost curious in his advance. The hound watched it all with a languid, but watchful, eye.

"I've never known a man to be in such a hurry to die," he said. "Who are you that you would visit a witch of Lilah's caliber? Not a client, surely. Not a mercenary." His gaze roamed my face. "No mercenary would dare storm her sanctuary for any amount of money." His eyes narrowed, and the purple sparked within the depths. "Not a witch, either." He sniffed. "Or fae."

That last was said with a taint of relief as though he'd worried fae was something I could actually be. I shrugged as I took a subtle step backward.

"I should ask you the same question," I said in a scolding tone. "No good can come from ambushing a witch like Lilah here."

I gestured toward the witch's body with the karambit, and repeated the name so I could add it to the list I kept rolled into a scroll in the deepest part of a hidden cupboard along with a wooden chest that held some more grotesque items than a bit of paper. Stuff that would go to my sister upon my death because in the end, I'd want her to know I'd done something with my miserable life. "Maybe it's not me who's feeble-minded."

"Who said it was the witch I wanted to ambush?" His grin slid over his expression like an egg over a greased skillet, and I knew at once that I could not take on this fae and his cronies and live.

A smile, probably too confident, maybe a little too casual, tugged at my lips. Relief, then. That's what the smile was. A flat out suggestion of joy.

I might not make it out alive, but damn, it was going to be a hell of a fight.

CHAPTER 5

It wasn't every day a hunter got a chance to spar with a hellhound. But the moment the beast took a purposeful step forward, I knew that was exactly what I was facing, and if the fae beside it could command it at will, then I was in for a hell of a fight. Fight or flight energy coiled into my chest.

"Well, human?" the fae said, his advance a slow but methodical one. "Do you want to try us all on at once?"

I jerked my chin toward the hellhound. It hadn't moved a single inch despite its owner's advance.

"Are you saying you're the kind of man who likes to share?" I countered with a side eye toward the hound that was already padding its feet in anticipation. "Because I'm not into doggie porn."

The hound growled, and the sound of it raised the hairs on my arms. Beneath the fury of that rumbling vibration hunkered a sort of indignance, an impatience. And what I was sure, was invitation.

"I'm not into men, either," the male said with a curl of his lip, and that was the moment his previous comments about me being male slammed home. The hateful lace corset had glamored me into looking like a man. That meant if I got out of there with all my skin attached to my bones, it wouldn't be Ava Ashe with her long black ponytail and telltale tattoo they looked for.

Score one for the itchy damn corset. I rolled my shoulders, suggesting I didn't care what he was into.

"Mind you," he went on. "Man on man violence isn't my digs either." He raked me with a glare. "I like women. And I like them bloody and running in terror."

A knot clogged up my throat at his words for all the faceless women he'd probably tortured over his lifespan.

"Well?" he asked again. "I know you want to fight. I can smell the magic coming off that blade behind your back."

I clenched the handle tighter, biting back against the heat of the blade as the black magic tried to worm its way inside me through dozens of tiny heat blisters. As dark as that power was, I'd just need an instant of opportunity to unload it on the fae. I was quick. I could lunge and sweep out with a roundhouse kick, take him in the ankles, and hamstring him with a swipe.

Or...

I could run like my brain told me the smart thing to do was. There was no way this fae and his hound and his shadowed cronies had come for tea with Lilah, the black magic witch. If I fought and lost, these cursed objects would find their way into the mortal realm before long. I wasn't going to let that happen. Didn't matter what it cost me.

So, I did the right thing, not the thing I wanted to do, and I grabbed for the pouch with a lightning quickness that astounded me.

It was too light to hold the sheer number and size of the things I'd seen her stuff inside, and for a second, I second-guessed what she'd been doing with it.

Then a ring fell from a gap in the mouth of the bag and rolled into one of the cracks in the floor gouged out by the black magic, and for a second, the bag seemed to grow larger, heavier. I clutched it tighter. In my grip, it shrank again. At the same time, the Fae whistled, and a blast of purple fire streamed across the room and struck the pantry shelf. It roared to life as though it had been soaked with accelerant. Dozens of vials and tubes exploded from the heat. Shards of glass rained down, peppering my bare arms and biting into my skin.

I bit back a cry of surprise as the vials unleashed a barrage of spells all around me. Two chairs leaning against the walls suddenly transformed into peculiar hunch-backed creatures with razor-sharp claws.

I leaped out of the way of them as multiple spirals of energy scored the air and spun out of control. The energy collected glasses, pans, pots, and some shadows from the doorway like miniature black holes gobbled up everything in their path.

Fires broke out. Ghosts popped into and out of being with such electricity. My hair stood on end.

And it got worse with each second that passed. I didn't think the fae expected such an explosive blast of magic, and even the hellhound reared back at the onslaught of power, one foot held aloft as its gaze narrowed at the sudden over-abundance of supernatural activity. Those beams of light within their sockets fell on me just as a tide of demons rose from one of the crevices left by the magic that had torn the floor into a minefield of cracks.

The intruder neatly side-stepped a tentacle the size of a dinosaur tail as it slid in a window and tried to curl around his legs. I recognized the stink of sulfur.

I half-grinned at the thought that all that magic was left to run amuck without the witch to control it, leaving these fae to face it all plus the creatures whose spells I'd broken.

"That kraken is a real bitch," I said, backing away from it all. "But the boggart is where the real action is. Enjoy."

Trapping myself deeper into the interior when I didn't know the layout was suicide, and suicide wasn't on the agenda right then. But going forward was also impossible. So, I backed up to avoid the chokehold the ambush had made of the foyer. I needed space to move and maneuver. Escape if I could.

If escape became impossible, then his heart would get the spelled blade, and I'd bolt past him.

With my karambit clutched in my grip, I made an awkward, ineffectual slice toward the fae's side. I kept the spelled blade close to my hip as the karambit spun in my other hand, pointing out instead of along my forearm the way it should be.

He laughed out loud as the blade caught on the leather of his pants and tore a small hole. I pulled the knife back to my side and danced clumsily three steps to the left before I dropped my arms.

"You'll have to do better than that," he said with a sneer.

I gawked at him. All the muscles coiled in his shoulders relaxed. Easy prey, he thought so clearly; it was written in the language of a cocky posture.

Well. Score one for the dumb human, then, because I was going to use that arrogance of his to leverage his outstretched arm in my escape. A dozen years of gymnastics training had saved my ass a good number of times. I hoped for one more happy intervention.

I might have made it too, except I stumbled on the witch's legs when I jumped for his shoulder. Witch's legs. Legs that shouldn't have been there when I'd left her paces behind me beside the pantry where she'd fallen.

I bumbled forward and only kept myself from falling flat on my face by pin-wheeling like an idiot. Shame would have colored my face if I wasn't so deadly earnest about getting the hell out of there.

Instead, I spun around, backing toward the exit, my hands up in surrender. I had one last trick up my sleeve, and I wasn't too proud to use it.

"Don't hurt me," I said, injecting my most pitiful human tone to my voice. The pouch hung from its string on my finger. "I just came here to deliver something. That's it. That's all. Please. Please don't hurt me."

The fae's expression became a muddle of confusion. He hesitated. Should he show mercy or violence? He wasn't sure, and I took that indecision as my cue.

The karambit came out swinging as I looped the strings of the pouch over my head. The fabric and all the weight from inside it settled over my chest. With an ease born of practice, my leg shot out in a sweep that took out his feet while he was still working out why I was attacking when I'd already surrendered.

I executed a perfect swing and slice, my legs pivoting me perfectly to avoid the blast of purple energy that burst into the wall from the fae's hands. Chunks of plaster rained down and turned to dust long before they hit the floor.

The men I'd heard earlier cracking open windows all over the building came then. Moving like a phalanx well-trained and hardened to battle, they fanned out and made a barrier out of their bodies.

I'd lost sight of the hellhound, but the fae was directly in front of me. Somehow, we'd swapped positions, and he was closer to the witch. I was closer to the door.

I should have been able to turn tail and run straight through the exit and out into the yard.

Should have. I couldn't. And it took me long, wasted moments to realize the witch had spelled the door to keep whoever dared attack her within her reach and trapped. Tentacles covered in black suction cups whipped about in front of the door.

The hellhound crept out from a shadow built by the magic whirling around the room. Its eyes landed on me as its lips curled back to reveal glaringly bright teeth.

"Okey doke, then," I said to it. "Let's see what you've got."

I brought the karambit to the fight, but it didn't obey me. While I sliced sideways, it stabbed straight ahead as though someone else's hand guided its arc.

Missing my mark, I fell to a squat. If I couldn't stab it, I'd have to roll between its wide-planted front legs and slit along its belly with the spelled blade. Hope that the magic unburdened itself into the beast's viscera.

But even as I leveled the knife at him, it burned so hot in my grip that my fingers opened, leaving it to clatter to the floor. I gawked at the blade winking in the light. It phased in and out of sight for a moment before it disappeared. The pain in my palms receded.

Wherever it had gone, the blade had taken the blisters with it. Small comfort when I was about to face beings who owned magic like breath armed with nothing but a regular blade and a few quick reflexes.

Except that wasn't all I had, was it? Magic was a chaos in the kitchen. Creatures, objects, and blasts of stinking air and fire swirled about so fast we were all dodging and weaving as we held our ground. There might be a chance, a way to turn chaos to opportunity. I just had to focus. And I needed it. Because everything moved like water, then, rushing as though unleashed from a tank split by a massive axe. The phalanx of fae came at me. The hellhound snarled and leaped. The greasy-looking fae advanced.

I didn't dodge artfully so much as scramble to the side. The rivers of broken floor, small tributaries that made a web across the floor, all aimed for one broad crevice. I was several feet from it. I glanced up.

The hellhound was in the air again. I was sure I saw a smirk on its face.

Dragging in one long draft of air, I lunged for the hole in the floor, measuring its width as I sailed through the air, praying it was wide enough for me to fit. That the great fissures would repel the hound even as it admitted me.

It wasn't a clean jump. My shoulder caught on the edge, and the contact knocked me sideways before I dropped at least five feet to a dirt basement. The landing came with a thud that sounded as hard as it felt.

Air coughed from my lungs along a thread of blood. The taste of it was like a battery post in my mouth. Panic flared in my chest at the thought I might have blown a lung.

I shifted my jaw sideways, testing, tentative. Ran my tongue along the inside of my cheek as I inhaled cleanly.

Blood, tangy and thick, made the touch greasy. Not a lung. Just my cheek. I'd bit down hard when I'd landed.

Black smoke billowed above me, a mercy of black magic that apparently had swum over the currents of air when I'd jumped. I looked up from my back, noting the way it swirled into shape. I thought I saw dark eyes peering out from the mass of it. A chuckle of dark humor rumbled down toward me.

For a second, I thought I'd die there. I hurt everywhere. I couldn't breathe, and it felt like someone was strangling me. Rope razed into my skin, cutting off my air. I was choking. Strangling. Dangling on a long hemp line with no one to care if I lived or died.

Then I remembered the little bag. The ties had wrapped around my neck as I'd leaped for the hole. When I'd fallen, they must have tightened. That was what was cutting off my air. That was what was digging into my neck.

Knowing that should have calmed me, but I was in a panic, too blind to see reason. I writhed about, twisting like a gator, the memories overwhelming me as I dug into the cords and yanked. Hard. Harder.

It took the slamming of my hands on the dirt floor to fully let go the image of hanging from a rafter in an abandoned gymnasium that somehow still smelled of sweat and shoes. I was here. I was alive. I was not strangling.

My fingers scrambled for the threading and loosened them. I gasped for air. Swallowed it down like it was manna from the gods.

With the oxygen came a renewed alarm. I might not be at the end of a noose, but I was still in danger. I had to get out of there. The fae and that damned hound would come for the dark objects. It made sense now why they were there. Why the witch was packing when I'd found her.

Like me, they wanted the witch's cursed relics and had ambushed her for them.

I rolled over to my side, coughing dust from my mouth and hauling in threads of air that weren't nearly enough to fuel the motion I needed to find. It took monumental effort to force myself to calm down. To get to my knees. As I cracked my neck sideways, freeing my throat from the last knots of the golden strings holding the pouch around my neck, a miracle presented itself.

A light. Far away but a light. And beyond that, the shadows of trees.

A window.

My legs were going long before I could get my hands moving, and I ended up awkwardly trying to get my top half out of the way of the bottom. Luck held, and I got all my body parts working in synchronous motion.

I kept my gaze on the light, and the window, and the trees beyond, and I ran like hell. Like a rat from a sinking ship, I streaked across the basement, arms pumping, legs burning, until I tasted fresh air wafting in through the broken window.

But even that gust had the stink of death.

CHAPTER 6

IF I DIDN'T GET out of the basement and onto my motorcycle, I was going to die. If I died, untold innocents might come in contact with the objects held around my neck in that pouch, and the deaths wouldn't stop with me. The thought of the harm it would do to those unknown lives was the only thought that kept me going.

Past the exhaustion. Through the burning lungs. I wasn't a hero by any stretch. I was a horrible, unsalvageable person, but that kid, and the world around him, deserved to live without supernatural interference. I considered doing a run-up parkour pull to the window, but it had been so long since I practiced or had a chance to use it during a hunt that I reconsidered almost as soon as the thought entered my mind. With lives on the line, I didn't want to risk falling and getting chomped beneath those large teeth. I needed something to climb onto.

With the noxious smoke unfurling all around me, trailing me like a foul smell, I scrambled to find enough boxes and crates to pile in front of the window. A battered old desk hunkered beneath a pile of old rags, and I raced for it. I dragged it, rocking and rolling it beneath the casing.

The stink of wet dirt and mulch wafted up at me with each push and shove of the desk as I manhandled it into place. At least twice, a claw of smoke scratched into my lungs as I worked to position the furniture. I didn't want to think what the magic within it might be doing to me.

The desk fell short by at least a foot, but it would have to do. I hopped on and fumbled for the lock on the window, knowing that I could at least pull-up that far.

Turned out, the hole in the window wasn't big enough to crawl through, and someone had painted the damn window shut. I scoured the area, looking for something to break through the glass. By the time my gaze fell on a heavy foot-high candelabra, shouting had begun upstairs. Heavy footfalls across the floor above me told me the ambush was heading for the exits.

They would fan out long before I got clear, and they'd be waiting for me around the perimeter of the house. It was now or never.

Frantic by now and feeling like someone was watching me, with the black smoke filling the basement and all but cutting off my air, I jumped down and sprinted for the candelabra. My lungs burned enough to sear my throat with each exhale. It was sheer determination that drove me, and by the time I had my hands around the candlestick and was hoisting it against my chest, the low-throated growl of the hound shuddered through the basement.

The distinct smell of grass on fire filled the space. I expected the hound to smell of sulfur and brimstone, but this scent was pleasant. It reminded me of spring visits with my country cousins who burned their fields to keep the soil fresh and avoid out-of-control burns later in the season. As though wafting through long fronds of ferns and dried grass, a cinnamon fragrance rolled across the dank floor toward me. Such peaceable scents. Such a sense of comfort.

But it was all a ruse, like the witch's rolling thunder and kraken. I knew if I turned around, that the hound would be right there behind me. I knew I shouldn't look.

Except I just couldn't help myself.

The beast was larger than it seemed upstairs. The thing stood several paces away but within easy swatting reach. It would just have to swipe its front paw lazily at me, and its claws would tear my stomach to tatters.

It watched me swallow as fear swamped my mouth, and when it licked it lips and—I swear to God—leered at me, I shuffled slowly backward, cradling the candelabra as I moved. I wished I'd taken that chance to run up to the window and pull myself up, parkour style, because now, I realized I'd wasted far too much time messing with the desk and cartons.

"Easy," I whispered to the hound. "We don't have to do this."

Its hackles raised at the sound of my voice. The gaze that had seemed to glow earlier like embers in a dying fire was now blazing with a sort of intelligence. Smoke and cinnamon and some other spice I couldn't name coiled in the air, an invisible pheromone that I knew was meant to draw me closer. To lure me the way a siren's song did a sailor. It blinked. Cocked its head.

Why in the hell wasn't it attacking?

At the same moment, the fae from above leaped down into the basement. The sound of his boots crunching on gravel and dirt freed the hound from its silent contemplation. I saw in its gaze the moment it decided to leap for me.

I pivoted sharply. Whether I was too quick for the hound or it had only given it a half-hearted effort, the beast managed to snap out and catch my arm as I pumped it backward in a bid to race for the desk. A trickle of blood, not a gush. Not a bad wound. Hopefully just a scratch. I kept running, hefting the candelabra above my head to borrow the energy of gravity for the moment I heaved it into the window.

By the time I landed on top of the desk, I was striking out with it and simultaneously covering my face with my other arm. Glass shattered, bringing with it a hail of shards and a tinkling sound as they struck the desk. Sharp pieces bit into my chest and scored my forearm.

There was no time to worry about cuts and abrasions. I hauled my ass through the window and heaved myself onto the grass. The pouch nearly strangled me again as I scooted along the turf on my belly to get my legs free.

Shadows moved with time-lapse speed over the tree line as those intruders raced to fan out around the house. For one second, the air felt charged with electricity. As I glanced toward the house, I saw one quick burst of purple light before the hound's face filled the broken window.

I rolled onto my shoulder, yanking at the pouch to pull it aside so I could push onto my feet without it tangling around my throat again. I caught the hound's eye once more before it forced itself through the window to chase after me. It shouldn't be able to fit. I was frozen for a moment, watching in horror as it squashed down like a mouse collapsing its frame.

By the time it managed to make it halfway through the window, I was already uncoiling my limbs and scrambling to my feet. My gaze cut a line straight to the nearest tree. My legs followed it unerringly without having to think.

It would take at least five minutes of a hard run to get to my bike. Five minutes with the hound chasing me the entire way. With fae fanning out around the grounds. With that purple blast of energy seeking me if I fell into a stray stream of light. But those five minutes were all I had.

My mind sped me along the same trail that had brought me to the witch's house way ahead of my legs. There had been an extensive herb garden. A gardening shed. I hadn't expected to carry back a cache of objects, and no matter that they were stuffed neatly into a magical bag; I wasn't entirely sure the pouch itself wasn't cursed too.

"Damn," I said, because it hadn't occurred to me until right then what I might do with the artifacts if I killed the witch making them. No telling what the damn things would do to me if I kept them in my possession too long. But I couldn't just drop the bag, either. And with the hellhound chasing me, I couldn't risk getting caught and having it taken.

I'd have to use my own terror-stricken streak across the property to distract the creature. But first, I'd have to stash the bag somewhere safe. Somewhere I could get to it easily later. If I lived.

Scanning the area as I sped across the turf to the garden, I scoured the troughs of soil in the hopes the smell of herbs would distract the hound and throw it off. Give me time to find a place to hide the pouch.

With the weight of the karambit against my thigh reassuring me I wouldn't be caught completely vulnerable, I paused for one moment, sighting the grounds, surveying everything in the time it took to gulp in one drag of air.

The city scape rose to my left, the glow of streetlights a warm invitation that ruined the star scape above it. Light pollution might be a hateful thing to stargazers, but at that moment, I was grateful to have it guide me through the property. As long as I stuck to the shadows, I didn't have to worry about the hound sighting me.

There. A garden shed cast a long shadow on the edge of the tree line. With an oblong shape just large enough for a full-grown woman to stand inside, it would be the first place they'd look for me, but that didn't mean it was useless. My initial inspection of the property had indicated a bin of some sort around the back.

In a burst of inspiration, I tore the lace corset off and scraped it over my skin, wiping away the goo left by the kraken as best I could, then tossed it to the side long before I met the shed. My breasts goose pimpled as the air hit them. I didn't relish speeding across the grounds with them jostling like puppies wrestling each other, but that was the least of my concerns.

I just hoped the hound would follow that scent of me left on the corset and give me the time I needed to get to my bike and motor away.

A quick glance over my shoulder as I ran, breasts bare and prickled with cold, I raced for the shed. The pouch had pulled off into my hand as I'd slipped free of the corset, and it dangled from my fingers. The shed smelled of rat shit and urine, and its door was a wide open invitation, a block of shadow in an already dark yard.

I had no intention of going inside the shed. Inside, I'd be trapped.

Too many scenarios flitted through my mind about what they might do if they caught me, but one thought overrode them all. The objects had to be disposed of. Now.

My fingers ran over my pants as I moved. I needed to empty my pockets of anything I'd taken from the witch. The stone I'd snatched from hand as she died was still tucked inside somewhere. I'd have to drop that into the bag and leave it behind too. With any luck, I could return for everything later.

I ducked behind the building, searching frantically for the plastic bin I'd spied during my initial survey.

The bin was still there. In the shadows, it had no color, but it looked like any other garden variety storage bin available from garden centers. I yanked open the cover and blew out a breath of relief to see simple grain and bird seed, and as luck really would have it, a sweater on top. With the disquieting thought that Lilah probably used the sweater for cold nights as she gathered ingredients for her spells, I opted to believe it was free of black magic.

I'd not seen a single bird on the property, so I doubted the witch had been a bird watcher of any kind. I didn't want to think of what she might be baiting with the seed. I didn't have the luxury of questioning anything right then except whether I could yank it over my head fast enough to get the hell out of there before the hound caught my scent again.

I pulled out the sweater and hauled it over my head. One more plumb into my pocket to extract the stone. I jammed it into the pouch, opening it just enough to push the gem through the mouth, then cinched it closed. I shoved the whole thing into the depths of the bin, scooping seed over the top for good measure.

All of it, the burying of the pouch, the dressing with the sweater, the frantic look over my shoulder, all took mere seconds, but it felt like forever. My breath was a rasp in my ears. Everything had grown too quiet.

Ears straining for any telltale sound that I'd been spotted, I eased the bin closed. The hiding spot wasn't great, but it was the best I could do under the circumstances. If I got caught, at least the relics would be safe. I hunkered low beside the bin, confident I'd done what I could, scanning the grounds for any signs of ambush.

A snuffling sound came from beyond the shed around the garden. The hound must have taken the bait. I hoped it had found the corset and tore it to shreds. The damn thing still made my skin itch just thinking about it. I could almost feel the tightening of the laces cutting off my air.

But at least without the corset glamoring me to look like a man, I might just be able to pass as an innocent passerby and not the person they'd faced in the witch's lair. Providing I got to the edge of the property without being seen. Then, it was all promised land.

I scanned the yard from behind the shed. Shadows crawled the property as the men searched for me. The fae with the greasy smile stood on the stoop with his hands planted on his hips, confident his pet would bring me to heel. Watching. Waiting.

But there was no sign of the hound breaking free of the garden. That sent a tingle of warning prickles up and down my spine. My gaze trailed to the house one last time. It no longer looked like a bungalow. Instead, a mansion stood in its place, sporting glass from top to bottom, providing the witch a full view of her property on all sides and all levels.

The windows I'd heard breaking now proved to be large banks of floor to ceiling plate glass.

"Seen me coming, did you, bitch?" I muttered beneath my breath. No wonder she had time to conjure up that kraken and boggart.

It didn't matter now. She was gone. She couldn't harm anyone else. Whatever happened to me now didn't really matter. If I lived through the next few moments, I'd come back to retrieve the sack and destroy the contents. I told myself I needed to live that long, at least. Maybe I'd send Gideon and Shea to dispose of the body if the fae hadn't befouled it already in some way.

When I thought they weren't looking in my direction, I loped low and fast over the rest of the property without looking back. In moments, I'd retraced my steps all the way to where I'd parked my bike. A quick, rifling check for my karambit to satisfy myself it was still sheathed to my thigh. I straddled the seat and rolled silently out of the cul de sac. I wasn't about to take the time to pull out my bra and jacket from the saddlebags. I wanted out. Clean.

I only engaged the engine when I was sure I'd look like any other motorist to those who no doubt still roamed the property looking for a human man.

I grinned as the engine growled its agreement. I'd done it. It had been a tricky job, but I'd taken her out. By myself. No need to call Gideon. No need for the Graves chick or her partners. Me. Alone.

Part of me wanted to gloat, and part of me just wanted to sit back and sip on a good dram of quality tequila, grease the internal gears that were grinding away like rusty hinges.

What I really wanted was something stronger than booze, but that was the old Ava. I hadn't had a hit of anything stronger than tequila in months. Long enough to recognize and avoid my triggers, but not so long that my mouth didn't water at the thought of a hit.

I didn't think there would ever be enough time between that moment and this to never want a hit of Bloodmist again. But I persevered. Every day was a victory.

So, as though the wheels beneath me knew my mind better than I did, the bike angled itself automatically toward Gideon's house. Gideon had introduced me to Bloodmist. Gideon was the one I'd want to gloat to.

He deserved a visit, I thought. After all he'd done to me tonight, these weeks, my entire life, he deserved to hear how I'd taken out the witch he thought needed an army.

Maybe Shea would be there with him, cuddling on his ratty sofa because I'd been foolish enough to push them back together. I even hoped she'd be there. Maybe then they could both see it would take more than a sex kitten with a little gymnastics training to replace Ava Ashe.

And if I found Gideon's stash of Bloodmist while I was shoving it in their faces, all the better.

I took back streets and back-tracked several times before taking the final, direct route to my ex's place. Just in case the hound was still on my trail. Gideon also lived in a cul-de-sac, same as the witch, but unlike Lilah's property, his was one of several ranch-style houses on the outskirts of the city. I had to cross my own scent trail several times and used up at least twenty more minutes of my time doing so, but I didn't mind. Whatever it took, I was willing to do it. It was a chance to clear my head. One more opportunity for me to undo the knot in my chest.

But for the entire ride, my entire body crawled with the sensation of being watched. Like God or Kit was waiting in the shadows for me to pick up a joint or a drink and leap out at me to yell they'd caught me. Or maybe it was the hellhound, finally scenting the real me after abandoning the chase of the hatefully itchy corset.

Whatever it was, by the time I pulled onto the street that would take me to Gideon's, I had seriously creeped myself out.

It didn't help that the witch's sweater I'd found and pulled on was itchier than the damn corset. First thing I was going to do was burn the thing and dig out my own T-shirt. Or maybe I'd burrow in Gideon's closet and find something there. It just might be fun to think of Shea watching me make a beeline for her lover's bedroom closet, showing I knew him as well, if not better, than she did.

I cut the bike's engine when I pulled up to his garage. A light came on inside. I knew it wasn't Gideon turning on a light, but rather a spell he'd purchased to make it seem like he was in one part of the house when he was in another.

The strategy had saved his life plenty of times already. One of those being from me the day I'd found out about Shea in the first place.

A breeze lifted the wet hair off the back of my neck that had come free of my ponytail, and I blew out a long breath. He was going to be pissed I was here. He was always pissed when someone intruded on his privacy. And after I'd lifted his corset from his bag in the bar, I doubted he'd be anything but surly.

Except for me and Shea and maybe one or two other trusted people, Gideon kept to himself. It had taken me months to convince him to take me on as a trainee, and months after that, to seduce him. My lips pursed at the thought of how hard I'd had to work when this Shea seemed to get into his pants with a wave of her glorious blonde hair.

If I was honest with myself, I'd probably only thought I was seducing him. The whole time, he was probably grooming me, and I'd not realized it. Not that it would have mattered. I was hopelessly in love with him the moment he staked the vampire that had cornered me at a stoner party. The loner, hermit habits he kept were just a bonus.

He surrounded his property with cedar trees and flowering shrubs that grew thick and high so that no mundane part of society would guess what went on in the confines of his property.

Now, at mid-summer, those bushes held lush foliage and flowers that emitted a fragrance so thick they would cause an instant headache to anyone sensitive to florals. Beyond his property in the back, several empty lots stretched out into a lush thicket of trees. I knew he'd used his inheritance to buy all that space, and he'd paid dear money to have it all spelled by a goblin into discouraging visitors. Past that, the perimeter of the city's massive park stretched out long enough to give him more privacy than a man of his means should have.

I had a feeling he wouldn't let me in. No matter. I was practically boiling to see him.

I strode with purpose toward his garage and not the house because I knew he'd be hunkered down in his hunter cave like he often did at this time of night, video chatting with the members of the hunters' network led by Joy and Terry Sharpe. Two pretty uppity hunters who didn't think I had what it took to be part of their gang. Leaders who thought Shea would fit right in.

To hell with them. They were all the way in Lincoln, Nebraska, and I was here in Manhattan. And if Shea was inside, I was going to give her a piece of my mind, too. In fact, I hoped she was there.

I was almost halfway to the garage when something caught my eye several yards away. A shadow that shouldn't have been there. I knew the area well. Hell, I'd ran naked in it to the hot tub out back so many times I knew every current of air.

That shadow was not part of the neighborhood.

When it blinked and red coals burned out from the hulking mass of it, I knew exactly what it was.

Somehow, the hellhound had found me. And I'd drawn it right into Gideon's safe haven.

Chapter 7

There should have been no way that hound could track me, and yet there it was.

In the seconds I caught sight of it moving from the trees, my mind raced through the path I'd taken to get here, and came up short of any evidence it could follow. It shouldn't have been possible. Not all this way. Not after all the streets and side turns I'd taken.

As slowly as I could, I reached for my karambit, knowing if it came to hand-to-hand battle, I was sorely under-weaponed to fight that thing. It was huge. If it was the same size as it had been in the basement of Lilah's mansion, I'd eat the damn corset that I'd dropped back in her garden. I didn't need to measure. I knew it was bigger. Growlier. Angrier.

I needed magic.

Or I needed speed.

I only had one of those things.

In the milliseconds it took me to assess that, I also knew that I had just enough time to know that no matter how close I was to the door of the bunker beneath the garage, I wasn't near enough to make it inside.

Racing for the house would be suicide. I had no doubt the door was locked and I'd be left on the step, hammering away while Gideon watched me from the monitors in his bunker. I had to run for the garage or not run at all. And then I'd have to hope Gideon would pull the latch and let me through.

"Alright, big boy," I muttered to the hulking shadow of the hound as it closed in. "If you're coming, then you best bring your A game."

I slid the knife from its sheath with no more sound than a whisper in the dark. Pivoting to face down the shadow still creeping from the bushes, I scanned the tree line to make sure nothing else waited within the shrubs. The hound had cleared the trees by then, as well as the flowering shrubs, and was advancing with a confident air reminiscent of a man striding into a room where everyone knew him.

I waved the beast forward.

"Come for me, then," I said.

It paused, one leg lifted like a hunting dog, and I could swear it canted its head at me. Sentient, my brain whispered. That damn thing had human faculties.

Years of training and instinct opened up the entire world of Gideon's yard for me in the next moments. My vision expanded so that the fronds of the cedar trees at the property line to my left waved gently in my peripheral vision. I memorized their movements so fast, I'd know the moment they let out a second intruder, should the fae who owned the hound decide to stroll on through.

My nostrils flared to catch the scent of flowers and separate them from that of hound. I heard the crunch of its teeth as they ground together, clenched to keep all the tension tightly wound, the energy stored until it streaked for me.

Swinging the blade to its balance point, I let it lay backward in my grip, the blade tucked against my fore-arm, as I considered the reason the thing might not smell like sulfur the way a hellhound should, why it was wait-ing with its teeth clenched in an expression that looked very human and very much like it was grinning.

"Well," I said to the hound. "What are you waiting for? A red carpet?" I planted my feet. Braced myself, letting my knees stay elastic so I could pivot or kick when need-ed. Hands up, chin down. Gideon's voice played in my mind, correcting my posture real-time.

The hound's hackles bristled. Its foot fell to the turf. A short of chuffing laughter came from its throat. My heart stuttered, but I didn't move. Not yet. Moving now would just tease out the predator in it.

The embers of its eyes flared. I sent all the energy I had into the muscles of my thighs. I put my weight on my heels, balancing there. Waiting. Breath coming in long, slow, focused intakes.

I held my posture, waiting while the currents of fra-grance danced around me. My blood pressure squeezed out several fast rushes of blood into my veins, and I heard the work it was doing by the thudding behind my ears. When I swallowed, there was no liquid to dispel.

I knew the instant the wait was over. The air shifted. A sort of electricity crackled all around me.

Bouncing onto my toes like a boxer, I braced myself.

Unexpectedly, instead of rushing me, the hound took measured steps. Strong, muscled legs and massive forepaws ate up the distance between us as I wavered, the deliberation of its movement holding me fast in indecision. Should I stand my ground or run for it?

Through the darkness of the evening, those eyes glowed, and damn if they didn't look like they knew me.

My fingers uncurled and curled again around the handle of my knife as I eyed the creature. Maybe it wasn't sure I was the same mortal it had chased from the witch's house. Maybe without the corset, without the magical bag, I just looked like any other human.

Before either of us could decide, the door to the garage flew open, and light flooded the driveway.

"What in the hell is going on, Ava?" Gideon demanded.

I didn't have to answer. The moment he saw my rigid posture and the way I was angled toward his yard, refusing to give him my full attention and tear my gaze from the hound, he cursed.

"Oh, shit on a stick," he said. "You brought company."

I kept my eye on the hound, deciding it was indeed sentient, and was ruminating over whether it should eat me or run.

"I hope you have the kettle on," I said without turning around.

"Filled with a steaming pot of whoop-ass," Gideon drawled.

I raised my hand with the blade to my lips, touching my finger to my mouth. The hound's head lowered as though it were listening. It blinked, shutting out those lights in his eyes for a second before turning them onto Gideon. I didn't need the full light of day to know what sort of expression played over my ex's boyish face. He scraped back his brown locks with a hand I knew was calloused from hours of training and years of fighting. He'd be scowling if his tone was any indication.

"What did you do to have a hellhound on your heels, Ava?"

As if he didn't know. He'd practically goaded me into killing the witch. With Gideon standing there as backup, I felt confident enough to take my eye off the hound and look his way. Gideon's eyes were glued to the shadow that had just then begun to back away into the thicket of trees around the property. Retreating.

"Oh, so now you're scared," I muttered to the disappearing bulk. I turned to pull my shirt and bra from my saddlebags because the witch's sweater was almost as itchy as the corset. A rummage through, though, proved the garments were not inside. I sighed. Probably fallen out when I'd yanked out the damn corset, and lying right out in the open on the cul-de-sac's pavement. No wonder the hound had my scent. I'd given it everything it needed to track me.

I was straightening up when I noticed Gideon had stormed into the driveway, aiming all his ire at me with an extended hand that suggested he planned to yank me by the elbow.

Right. And I was going to just let him do that.

I met his thrust and twisted along with him, using the leverage of his movement to heave him sideways and to the ground at my feet just the way he'd taught me.

He landed with a thud on the grass, his knees splayed outward. His slouch hat slipped free and lay beside his hand. With a grunt, he grabbed for it, bunching it against his chest.

I planted my hands on my hips as I looked down at him. "I know your moves, remember?" I said.

He looked up at me, draping the back of his hand over his forehead. the material of the hat all but shielding his face. "You used to love my moves."

"Don't turn this into something sexual, Gideon," I said. "Not now. Not with...Just don't."

I meant to bring Shea into the protest, because I knew she was probably lurking behind the curtains watching every move, but then my mind wandered to a delicious memory of him and me in his six-foot tub, a bottle of champagne and a tray of strawberries between us. And the hurt and fury all welled up into my throat, choking off my air.

"You think I'm flirting?" he said in a wheezy voice. "When you attack a man for trying to distract the beast about to munch down on your ragged ass?" He tried to roll over onto his side, but it was obvious I'd knocked a bit of wind out of him.

The man was a callous bastard at times, and he'd broken my heart in more ways than I wanted to remember, but he looked so damned feeble lying there, all the guilt and shame and—dammit—still hot as fuck energy wrapped around him. I couldn't help the twinge of sympathy, no matter how mad I was at him.

I reached down to offer him my hand, regretting my hasty attack. "Come on," I said. "You know you're getting too old for this shit."

He swatted my hand away, and as if his forty-year-old self had something to prove, arched his back and flipped onto his feet to face me. His scowl was clearly on display in the light that spilled from his garage door. He yanked the hat onto his head, pushing the cuff of it so that it landed mid forehead.

I waited for him to pull his T-shirt down as well, give him some dignity before I said, "You practically tasked me to go after that witch."

"Why would I do that, Ava?" he asked softly.

I bristled at the insinuation that he was innocent. "Oh, I don't know, maybe to teach me a lesson. Maybe because you're screwing the new girl and want her to look good to the Network. You told me she's got mad skills. That she's younger." This last hurt my throat. "You said she was better than me."

"What I said," he growled in that smoky voice of his that sounded as raspy as the stubble he wore like a uniform on his chin. "Was that some dark magic witch was going to get what was coming to her."

I nodded. "And she did." I rubbed my knuckles over my chest.

"And brought her damn hellhound here to my place like a rookie. What the hell, Ava? Because you're jealous of a girl I'm helping. Helping—" He sliced the air with his hand to make the point. "You go off all half-cocked—like you always do, might I add—and you nearly get yourself killed trying to take out a witch who by all rights would need an army to kill. And you have the nerve to blame me? It's your own guilt that sent you there, not me. You ever think how badass a witch has to be to have a hellhound for a familiar?"

I crossed my arms over my chest, tired of placating him already and refusing to take the bait of what, exactly, Shea was or wasn't to him. "That hound was not hers," I started to say, but then decided he didn't need to know the details.

He hadn't earned them. "What's the problem, anyway? You scared the beast off, didn't you?"

"Actually," said a voice from behind us. "I think that was me."

Every inch of my spine tried to crawl out from beneath my skin at the voice. For an instant, I was sure the fae from the witch's house had found me.

I pivoted fast, my hand on the karambit, sweeping it in a neat arc around to my chest, sharp side out. Ready to strike.

"Stand down, Ava," Gideon said.

My feet shuffled back together immediately, the result of a long habit of taking orders from Gideon without question. A scowl of self-recrimination tugged at my lips. In the early days, that reaction might have saved my life. Now, it pissed me off. I hadn't realized it was still so ingrained that I'd respond so swiftly. I gave him a long side-eye before sliding my gaze over the stranger.

I recognized in him the same energy as the fae who had ambushed me at Lilah's, something I'd somehow missed when I'd met him in the tavern with all the predatory energy of vampire stink cloaking my senses.

Backlit just enough to show red highlights in his chestnut hair, the rest of the light spilled over his face in ways that any woman would want to be seen by a lover over a candlelight dinner. A warm glow clung to all the right curves in his face. Blue eyes looked charged with internal light.

I almost gasped in pleasure.

"You," is what I finally decided on.

He stuck his hand out in greeting, and I found myself reaching for it without thinking. Yup. Those callouses were hard and deep as they met the toughest parts of my skin, whispering over places that were still soft enough to feel touch at all. A warrior's hands. Bigger than Gideon's and covered in battle-hardened flesh. Despite myself, I imagined each callous scratching over my bare body.

Except I'd sworn off men, hadn't I? Swallowing down the rush of lust was a matter of self-preservation.

The stranger grinned at me, showing a glimpse of slightly pointed incisors, smaller than a vampire's and more like a cat's. If he understood the effect he was having on me, he was totally milking it by flashing me that smile. Not that I minded; It lit his face and chased away the brooding expression that made him look almost brutal and boxy. Like a brick shit house, my father used to say.

"Stone," he said, giving my hand a gentle pump. "I remember you from the bar. I hope you don't mind that I asked the hound to leave. My natal magics hold sway over feral animals. I thought he seemed a bit too obsessed with your scent."

"Mind?" I said, shaking my head. "I'm god-damned grateful." I was aware that I was still holding his hand, but I couldn't let it go for the life of me. I tried to tell myself it was because there had been a peculiar note to his tone when he'd mentioned the hound's reaction to my scent, but I knew better.

Gideon slammed his shoulder into mine. "Jesus," Gideon said. "Wipe the drool off your mouth, Ava. And for Pete's sake, don't thank him. You wouldn't want to be indebted to any fae, let alone this one.""

I rolled my eyes at my ex, but he was right. I did need to rein in the gawking teenager vibes. I was about to shoot back some scathing retort, but he was already turning his back to us and heading toward the door to his garage. He waved at us to follow. A quick glance sideways, and

Stone's grin seemed much different. It was frozen there as he watched Gideon's back.

I had the feeling he didn't like Gideon much. Or maybe he didn't like Gideon's honest assessment. Whatever the reason, I pulled my hand from his. Hot or not, Stone hadn't saved my ass or knew the scars it wore. Gideon had. So Stone's reaction to my mentor raised a few alarm bells.

"I know better than to thank a fae," I said, more to Stone than to Gideon, because the fae was watching me, a general assessing his quarry. Or was that a predator eying its prey? I wasn't sure. All I knew what that my spine was doing all sorts of different kinds of tingling. And that, too, raised alarm bells.

"Smart woman," he said, the corners of his eyes crinkling. A punch to the gut was what that look was. By the time Stone offered a casual shrug as though he was apologizing for being Fae but couldn't care less about being brutal enough for Gideon to have shot out a warning flare in my direction, Gideon was already reaching to adjust a camera in the soffit.

It was my turn to watch him. "After you," I said to Stone, because for some reason, I did not want him behind me.

Gideon turned around at that and halted with his hand on the camera. "Think again, Ava," he said as he caught me angling myself to pass by him. "I didn't invite you in."

My brow furrowed over my eyebrows. "I'm not a vampire, Gideon. I can come and go as I please. Besides, you did so."

His eyebrows climbed nearly to his gorgeously wavy hairline. "I did not. And it was intentional."

"Because Shea is inside and you don't want me to see her, maybe?"

I thought I'd get a rise out of him with that, but he merely waved at my bike. A most unsatisfying reaction. "Stone and I have business. Now, get on your silver bullet and get out of here. I should shoot you for bringing that beast to my property."

"If you're thinking of putting bird shot in that rusty over-and-under again, you can forget it. I dunked the hot steel into a tub of cold water. I'm surprised you didn't notice the banana peel barrel on it."

He glared at me, his jaw tight. "I noticed."

My arms went out sideways, innocent and confused. "So, what are you saying? I should have let that hell-hound follow me to my apartment? Let it tear some poor innocent resident to bits?"

His glower rivaled the light from the door. "Go home, Ava."

I cocked my hip, one more spiteful jab to the ready because he still hadn't answered and I was dying to know. "Too busy showing Shea the ropes to shelter an ex?"

He sighed. "Shea is not here. I don't know why you dislike her so much."

My mouth worked with all the things I wanted to say, but I abandoned the argument because I was just so damned happy she wasn't hiding behind the curtains watching me.

"You're going to send me home, knowing that damn thing has the scent of me? Knowing it's still out there, probably lurking in the shadows, waiting to jump me?"

"You're a big girl," Gideon drawled, his hand dropping to scrutinize the data card in his palm, something he'd obviously pulled from the camera. He peered up at me briefly. "I'm sure you can handle it."

My lips pressed together. Whether I could handle it or not, wasn't the point. "And what about those cursed objects the witch was spelling?" I asked. "Are you sure you don't want to know what I found?"

He paused in his inspection. Stone's gaze slid over me surreptitiously, a look of surprised interest on his face. He did a good job of catching it and reining it in, but I noticed just the same. Some communication moved between the two men. They obviously thought I didn't notice. I held my ground.

"Come on, then," Gideon said.

I followed behind them both, pulling the door closed behind me. Gideon nudged us ahead of him with a jerk of his chin. I knew he didn't want us to see the spell he put back in place over the door lock. He trusted no one. Not even me.

The garage was a misnomer. Gideon didn't own a car. The inside had concrete floors and reinforced walls. Work benches lined the far wall as though a mechanic worked there, but they were loaded down with tech. Shelves lined another two walls with pegged weapons that hung on boards outlined in black. Gideon's OCD was bad enough that my seat-of-the-pants style of hunting made it even harder for us to get along.

The remaining wall was clear of anything but the man-door and the garage door. I waited till Stone moved in front of me to stride up toward the corner of the garage where I knew a glamored staircase would lead us to the tunnel that housed Gideon's real man cave. That was an underground bunker with several tunnels leading to strategic parts of the city and various manholes and drains.

Gideon trailed along behind us both. The back of my neck tingled in warning. Just who my cells thought was a threat, I wasn't sure, but I hung back and let him pass me because...well, because I didn't trust anyone either.

"You see your sister lately?" he asked as he brushed by.

It was a jab with enough force to almost stop me in my tracks. Intentional. Aimed. But I refused to take the bait, no matter how badly my chest burned at his off-hand comment. Instead, I rolled my eyes as though I'd expected the barb.

"If that's the best dig you can think of to spite me, then please do. Bring it on."

His dark chuckle did nothing to assuage the immediate pang of guilt and shame that he knew his comment would raise. I couldn't let that particular sleeping dog lie. Maybe he knew that, too.

"You know we don't talk anymore because she hates you, right?"

He said nothing to that, because he knew it was true. I'd been a handful before my parents died. When Kit took over my guardianship afterwards, I was worse. A teen with a penchant for pot and a wild streak was nothing to the grieving seventeen-year-old who developed a taste for harder drugs and street fights.

My pursuit of a man twice my age did not endear Gideon to my sister after all that, especially not when he took me up on my advances after I dogged him to near exhaustion.

I examined my nails. "Kit thinks you're a pedophile."

He swung around at me, a familiar-looking hatchet in his grip. "Say it again and I'll take your head off."

I blinked at him, aware that Stone had paused and was watching with interest. "Reason number two for why she hates you," I said, without a lick of fear in my voice.

"Being?" he asked, as though he wasn't brandishing a sharp weapon at me.

I lifted one eyebrow. "You're too violent."

He harrumphed, but dropped the hatchet to his thigh. "She knows you, right?"

All during the exchange, Stone watched quietly, no doubt trying to decide if he should excuse himself. That he didn't, made me even more suspicious. "Do you have siblings, Stone?" I asked.

He hesitated long enough that I had a feeling he didn't want to give up any information about his personal life, but then he said, "I have brothers."

"Are any of them prudish assholes?" I asked, thinking of the last words I'd leveled at my sister before she told me not to bother with her anymore.

Stone grinned broadly, showing those teeth that had just a hint of sharp point to them. "We're all assholes," he said.

His gaze lingered on my throat, and I wondered if he was thinking about burrowing those little fangs into my neck. I felt my stomach tighten reflexively.

"But I wouldn't call a single one prudish," he quipped. "Why do you ask? Are you in the market for a lover?"

CHAPTER 8

I WOULD NOT GET into a battle of barbs with a fae who was so obviously goading me, I was sure he wanted to see how fast I'd grab the bait.

Instead, I hemmed quietly to myself and waited until he had fallen into step with Gideon, so I could watch him move.

Yup. Definitely a warrior of some sort. His muscles bunched under his shoulders, knotting together and uncoiling with each stride. Ahead of him, Gideon had the same sort of movement going on beneath the gray T-shirt he favored, but his neck was smaller, with obvious hunching that came from drinking too much and folding over monitors day in and out. It had been years since he'd gone on a hard hunt and it showed.

It struck me that he was aging. A sort of pang tightened my throat.

Gideon yanked open the door and stepped aside to let Stone pass. He waited until I stopped beside him before he held the hatchet out to me.

"Where's my shirt?" he said.

I took the hatchet and let the heft of it sit in my grip for a long moment. It was a weapon he'd gifted to me at the end of my training, one he'd taken back when I left him. I was surprised he was giving it back now.

"Well," he prodded.

I lifted my gaze to his. My mind ran screaming toward the moment in the tavern when I'd stolen the thing from his duffel bag. "I don't know what you're talking about."

"My shirt. The one I showed you when I ran into you at the tavern. The one I paid a ransom for from a goblin. Where is it?"

"You said you stole it," I countered.

His mouth twitched. "Where is it?"

"Maybe you gave it to Shea," I said, eyes narrowed and voice filled with heat.

"Is that what this is all about, Ava?" he asked. "Is that why you stole my shirt and rampaged over to Lilah's house when you should have waited for reinforcements? Because you're jealous?"

I sucked the back of my teeth. "I'm not jealous of Shea. She's not half the hunter I am. I went because you taunted me with that witch. Saying she was so powerful she'd need an army to take her out, that if we didn't do something soon, we'd all be in a mess. What did you think I'd do? Sit back and let the bitch hurt more kids?"

"I thought you'd do the sane thing and wait for more hunters."

I snorted. "Right," I said. "That's exactly what you thought when you started filling my head with all the nasty things that bitch was doing. It had nothing to do with the fact that you wanted me to fail so you could send Shea in to help me." I waved my hand in the air, mimicking his dramatic style. "Dear Gods, Shea, if we don't get to Ava, she's going to out and out get herself killed, and the last thing I need is for the ghost of a rogue hunter with a death wish haunting my lair." I planted my hands on my hips as I glared at him. "Well, I didn't need Vicki Graves and her boy-toys and I didn't need Shea. I took care of Lilah all by myself."

His eyebrows climbed an inch up that flat brow straight to his buzz cut. "Oh, my God. You waited till I had to piss and then you stole that shirt right out of my duffle bag so you could go out and be a hero."

"It was a fucking corset, Gideon," I said, matching the in his tone. "Your shirt was a lacy, beautiful, and itchy piece of fabric with boning that I can still feel digging into my ribs. Is that what you're into now? Women's clothing? Or was it for Shea? Because if that's the case you can have it back. I'd love to see her traipsing into a nest of vampires scratching her boobs bloody."

"People," Stone said, interrupting my tirade as he poked his head back into the garage around the door frame. "Does it really matter right now?"

I cut him with a look. "Stay out of this."

Gideon, however, clamped his mouth closed and held up his hand in surrender. "Just tell me where it is, Ava." His voice was weary. Resigned.

I wasn't satisfied, though. Not with resignation. I wanted victory. For once. Just once, I wanted him to admit defeat.

He certainly never made me feel as though I was Network material. He always kept us, kept me in the shadows. "Is that why you're giving me my hatchet back?" I asked. "Because you think I'll cough up your precious corset quicker if you show me you're not a petty bastard?"

I brushed past him, holding the hatchet at its balance point, and scanned his training room for the sheath.

"The hatchet was mine before it was yours," he said, that same resignation in his voice. "But yes."

"What was it doing in the garage in the first place?" I asked. "And why is it out of its sheath?"

He sighed. "I had some trouble with a few fae," he said and looked pointedly at Stone.

Without meaning to, I followed the direction of his gaze. Stone stood in front of Gideon's rock wall, a gargantuan thing that I'd hated with enough energy to incinerate an entire city during my early days. But one that seemed to interest Stone enough to have him staring up at it with his back to us. Listening, though. The very cant of his head suggested he was most eager to hear our discussion, no matter how much he protested that it was an annoyance. I knew Gideon had trailed my gaze with his, too. And that rankled for some reason.

I nudged Gideon, spite moving my arm. "Tell me he's single."

Gideon sighed. "Don't, Ava," he whispered. "It wouldn't be smart."

I swung my gaze to his. "Seriously, Gideon. Your shirt was a lace corset," I said, avoiding his comment. "It itched like hell." I rubbed my boobs with the heels of my hands for emphasis and his eye trailed to the witch's ugly sweater I'd pulled on when I stuffed the bag of cursed objects into the seed bin. I'd have to go dig out my T-shirt and replace it or I was going to have nothing left of my double-Cs by the end of the night.

"It was cotton," he said, correcting me. "And it was a shirt."

I eyed him, narrowing my gaze and holding his eye for several long moments.

"You cheated on me several times," I said in response. "And you still can't handle me wanting to screw another man."

"Where is my shirt?"

"What were you planning to attack with my hatchet?"

He tugged on my elbow, pulling me away from the rock-climbing wall and toward the heavy bag on the other side of the room. He watched Stone testing the foot and handholds as he spoke out of the corner of his mouth.

"I've got myself into a pickle. I need that shirt."

One of my eyebrows raised a half inch. "Is a pickle a little bit of trouble or a lot?"

His jaw seesawed back and forth. "It's quite a lot, actually."

I placed the hatchet on the workbench beside him thoughtfully, giving the room a scan as I checked for evidence of this pickle.

Beyond his shoulder lay his entire training room. A spar mat covered the corkboard floor in front of the boxing ring. On one side of the room, to his right and opposite the rock-climbing wall, he'd installed an ax throwing gallery with a wooden target and several dummies of various heights. A huge, ballistic mannequin swallowed dozens of wooden bullets and cold iron bullets alike. A knife stuck out of its shoulder, showing half an inch of a blade made of what I supposed was blacksteel, a type of metal I'd heard him speak of before but had never seen.

He'd been training Shea recently. My throat started to hurt.

I slid sideways an inch to take in the virtual reality equipment that he designed to simulate fighting various monsters. The goggles lay askew on the rack. But the strap was set too wide to fit a woman.

"What's going on, Gideon?" I asked.

Before he could answer, Stone approached us, his gaze locked on my face. I felt a flush creep up my neck, the likes I hadn't felt since I was a teenager. Since Gideon had come riding on a white horse to save me from a big, bad vampire. My heart squeezed at the memory, even as my mind whispered that the vampire hadn't been all that cunning. A few months of training and I could have easily taken him out.

"So, do we have a deal or not, Gideon?" Stone asked, his eyes only leaving mine to dip to my throat. Yup. Definitely sexual tension there.

The temperature in my cheeks rose enough to fry an egg, and because it flustered me more than I wanted to admit, I couldn't help plunging into the discussion as a distraction.

"Gideon doesn't make deals," I said, swiveling to take in the way he was fidgeting. "At least, he never used to." I turned on my mentor, eyebrows lifted in query. The least the man could do was explain himself.

He sighed pretty theatrically for a guy who didn't sigh very often. He was a do-er. A put your head down, eyes forward, kind of man. It took a few moments of awkward staring before he finally waved the both of us toward the inner sanctum of his man-cave, a place I never got to set foot into lest he take his favorite cattle prod to my legs.

Inside the four-by-six room, he'd installed several more monitors since the last time I'd been inside. The only difference between these and the ones spying on his property was that this one showed a cozy interior with warm, tobacco-colored walls.

"That's Slow Smoke," I said, crossing the space to tap the monitor that showed Joy Sharpe making one of the hunters a latte.

Her froth-art left something to be desired, I noticed. The ghost carved from the milk looked decidedly lop-sided. "Does Joy know you're spying on her?"

Stone came up behind me. The smell of him, like warm caramel, enveloped me like an embrace. I fought the urge to inhale deeply and drop my head back.

"Who is Joy Sharpe?" he asked almost too casually, even as he craned to look over my shoulder at the forty something redhead who owned the coffee shop beneath the Rio Grande.

I had no love for Joy and her merry band of monster ass-kickers, but I wasn't about to rat the network out to a fae I didn't know. Or any fae. If Gideon wanted to do that, it was his business. The last thing I needed was for one of the hunters to come hunting me out of vengeance. They already hated me.

Gideon snapped off several other monitors as he hustled around the room. No matter how fast he moved, he wasn't quick enough to keep me from seeing it wasn't just Slow Smoke he was watching. He had cameras rolling tape upstairs at the Rio Grande, a clubhouse right here in the city, and the Rot Gut Tavern where I'd run into him earlier in the day.

The fae's eyes narrowed as he spun to face Gideon along with me. "You asked me here because you said you were ready to pay. Is this ludicrous bit of espionage what you consider your payment?"

Stone's expression went hard, and I could swear Gideon's face blanched. He held up both hands as if in surrender, which made me triply suspicious. The Gideon I knew would eat glass shards before he surrendered to anyone.

"You've got me all wrong," he said. "Let's have a shot, OK? Calm down. Realize we're all on the same side here. Want the same thing?" He made a move to an in-wall cupboard and pressed the corner. It popped open to show a dark bottle of mezcal with a skull-shaped cap.

"What the hell is going on, Gideon?" I asked.

I was aware I'd taken several steps toward the door. Something was off. Something big. And my instincts had set my feet into action. Maybe he wasn't thrilled to see me, not because I'd brought the hellhound to his door, but because something had started to stink in the Denmark of his little haven.

Stone noticed the distance I'd moved before Gideon did. Another red flag. Noticed, and barred the door so I couldn't get out.

"Get out of my way," I said to him.

He canted his head. I felt a swirl of energy coiling about me, not unlike the time I'd met up with an incubus demon.

"I told you to move," I said.

"Ava," Gideon said, drawing my eye to him. He'd poured three shots and held them all bunched together in his hands. The blunt fingers corralling them neatly. "Have a shot. Ask your questions. I promise I'll answer."

I ran my gaze over the fae, who seemed nonplussed at my bristling glare. I noted he hadn't moved a single inch. The muscles in my jaw ached from clenching my teeth.

"Please, Ava," Gideon said.

I scored him with a suspicious glance. "You've never said please to me in the entire time I've known you. What's going on?"

He inclined his head toward Stone. "He's dark fae, Ava. Mafia. Shadow Court."

I dropped my head back, understanding dawning finally. I'd not met a fae before this one, but Gideon had not been lax in his lessons. He'd schooled me well. I didn't need more information to know this fae was dangerous.

"The damn glamor corset," I said.

The sound of his ass striking the soft cushion of the swivel chair confirmed my guess.

"I'm right, aren't I? This has something to do with that itchy damn bit of goblin-spelled lace."

Stone cleared his throat, drawing both Gideon's eye and mine to him. "It's fae magic," he said. "Not goblin. We just arranged for a goblin to sell it to him."

I swung on him. "So, go get it. No one here will stop you."

"You misunderstand," he said. "We don't want it back. I gave it to Gideon in exchange for a favor."

My spine went cold. Gideon looked feverishly miserable. "Favor?" I said in a pitch very unlike my usual timber. "From a fae? What did you do, Gideon?"

He shrugged. "A bit of trouble is all. Nothing I can't manage."

Stone's snort was barely audible, but I knew we both heard it. I stormed the few feet to Gideon and spun him around in the chair to face me. He didn't resist when I planted both hands on his forearms, pinning him there. If he saw the rage in my face, he didn't react.

"I'm not going to ask questions," I ground out. "You're just going to volunteer the information. You understand? Because I have a feeling Joy and the gang will happily put you to pasture once they hear what's going on here."

He shook his head. "You have no idea what's going on, Ava," he said. "I'm doing it to protect them."

My hand went to his throat so fast, I didn't realize I was going to move until his face started turning red. "This isn't protection," I whispered. "This reeks of extortion."

Stone snorted even as Gideon's gaze locked on mine. I squeezed again. He didn't resist.

He. Didn't. Resist.

"Fuck, Gideon," I said as I released my grip on his throat. "What have you got yourself into?" Pissed as I was at him, I wasn't angry enough to want to see him dead.

His hands remained on the armrests instead of rubbing his neck, which had to hurt. But that was Gideon. He wouldn't show me that weakness. "It is extortion, Ava," he said. "You're right about that. But it's not coming from me."

I straightened up as his gaze flicked over my shoulder toward Stone. Understanding lit its way through me. I swung slowly around to see the fae standing there with his arms crossed, a sly grin spread over his face. All of a sudden, he didn't look so attractive.

"Yeah," he said. "It's me. I made sure he had the Raiment of Roman because I thought he could use it. But it seems we have another candidate. A better one." He raked Gideon with a disappointed glance.

Gideon bolted from the chair then, all his natural bluster bristling over his entire body. "This has nothing to do with Ava. Leave her out of it."

Stone didn't move a single muscle to show he was the least bit affected by Gideon's anger.

"Your ex here owes the Shadow Court, Ms. Ashe," he said to me. "He agreed to complete one task for us, one that the Raiment of Roman was going to help him accomplish."

I shrugged. "His business, not mine," I said, trying to inflect a note of casual disinterest. Never show your cards, is what Gideon always told me. Hard as it was not to beg for more information, I feigned the apathy, all the while hoping that Gideon realized I wanted desperately to know what was going on.

"It was supposed to glamor me, to keep my identity secret," Gideon volunteered, but there was shame in his voice. Uncharacteristic and unnatural for him. I waited for him to clear his throat. "I need you to fetch it for me, Ava." He wouldn't hold my gaze. Not at all.

"Fetch it," I repeated in a tight voice. "As though I'm some common intern? Sure. I'll rush to do that right after I make your coffee. But tell me: exactly what are you going to do with it after I fetch it, Gideon?"

Stone was the one who answered. "He's not going to do anything with it now."

I pinched the bridge of my nose. "Seriously," I said. "The two of you are giving me a headache. I haven't slept for almost eighteen hours. Think we could move this confusing muddle along so I can hit the hay?"

A grin slid over Stone's mouth as he inclined his head with such grace he might have been an old world courtier. "Sure," he said. "It's really very simple. I need an assassin."

"An assassin?" I looked from him to Gideon and back again. "That's what he's going to do for you? That's the price of his favor?"

Gideon hung his head at the word favor because we both knew it was a euphemism for extortion, and the Network's safety was the price. Whatever he'd done to me, he was loyal to the cause. I knew he'd do anything to keep hunters everywhere safe, so that had to mean the Shadow Court had threatened to take out the entire network if Gideon didn't complete their one task.

As I mulled the information, sorting and discarding bits of detail to come to the conclusion that Gideon was indeed in a pickle, Stone had closed the few feet between us. It was fast. So fast I didn't see him move until he was there and that caramel fragrance washed over me again. I tasted it on my palate. Too sweet, I thought.

"He was going to be our assassin," Stone said. "Until about twenty minutes ago." He brushed at the sleeve of his suit as he watched me. "But not now."

"Because the ramen noodle vest of Ronnie is gone?" I asked.

Stone's expression went tight at my dry reference to his precious garment, but there was no evidence of his displeasure when he spoke. In fact, when the words exited his mouth, they sounded downright cheery.

"No," he said. "Not because it's gone, but because I've found another assassin."

"Oh," I said, thinking that things were coming up daisies for Gideon after all. With any luck, he'd have tossed Shea under the bus.

"Yes," Stone said. "Don't you want to know who?"

My eyebrows climbed to my bangs, and he smiled that same cocky smile.

"You," he said. "Since you took out a dark witch who, by your very account, required an army to neutralize, you'll be perfect."

CHAPTER 9

I WASN'T AN ASSASSIN; I was a hunter. Anyone who didn't understand the difference was going to get schooled. Jabbing my finger into Stone's chest, I tried to ignore how hard he felt beneath my fingertip.

"I kill creatures like you," I said. "I don't kill *for* you."

He grabbed my fingers, exerting enough pressure to ball them into a fist. I felt the buzz of a fine electrical hum all the way up to my elbow.

"Fine line," he said. "When you kill creatures like me, are you not a killer just the same? Some might call that an assassin."

That gaze was hard as diamonds, but I refused to back down, choosing to hold that gemstone gaze with a flinty look of my own.

"Fine line, but big difference. Assassins are sneaky pricks. When I come for you, you see my face."

He let go my hand and straightened his sleeve cuffs. "That's the point," he said. "It won't matter if the target sees your face. You'll be wearing the raiment."

Wearing that itchy piece of clothing? I'd rather go nude to my death, and that might just be what happened if I accepted this foolish job.

"Hell nope," I said. With a gesture toward Gideon, who was watching with interest and not a bit of indication that he would help me. "I wouldn't work on *his* terms, and I loved him. What in the hell makes you think I'll work on yours?" I sliced my hand through the air. "Forget it. Gideon is the better choice. Keep him onboard."

That was the time Gideon decided to lift his ass off the chair. "She's right," he said. "You can't trust her. And she's for shit when it comes to taking orders."

I swiveled my head in his direction, annoyance working its way through my nerves at his assessment, however accurate. "I'm going to ignore those comments because it benefits me."

He shrugged. "We both know it's true. You are shit at following orders. You went off half-cocked to the witch's house when I explicitly said—"

Before he could finish his sentence, I stormed the few feet to jam my finger into his chest, slamming him back down into the seat with a whoosh of air.

"I took that corset because you left it sticking out of your duffel bag when you went to take a leak. And as for what you explicitly said: I seem to recall you saying someone should take out that witch. Someone. Me." I thumbed my collarbone. "You were practically begging me to do it."

"I said the Hunter Network was on it. I said Vicki Graves and her reckless partners were on the case."

"Right. Reckless partners. I remember you saying that." I ticked off a checkmate in the air. "You might as well have waved a red flag in my face."

"You're not going," he ground out.

I gripped the armrests as I braced myself, all the better to aim my anger at him. "You don't tell me what to do anymore."

He shifted his weight from cheek to cheek, a sure sign he was doing everything he could not to point at me and force me to break his finger. I stepped back from the cage I'd made of the chair and he got up slowly, tugging down his shirt.

"No one tells you what to do, Ava," he said in a low voice as he shouldered around me and headed for one of the monitors. "That's your problem. It's what drove us apart in the first place, and it's what made Kit throw you out."

Fury licked at me as those words sunk in. He'd gone too far. It wasn't just the inference that our failed relationship was my fault, but that he'd bring up my sister meant he wanted to die.

I lunged at him, going for his balls with one hand, when he heard me coming and spun around. His defenses were almost too slow, but I expected he'd drop his hands to protect himself. His most prized possession. But at the last second, I spun, using my movement to hurl all the force I could into a clothes-lining motion with a snap of my elbow. He fell sideways with a grunt, catching himself on the counter that held the bank of monitors. One more shot, this time, a sweep of his legs and I threw my weight on him, straddling him and grappling his head between my hands.

His arms pinned beneath my knees, he did his best to buck me off. I might have slammed his head into the floor had Stone not plucked me from Gideon's supine form. I flailed, fighting to remove myself from his grip. The fae was damnably strong. And silent. I'd not even heard him come up behind me.

"Let me go," I growled.

He did, shoving me to the side and into the wall with enough force to make my teeth clamp down on my tongue. I tasted blood. Something flashed in Stone's gaze when I touched my lips to test for cuts.

"It's done," he said, his fists clenched at his sides. He dropped his gaze from mine. "I've chosen you." He sent a surly look in Gideon's direction. "I need the raiment."

Gideon glared at him and snorted. "You think she's the better choice because she sucker-punched me?" He rubbed the back of his head. "I wouldn't recommend her. She's uncontrollable. Reckless. She doesn't care if she lives or dies. You can't trust an assassin like that. You might as well serve her to the dark enforcer right now as send her in."

He probably expected me to feel stung over the assessment, and I did. Just not as badly as he might have wanted. Whoever the dark enforcer was, the threat meant nothing to me. It didn't seem to faze Stone either, except for the flare in his eyes that suggested he didn't like the enforcer. Not one bit.

Nevertheless, I lanced them both with a look that should have peeled the skin off their faces.

"And I refused." I crossed my arms over my chest. "It's your problem, Gideon. Not mine. Whatever you owe them, pay it like you agreed. Like a man."

His lifted brow said more than his words could. He thought I was being foolish. I didn't care. Running my hand over my shoulder to test for soreness, I pushed away from the wall.

"I'll get your damn shirt for you tomorrow. I'm exhaust-ed right now." I spared a glance at Stone, who was watch-ing my mouth move with every syllable. "Whoever Gideon is supposed to assassinate, he'll have the vest to protect his identity as you wanted. Just give me a beat, will you?"

"You're not listening," Stone said and Gideon snorted beneath his breath. Both Stone and I cut him a look before he turned back to me. "I've changed my mind. I want you."

My arms flew out to my sides, frustrated. "You're the one not listening. I pick my own hits."

"Spoken like a true assassin," Stone said.

I'd had enough. A glance at the only monitor still turned on showed the time by way of a bunch of swords spinning in circles around a clock face. It was nearly dawn. With any luck, the fae surrounding the witch's property were long gone. That meant I had to leave. Now. Tired as I was, I needed to get that sack of cursed items before some inno-cent found it and started handling all the goodies inside.

I ran my hand over my ponytail, smoothing out the hairs and tossing it over my shoulder. A long exhale. Planted my hands on my hips. "Listen, why don't we take a break? I shouldn't have come here, I admit. But now, I'm tired. If you're not going to give me a bunk for a few hours, then at least let me look for a new shirt so I can be on my way." I plucked at the sweater. "This one is giving me hives."

Gideon's surly look punctuated his tone. "You don't have anything left here," he said. "I burned it all."

I dropped my head back with a chuckle. "Oh, please. You don't have the stones to burn my clothes. We both know you run the dirtiest of the lot all over your nose on a daily basis."

Without waiting for him to give me permission, I strode from the bunker up to the garage and then headed for the lawn leading toward the house. He let me go. Whether it was because he was still lying on the floor or because he was tired of arguing didn't matter.

Pre-Dawn had pulled a pink boa over the tops of the buildings by the time I reached the yard. A squirrel skittered past the garbage cans. The air felt light and fresh. I inhaled deeply, filling my lungs with the rawness of dawn before too many vehicles could pollute the air with diesel and gas fumes.

It was during this rather large lungful that my lungs...hitched. For a moment, curiosity lead the panic, and I waited far too long to realize my lungs weren't expanding as fully as usual. My hand went to my chest instinctively, then climbed to my throat when I realized I couldn't take in a breath at all.

I stopped mid-step, several paces from the house, and tried again.

This time, every muscle in my throat strained to suck in drafts of air. Tried. And failed.

My lungs burned. Prickles of black sizzled behind my eyelids.

Oh, my sweet baby Jesus. I was going to pass out. Shadows crept in from the sides of my vision. I had just enough time to pivot, thinking I could run back to the garage to get Gideon's attention before I crumpled completely onto the driveway and hurt something bad.

In that short time, I had one thought. Stone. He'd done something to me.

A croak for help was all I could manage before I sank to my knees to cushion the complete collapse. I fell hard, and I fell fast.

There was one instant when I had a chance to brace for the crack to my cheekbone that I knew would come when I struck the asphalt. Because I was going down.

I didn't feel a thing. At least, not until I woke. And then, it wasn't pain, but a sense of warmth that enveloped my entire body. I almost curled into it the instinctive way I did when I woke too early in the morning and my legs and flung free of the blanket of warmth. Then I remembered I'd fainted cold in Gideon's driveway. And I hesitated.

I blinked my eyes open to discover I was being cradled in someone's lap. The scent of warm caramel encouraged a large gulp of air. I took it greedily, autonomically.

"There she is," Stone said, his voice as warm as hot butterscotch.

I looked up into his face. His eyes flared from blue to purple. His lap. That's where I was. That was who held me. The fae who'd just tried to kill me. I considered gutting him right there but realized he was holding onto my hands.

"Let me up," I said through a dry throat.

He canted his head sideways, taking in my entire face before letting his gaze drop to my...chest? Was he actually trying to steal a look at my boobs? After he'd squeezed my lungs free of air with his magic to try to force me to agree to helping him?

"Let me up," I said again.

"We saw you on the monitors," he said but didn't take his hands from mine. Instead, he seemed to hold them all the tighter against his chest. "You fainted."

"No shit, Sherlock," I said. "Because some kind of magic—fae magic, no doubt—stole my breath." I glared at him. "You've got a hell of a nerve playing the gentleman when you blasted me with magic for refusing to do your dirty work."

Gideon's face came into view over Stone's shoulder. "It wasn't him, Ava," he said. "That wasn't fae magic. It was just plain old black magic," he said.

"Potato potahto," I said and tried ineffectively to pull my hands free. Stone was damnably strong. "Either way, if I have a concussion, I can't very well go killing anyone for you. So, there's that. Maybe I should thank you."

"I wouldn't do that," Stone said with a hint of humor.

My gaze ran to Gideon, who ran both hands over his hair. "Stone saw you go down. He caught you before you hit the pavement. If you have a concussion, it's from something you did before you got here."

My left eyebrow quirked up at the comment. "Before I hit the pavement?" I said. "That's impossible."

If he'd caught me before I fell, he was hella fast. A shiver took me as I tried to extricate myself from Stone's arms.

His gaze fixed itself pointedly on my face. "Speed is one of our gifts. At least, the High Fae." I felt his shrug. "Sometimes it comes handy, but I don't use it often. Drains me."

I narrowed my gaze at his confession. "Confiding your secret weakness to me isn't going to change things." I didn't want to admit that even drained, he was still too strong for me to pull myself free. I was beginning to feel far too uncomfortable.

I elbowed him in the stomach. "If I don't have a concussion, I think you can safely let me up."

His jaw seesawed back and forth, and over his shoulder, Gideon's eyes rolled. Something wasn't right. I just couldn't figure out what, and I certainly wasn't going to just lie there at someone else's mercy.

"Well?" I said. "Any time now would be nice unless you have some nefarious plans for my person that would make a less worldly girl blush...and trust me, if that's the case, be prepared to suffer later."

A sort of half-smile played over Stone's face. "Any nefarious plans I have for your person would be completely mutual, I assure you," he said.

Before I could respond, Gideon popped back into view over Stone's shoulder. "You should know something before you get up," he said.

A glance at Stone showed him averting his eyes, but a smile tugged at the corner of his mouth. Gideon, too, turned away. Both of them, far too shifty for my liking.

I pulled my hands free of Stone's. Neither one's modesty was the least bit authentic. I discovered what had them faking concern when I pushed myself upright and a cold breeze brushed over my skin, raising goose bumps all over my chest and arms.

I looked down at my chest. "I'm naked," I said in a flat voice. "You decided to take my clothes off? While I was out cold?"

I whipped my head up at Stone and backed away, my arms covering my chest. "Seriously? No alarm bells about consent ring in your ears at all?"

Stone crossed his arms over his chest in a ridiculous parody of me. "Not entirely naked," he drawled. "Just your top half."

"The sweater was cutting off your air," Gideon piped up. "Stone had to rip it off." He gestured to the lawn where a puddle of material lay smoking in the grass.

I edged backward. "You let me lie there for ten whole minutes naked and never thought to get me a blanket or a jacket?" I shook my head. "Bastards."

Gideon's brow furrowed. "Ten minutes? It's been less than two. There hasn't been time to get you covered up in anything."

I jerked my chin at him, indicating the lovely, warm-looking sweatshirt he was wearing. With a grunt, he peeled it off and tossed it to me. I caught it with one hand and turned my back to them, all the while feeling both gazes on my shoulders as I pulled the sweatshirt over my head.

I didn't bother with turning back to them once I was decent. Instead, I stomped toward my bike. Morning was coming, I had to get those objects back, and I was dead tired.

Stone was in front of me before I got more than ten paces. The solid squareness of his shoulders was a barrier reminiscent of a rock wall.

"Get out of my way," I said to him.

He shook his head. "I already told you. I need you."

I snorted. "And I told you. I'm not for hire."

He was tall, this one, at least three inches more than me, and I was a good five ten. He had to hunch over to look me in the eye but he did so without looking awkward. A tic in his left eye gave him the look of a mob boss and for a second, my breath caught in my throat. I just wasn't entirely sure it was fear.

"I don't plan to hire you, Ms. Ashe."

I snorted. "Then you best have a damn good reason to think I'd do anything for you."

His exasperated sigh was filled with such disappointment that he had to explain things to me that I couldn't help shoving him. It did nothing. Just made his hand snake out and grab my wrist.

"Listen," he said. "Your sister. Kit? Is it?"

Kit. How did he know about her? How did he know her name? I wrangled my expression into one of careful neutrality and refused to confirm or deny the information.

"What about her?" I asked.

"You know how the mafia works in your world, right?" he said and his voice was thick with threat. He didn't wait for my response because we both knew it was a rhetorical question. Instead, he went on, the threat gaining in his voice until the words came right out with it.

"I need an assassin, and I'm guessing you need a healthy, living sister."

CHAPTER 10

THE NIGHT MY PARENTS died, I was getting high. I was fifteen and rebellious like most teenagers, except I took it to the extremes. I'd always been a handful and aging to puberty didn't do that quality any favors. Every chance I got, I skipped classes. Stole money. I fought like a brawler for any reason that struck me, picking fights with the pretty girls and even some of the jocks because I knew they wouldn't retaliate.

My mom didn't know what to do with me. My dad had stopped talking to me. Kit ended up saving me from myself more times than I could count when I slipped out of the house and went partying.

I was too high to go to the funeral. And I was too strung out and lost to help Kit grieve. By the time a few months passed, I wasn't remotely salvageable. Not even by the time she'd found me strung out and strung up by a hemp rope as a dealer tried to kill me for stealing his money.

She'd promised the dealer anything. And she gave what he asked like a pro. He released me and her with a warning for me not to come back or he'd exact more than a blow job from a fat chick, and the reactionary cone of silence came down between her and me after that.

Surviving that encounter did nothing to prevent me months later from being lured to a party by a vampire looking to get blood-high. It was Gideon who saved me then, not Kit. And Gideon was Kit's last straw.

But she was free of me, finally. Seven years of living her life for herself and not her kid sister. It had to feel great. Liberating in more ways than I could imagine. I wasn't about to let this stranger change that. I might have been a shit sibling, but I would not be the reason my sister died.

I steeled my spine as I looked from one man in front of me to the other. "If you so much as exhale in my sister's direction," I said in a voice sharp enough to carve basalt. "I swear I will cut your nut sack from your crotch and use it to carry my lipstick."

He smirked, arms crossing like he had all the time in the world. "Sweetheart, your entire makeup kit would get lost inside." He crossed his arms over his chest. "Now be a good human and do what you're told."

I was still formulating a fuck-you response when Gideon said my name. A plea of sorts. Like he fully expected me to surrender. I spun around to glare at him as he stood in the shadow of his garage. Just seeing him lean against the building so casually, so unaffected made my blood boil. He'd never liked Kit. Hell. She hated him too, but this was unconscionable. I stormed across the asphalt, aiming the ugliest tone I had in my repertoire at him as I accused him of all sorts of things. Called him a dozen nasty names.

And he still just stood there. My mouth went dry. It was clear where he stood metaphorically. "You're going to just let Stone threaten Kit, aren't you, Gideon?" I asked.

He hung his head, and rage seeped up to my throat, burning the back of my sinuses. Even if he saw how furious I was, he kept talking, jamming the threat toward me with that calm, even tone he affected when he thought I was being unreasonable.

"You think Stone is a boy scout, Ava?" he said, peering at me from beneath shuttered lids. "He's a Shadow Court fae. Their version of the fae mafia. Crueler than their human counterparts."

"You never told me the fae had a mafia."

He glowered at me. "You think the mafia of any sort would spread word of their existence? Most barely know the fae exist, let alone that they have a cartel. But trust me. There is. And he is in it."

I stole a glance at the fae who had taken to inspecting my bike as it sat in the driveway. He certainly looked violent, predatory even, but I could take him if I had to. I'd taken out a plenty of monsters, predators, all. Seemed to me that Gideon should be helping me do exactly that.

"Why are you doing this, Gideon?" I asked beneath my breath. "Why involve Kit? She doesn't deserve that. You know she doesn't."

He splayed his arms out to his sides helplessly. "They have a list of all the hunters in the entire network. Imagine what they'll do with that information. You aren't on that list because you're rogue. You were safe, Ava. But now..."

"Now I put myself in their sights because I came here." My throat did its best to choke off the words. "You're saying I'm the one that put Kit in danger."

I gripped the hem of the sweatshirt, pulling it down further, even though it already reached my hips. A familiar panic bloomed in the pit of my stomach, a flash of memory from the night she'd tracked me down.

I all but closed my eyes at the image, the cell memory of kicking out hard enough to make me swing in the air. The sensation of the hemp biting into my neck brought my fingers up again now to test the skin. It had chafed me raw as I struggled. The echo of that was a warbled silver scar circling my throat now, faint enough to fool anyone who wasn't looking too closely, but a blatant, raw reminder to me every time I looked in the mirror.

He'd hoisted and lowered me from that rope at least three times that night, and I still remembered the sensation of strangling, the helplessness of it, the drive to breathe, the panic that stole air like a thief with full rein of a bank vault. Each time my sneakers left the floor, I was sure I was going to die. That last time, the bastard held me aloft a bit longer.

I'd thought Kit was a mirage when she arrived, a death dream, as she stood in the doorframe of that old gymnasium, holding out the rent money in a trembling hand.

Something in me cracked right then. It broke apart when she called my name and he swung around to see her standing, chest heaving with fear. I dropped to the floor like a bag of sugar as he let go, and I sprained my ankle.

Shame was the least of my worries as she crept forward, slippers still on her feet as she bargained for my life. What I flirted with up till that point became fully fledged vice afterward. Kit never had a chance to save me from myself.

But this fae had no idea where Kit even lived. It was a hollow threat at best. Gideon lived to protect the innocent.

He wouldn't give her up. He'd never tell Stone where to find her. And even if he did, I'd get to her before any of them did.

That didn't mean my heart wasn't in my throat as I spoke.

"I'll gut you without a thought," I said to Stone. "Just you try to find her and I'll feed your viscera to the fishes." I didn't intend for the mafia reference to infiltrate my threat, but there it was. I held my ground, doing my best not to so much as blink.

The relief that swam over Gideon's entire body put tension in mine as I realized the truth of what had just transpired. It wasn't much, just a flash of expression crossing Gideon's face, but I knew what it meant. Stone would never have known about Kit had Gideon not intentionally dropped her name into the conversation.

"You bastard," I said. "You knew exactly what you were doing when you mentioned Kit."

"It's your own fault," he said, then he leaned down and ran his hands into the pouch of the sweatshirt, pulling me close enough to rasp into my ear.

"You shouldn't have come here, Ava. It was a mistake to take on the witch by yourself. You're your own worst enemy. God knows what drives you to drive everyone who loves you away, but dammit, that's all on you. You're the one who put your sister in danger the moment you drew that hellhound here, not me."

I pulled back, hot anger curling my lip as I flipped them both a finger and stormed away. There was no way in hell I was going to get Kit involved in this. It was Gideon's mess. He had to clean it up.

If I had to convince her to leave town in the meantime, I'd do whatever I had to in order to manage it. A quick glance at the skyline suggested I had enough time to catch her before she left for work.

I angled myself so I could watch Stone out of the corner of my eye. He seemed to be doing something with my bike, and I shuttered my eyelids to watch him as I spoke to Gideon, low, a whisper, really.

"I took out that witch because it was the right thing to do."

"Right," Gideon said, extracting his hand and running it over the smooth stucco of the garage. "And it didn't hurt that it was the sort of job that might get you killed."

I laid my hand down on his, pinning it to the wall. "If that was my intention, then you goaded me into it." I squeezed his hand cruelly. "Is that what you wanted? For me to get killed?"

With a hard yank, he pulled his hand from mine. "Sometimes I wish you were dead," he said. "I could move on. But no. You're like a cockroach or a bad itch. Loving you is like playing the worst game of Whack-a-Mole ever."

If he thought that little declaration was going to change things, he could think again. I looked at him with a guarded gaze. His face was earnest and sincere, and I knew he meant every word. That was the thing with Gideon. He never worried about hurting my feelings. Not with truth.

"You're a bastard, you know that?" I said.

His hands went to his sides, defeated. "You knew what I was when you started chasing me," was his answer. "A bastard does what he has to do . Those hunters need to be protected. I tried not to involve you, but you had to argue. Now he thinks he's got the best of the whole damn lot, and maybe he does. Maybe you are perfect because you don't want anyone to love you. Maybe that's your ace in the hole."

I stole a glance at Stone, who was acting as if he wasn't listening. His index finger traced the line of my bike as though he'd never seen such a thing before and was worried it would burn him.

"Doesn't matter," I muttered, as I headed for the door. "I'm not doing it."

Gideon snagged my arm on the way by. Held it tightly, digging his fingers into my muscles pointedly. "Don't be thinking you're going anywhere with my favorite sweatshirt on your back," he said. "Take it off."

"You've got to be kidding?" I demanded, annoyed. "Right here?"

He jerked his head toward the garage, where I knew a tiny bathroom was situated between two large monitors. "There's a leather duster jacket and an old sweater hanging on the door. Leave my hoodie on the hook."

"Someday you're going to tell the wrong woman to get undressed, Gideon, and she won't be as kind to you as I am."

He rolled his eyes. "And someday, Ava, you're going to fall for someone with a heart as cold as yours, and you're going to appreciate what you had." He pointed at the garage again. "Now you can either swap my sweatshirt for the nice things hanging on the door or you can go naked. Your choice."

I rolled my eyes but did as he bid. Once I closed the door behind me, I peeled off the sweatshirt and dropped it on the floor. As my fingers moved over the material of the duster, they found a hard, tubular lump bundled into a pocket.

A hidden pocket, judging by how long it took me to find it with searching fingers. And then, as if not a single month had gone by since my long, drawn-out, and painful withdrawal, my heart rate ticked up.

Bloodmist.

The last time I'd used had been after weeks of gorging myself on it. The drug was a combination of magic and plasma taken from a certain species of vampires and infused with magic.

No one was sure who cooked the drug, but it was outlawed in the hunter community because it meant the vampires had to be alive in order to extract the plasma. And keeping any vampires alive, let alone the species that provided the key ingredient, was a violation of everything the Hunter Network believed in.

And yet, it added stamina as well as speed and strength, almost akin to a vamp's. A perfect vehicle to train a scrappy fighter who wanted more than anything to become a hunter. Gideon had a stash of it, and he used it to help me survive my first hunts.

I couldn't blame him for not realizing what would happen. After all, he'd only known me as a victim of a vampire, a young woman who dogged his steps afterward, begging to be trained so I could protect all humanity. Like he did. He didn't know the monster that lurked behind my gaze.

Like every drug I'd ever taken, it got hold of me with sharp, long talons and sunk them deep. It had taken weeks for him to starve the addiction and dependence on the drug out of me in his bunker below ground, leaving me sweating and aching and puking for days on end.

But here...right here, was a full canister already loaded into a vaporizer. Even knowing how bad my addiction had been, he'd directed me right to it.

I clutched the vape pen in a trembling grip. Bloodmist was a bargain with the devil. Gideon knew exactly how evil that demon was for me. If he was supplying me with a hit, then he knew very well he was risking my hard-won sobriety. And that was the strongest indicator of how much shit he was in, of how much I'd stepped in accidentally.

For a moment, I wondered if it wasn't a trap, some kind of dig or punishment. But then, I knew Gideon almost as well as he knew himself. This was his way of protecting me and warning me about the sort of threat I was facing. I saw the inhaler for what it was. A chance to even the odds.

It took every ounce of will not to inhale a jolt right then.

With a long, purposeful exhale, I shoved the vape back into its hidden pocket in the jacket, a black leather thing with buckles and pockets galore that would come to mid-thigh. I zipped it safely inside and patted it, telling myself if I needed the drug, I knew where it was.

I told myself I'd keep the vape as payment for his treachery, but even as I stood back and pulled the jacket and sweater off the door, I felt sick with desire.

I swallowed down the flood of water and slid my gaze to the sweater. It had to be at least ten years old and was horribly out of fashion, with sleeves that hung below my fingertips. I'd worn that sweater plenty of times after a hunt, sitting with him in the back yard, watching a propane fire, debriefing with a beer or a shot of tequila. I knew it was warm and soft. A reminder of better days. With a huff of resignation and a bit of nostalgia, I pulled it over my head and shoved my hands through the sleeves of the duster. I smoothed down the leather. Patted the pocket storing the inhaler once more to be sure it was there.

Satisfied, I exited the bathroom and faced the two men who watched me. Gideon's face was a little less pinched when he saw me wearing the duster, and I guessed he was relieved I'd found the inhaler. Not that it mattered because

I had no intention of becoming a disposable weapon for a dark fae no matter what he threatened me with.

Stone looked agitated. I didn't care. I was done arguing. With a flutter wave over my head, I left them there, both of them. If they stared after me, silently, or argued about it once I'd gunned the engine and gone, then that was their business. My business, right then, was to get to Kit. I knew she was home. My gut rolled around itself at the thought of facing her as I stood on her doorstep after so long, but it had to be done. Face to face. No matter how much my stomach bunched at the thought.

I had to at least try to convince her that her life might be in jeopardy even if I ended up lying and telling her it was from drug dealers trying to get back at me. Because that might be the only way to spare her. She'd believe it, I knew. It killed me that she would, but there was nothing for that. I'd do like Gideon did so often. I'd use the awfulness of the situation to my advantage.

I halted outside the door to Gideon's bunker and took a beat to inhale the early dawn air. First light. The moments before the sun fully cracked its eye open over the horizon.

That time of day always held a bit of mystique, and I often tried to be out on the hunt at that time, taking vamps by surprise as they hunkered down for their day's sleep. Most creatures did the same. Demons and werewolves and banshees all had different circadian rhythms that made me a night owl of me instead of an early bird.

But this moment came each and every day of my career, and I used it as often as I could to rejuvenate and clear the webs of the sticky residue of death and killing that always clung to some part of my mind. I was still inhaling the crisp air when I realized with a start, that Stone stood beside me, silent as the sun-stained skyline. I hadn't heard him follow me out into the yard. Hadn't even sensed him until I caught wind of a waft of caramel, sweet and enticing, and knew it was him. But there he was, taking in the skyline the same as I did, with a sort of reverence.

I thought of the times I'd tried to get Gideon to join me for those moments before sunrise. He'd always been too busy debriefing or falling into or out of bed to enjoy the moment.

No doubt, my mentor had already snapped on his monitor that watched the yard and was eyeballing me standing next to Stone. I resisted the urge to look up into the camera and make a face. He'd have his hands full trying to convince Joy Sharpe he hadn't sold out all the hunters in her network. He didn't need to worry about me too.

So, I shook out my hands and cracked my neck back and forth like a fighter. I had a sister to save. Wordless, and without a single look sideways at Stone because to do so would acknowledge his presence, I marched to my bike. If he wanted to stop me, he could have. But. He didn't.

I gunned the engine and roared into the slowly brightening streets, leaving Stone in the driveway, watching me pull away.

The rhythmic purr of the engine caught hold of the nerves the way it often did after a hard hunt and slaughter and bundled them neatly into a wad that could be tossed into a pile along with so many other emotions. Jammed into a deep closet that I expanded year after year. The guilt could come later. The shame that my sister hated me and the very worthy reason that she did. The memory of a woman's gaze behind a witch's eyes, begging to be seen once more as the innocent soul she'd once been. The knowledge that in the gray November of the night, I would ache over the piece of my own soul I'd scored away in order to do the horrible necessary thing that was my stock and trade.

For now, it was about Kit, and as the night air caressed my face, it offered a semblance of calm amidst the buffeting winds of addiction and regret. I took a shortcut to her apartment, not sure how long it might take for Gideon to finally surrender to the fae and confess where my sister lived.

It was as I rounded the block that I caught sight of them: a grouping of hooded figures clustered like an angry fist around a woman on the sidewalk.

These weren't leisurely teens smoking a bit of pot and hanging out. Their sneers and jeers echoed through the desolate alley and rose over the purr of my engine.

One look at those menacing postures and it was clear they were directing the abuse toward a young woman. Not a hooker. Not a gang-banger. She was too frail, this teen. Too hang-ass skinny to be anything but an addict.

The sight struck a nerve. A hot, bare wire of nerve that had me braking the bike to a fast halt. I dismounted. Hollered at them. A warning shot, like the stink outside the witch's house. Get moving. Take care where you step. Get out while you still can. I hoped they'd scatter. I didn't really have time to chase them off.

They ignored me. One of them actually turned his back to me as though I was nothing. I chewed my lip, considering my options. Kit would be about to lock up her apartment for the day. She'd be wearing her sensible sneakers for the hike to the bus stop. She'd linger over a few of her plants, maybe pull a few weeds from the tiny garden lining her walkway. I knew. I'd watched her enough.

I almost got back on my bike. She was running out of time. I couldn't dally. Not now.

A sickening thud grunted through the air toward me. A moan of pain.

I took a step and paused. Shit. Through a gap in the bodies, I saw the girl roll over onto her back and stare up into the face of a rather large army boot.

That sight was all it took before I started racing toward them. The echo of my footsteps on the worn pavement caught their attention, and they glanced at me almost leisurely. They expected me to move on by. Leave them to their business for the fear I'd be next. I might have. I should have.

I just couldn't.

"Back off," I said, sizing up the crowd and immediately recognizing the leader in the gangly youth standing just outside the circle. "Leave her alone."

"Keep riding," he said, with barely a glance at me. "This ain't none of your business."

This was the last thing I needed. But I wasn't about to keep riding. I knew the lay of the land now that I'd taken the time to look. These weren't teenagers like I'd thought. Each man in the four-cluster gaggle had to be at least twenty-five. The girl looked haggard, but it was her skinniness that made me mistake her for a young teen. She was more nineteen or twenty.

And this wasn't a simple bullying. It was retribution. A drug deal gone wrong. Maybe even a lesson being served. I was tired. Aching all over. I should just let it go.

I sent up a silent prayer to a deaf god that Kit had time to get on that bus and was on her way to work. Even as I marched into the fray, I told myself I'd still be able to find her later. There was plenty of time to warn her. Right now, this woman was in immediate danger.

"I told you to leave her alone," I said, my voice laced with a potent mix of authority and menace.

One young man's eyes widened, momentarily stunned by my audacity. "Who the hell do you think you are?"

So. He was the leader, then. Well, he'd have to take his lumps like any boss.

I met his gaze with an unwavering stare. "Isn't it obvious who I am?" I asked, my fists already curling into balls of hard rage.

He slipped his hand into the waistband of his jeans as he stepped closer. "Sure it is," he said. "You're the dead chick who's gonna be on the news tomorrow."

Chapter 11

Anger lit a fuse inside me, the kind that made me want to strike without asking questions. But I held my ground, unmoving, stoic. I stared him down, hoping it would be enough. I didn't really want to hurt him. He was human. Not a witch. Not a demon. These were bad people, but people none the less.

My jaw ticked to the side as I considered the gang and the girl in their midst. Her eyes were haunted and sunken as she peered up at me. The harsh light of the streetlamps and the buzzing, flickering neon sign above her did her features no great favor. The skin on her collarbones that showed above her ratty shirt was hollowed out. Long and hard into her addiction, that was for sure.

But for the grace of Gideon, that could have been me.

Or not. I'd found salvation in something other than drugs. That thing was just as dangerous, maybe more so, but it cracked through the hard shell of candy coating to give me the sweet release and relief of guilt and shame.

Hunting. That was my savior. The violence of it was the one thing that loosened the tight noose that always seemed to wrap my insides up into a snarl.

Seeing the poor creature of addiction in their midst, being assaulted and bullied, and harassed, gave that knot a yank. It demanded a response. If I didn't find a way to undo the knot, I was going to suffocate.

A moment of tense silence hung in the air as I weighed possible action against the bulge of the weapon I saw protruding from the dealer's waistband. I had to take one more to remind myself that while these were certainly monsters, they were also human. I'd need to resolve this without violence.

I huffed out a long, defeated sigh of disappointment and frustration as I turned to dig into my saddlebags. I knew exactly what sort of thing could fix the situation without them slipping in pools of their own blood. I didn't like it, but I had to do something.

The leader yelled at me to stop the moment my fingers slid inside. "Take your hands out of the bags." His order, curt and commanding, was a brutal scratch on an already reopened wound.

"Hang on a sec," I said over my shoulder. I rummaged about still, cursing beneath my breath as the stash I was looking for evaded my fingers. "I've got something that might help."

A barely audible sound of fabric rustling caught my ear. A click of a mechanism switching from safety to on. "I told you to take your fucking hands out of those bags."

I didn't have to turn around to know he'd pulled that bulge out from his waistband. I froze. My fingers finally touching the wad of cash I'd shoved in there. Slowly, so as not to alarm him, I pulled my hands free, sans the money.

Hoisting them into the air, I spun around just as slowly, letting him see me. No sense in getting shot in the back. A gun, sure enough. Pointed my way. The tension in the air was thick enough to chew on.

"You don't have to do this," I said.

Someone else stepped around the leader. "Fuck we do."

Of course they did. Because they were monsters and monsters did what they wanted. Except I knew they wouldn't shoot. Too noisy. Too messy. And far too unsatisfying. No. These monsters would make it personal.

My gaze skimmed past them to the young woman. She looked terrified.

"You're wrong, you know," I said, locking eyes with the one holding the gun.

He waggled the muzzle at me. "The hell are you taking about you crazy bitch?"

"The news," I said, lowering my hands to chest level. "You said I'd be on it tomorrow."

He snickered. "What's left of you will be," he said.

My grin pulled tight, strong enough to hurt. I planted my feet, rocked onto my toes. "Yeah, about that," I said. "You see, that's where you're wrong. You think there's something left to break. Truth is I'm already dead. And the dead don't fear the living."

He elbowed one of his nearby dudes and jerked his chin at me. "Stupid. Crazy. Bitch. Take care of it."

At that, someone stepped up behind me. I heard him coming and swung around, my fists ready. I took a glancing blow to the back of the shoulders as I spun and ducked. When I came up, it was with a hard punch to a flat masculine stomach. He let go a long groan that filled with air. Dropping to deliver a roundhouse sweep, I took his legs out from beneath him before he could react.

He lay on the ground on his ass for one second before the others swarmed me. I might have struck out twice. Pain came and went. Moments or hours went by before we all fell back. All of us panting. I noted three men holding their noses. One held his crotch.

The alpha in the gang didn't lift a finger. Instead he pinned the girl against the brick façade her throat. The gun tucked back into his waistband showed its butt as his jacket lifted.

I was about to launch myself at him, when the door to the building banged open and stopped me short. A burly gent with a bandana over his hair stood in the frame holding a bat and a cell phone.

"Little early in the day to be fighting like drunken idiots," he said.

I put up my hands. "Just trying to help a girl out," I said to the bouncer.

The bouncer looked me up and down, then spared a glance for the surrounding hoodlums. The look on his face spoke as loudly as the tone of disbelief and scorn in his voice when he said, "You?" He pointed the end of the bat at the gang of hoodlums gathering back into a pack.

I shrugged with one shoulder.

"Bat-shit crazy chick if you ask me," he growled and waved the phone at the dealer. "I've called the cops," he said. "Leave or stay. Your choice. But they'll be here in less than five minutes."

As if to prove his words, the night came alive with the sound of sirens. The leader nodded with a surly glance at me before waving his chums toward the alley. He pushed the girl ahead of him, herding her away from the scene.

"Leave the girl," I said.

A muttering noise filled with expletives before they tossed her back. She staggered for a second before she fell onto her palms. The bouncer shot her a look of disgust.

"Do your dealings on the other side of the building," he grouched. "This one's for patrons only."

She said nothing, her face aimed at the paving stones. But she nodded. The greasy locks of her bangs bobbed up and down.

I waited until the bouncer retreated into the building again before I turned to dig into my saddlebags again. I extracted the small wad of bills I'd been going for before the gang had attacked me. It was a small bit of cash I kept in a zippered pocket for emergencies. By the time I approached her, she was sitting with her knees up, arms circling them, back against the bricks.

"Here," I said, shoving the wad at her as I stooped over her hunched form.

She laid her head back on the wall, a lace of hair sticking to the grout from the static. "What?" she said.

"Money," I told her. "Probably not enough, but it's yours if you want it."

She eyed me suspiciously, and I crouched in front of her. She stank of sweat and fear. "No judgment here. You just look like you could use a break."

Her gaze flicked to the money clenched in my hand. I knew she would probably just use the money for more drugs, but I didn't care. It was her choice. It wasn't like I was handing over my body or my spirit, or the last hope I had in someone that they'd do the right thing, finally. I had money.

I could spend it and walk away. No harm done to me. It was easy. Almost too easy. My throat choked up as memories tried to worm their way out of the grave I'd stuffed them into.

"Take this," I said, pressing the money into their hand. "Grab a meal, find a safe place to stay, pay your debts or not. The choice is yours."

I knew what she was going to do even before she snatched the money out of my hand. I knew the path she would take before she pushed herself to her feet and mumbled a thanks. Before she felt her way along the wall and disappeared into the alley. I knew she had made her choice the moment she'd touched the money. But it was her choice to make, not mine, and I knew that too.

It still didn't ease the ache as I stared at the corner of the building where she'd disappeared. I ran my thumb over my lip and felt the telltale swell that told me one of the hits I'd taken had been in the mouth. My tongue darted out, testing. Blood, coppery and acid sent a tang into my cheeks.

My palm reached for the wall, and I closed my eyes, breathing long and slow. Just like I'd learned to do. In. Out. I'd done something nice for someone. That was what mattered. I'd used my body, my wits, my instincts to try to make a difference. What did it matter what path she'd chosen to walk down? It wasn't my judgement to make.

Even so, the tightness in my chest remained. I bit down on my lip, feeling the sting of the cut there. Grounding myself with something more acute, something more real than the airy fairy sensation of emotion squeezing my lungs.

But that didn't help anything. What it did was make things worse. It dragged out a shape and form from that moldering box and held it kicking and screaming in my grip. I thought of Kit and my stomach sank. I'd probably already used up all her precious time saving this filthy urchin. I couldn't guarantee that Gideon hadn't already sent Stone her way, that the fae wasn't already on her doorstep. Fuck. What had I been thinking?

My cell phone was in my hand before I'd realized I'd pulled it from my saddlebags. I ran my fingers over the screen. My mouth twitched. I prayed she'd answer as I tapped the numbers that made my chest hurt the most.

The signal chirped away cheerily in my ear for a mere five seconds before Kit's voice filtered through the tinny speaker. I knew my identity would come up as Private Caller. I used burners and replaced them every few months, and not just because I didn't want to leave a trail that monsters could follow.

A ragged sigh of relief escaped me when she answered. "Yes?"

I couldn't speak at the sound of her voice. Just like every other damn time I called her. My eyes squeezed closed as I listened to her breathing. I imagined Kit on the other end, sighing with frustration, and my eyelids tightened. She was safe. That was all that mattered. But finding the courage to speak, to break her heart again, was almost more than I had in me.

If I was smart, I'd just blurt it out. If I had any real courage, I'd beg her to get the heck out of Dodge without preamble, without this horrible tension in the air that held every single word hostage behind my ever-growing nausea at her disappointment. If I was any sort of sister at all, the words wouldn't matter. They'd just tumble into the breach and make everything alright. One more heartache and she'd be in the clear.

And I wanted to. I really did. But my throat was so choked up, I couldn't force out anything but a swallow.

A groan came through the phone.

"Again?" she said. "Look, I don't know what you want, Ava, but stop fucking calling me."

I expected her to hang up like she usually did, but she didn't. She let the air hang between us. My mouth watered even more, the ache for a hit lodging in my psyche like a dodge ball thudding into the softest parts of my belly.

"I know you're there," she said. "I can hear you breathing."

Breathing. That's right. I just had to breathe. I sucked in a hasty gulp of air and let it go with the words I'd been terrified to speak.

"You need to get out of the city," I said. "Some men are coming. I owe them money and—"

"Are you high?"

I staggered against my bike as the words hit home. High. No. Not for a very long time, but she didn't know that. She had to think it was true because that was the thing that would save her. I reached for the cold grip of the handlebar near me, swallowed.

"Please, Kit," I said. "You need to leave. Just for a few weeks. Go for a nice vacation."

There was a moment, just one, where I thought she might say something more. But then, like every other time, the line went dead in my ear. The cell phone shook in my grip as I tapped out the numbers again. I felt my breath quicken, my lungs flaring too fast for me to catch a good bit of wind. Her line rang. Three times. Four. The voicemail came on. Just like it always did until I got a new burner and she realized who was calling.

I let go a stream of obscenities as I shook the phone in tightly clenched fingers. There wouldn't be another chance. Not this way. Dammit. I should have just kept going. I shouldn't have stopped.

"I don't think I've ever heard language so vile," said a now-familiar voice. "Is that how your sister brought you up?"

I hadn't heard him approach. Too caught up in my own misery to realize Stone had crept up on me at some point. I shoved the phone back in my pocket. At least if he was here, he wasn't terrorizing Kit. My breath came easier seeing him lean against the building. I still had time to help her.

"My sister would run soap over my tongue and use it to do the dishes." I sagged against my bike, angling one foot over the other as I lifted my gaze to the gorgeous creature whose face was shadowed on one side because the sun was so low over the rooftops.

"I have a message for you from Gideon," he said, pushing off the wall and prowled toward me.

"I don't care what Gideon has to say to me," I said and spun on my heel, dismissing him in the hopes he'd leave me be. I swung my leg over the bike and made to start the engine. A moment more and I could be out of there, out of his reach and heading to Kit's.

"I think you'll want this message," Stone said, putting his hand on mine when it wrapped around the grip. Seconds. That's all it had taken for him to reach me. To *touch* me. He was so fast that I'd barely had time to swing my leg over the seat. I wouldn't even *think* about how his calloused palm felt on my skin.

I scored him with a pointed gaze. "I think you should get your hands off me."

He angled his head, giving me a very dog-like look of curiosity. "How long do you think I was listening to you talking to your sister?"

I yanked my hand from beneath his, feeling the chill of the air suddenly as I did so. I rubbed it over my stomach. "What's your point?"

"My point is you had no idea I was here. And if you didn't, I highly doubt your sister will notice the tail she has suddenly gained." He inched closer, the green gaze narrowing mercilessly. "She pulled three weeds from her garden before you called her. Tossed them into the compost, then picked a bouquet of black-eyed Susans to take with her on the bus."

I swore my heart stopped. "She's not involved in this," I said. "She doesn't even know I'm a monster hunter."

He crossed his arms. "That's what makes it so hard for me," he said. "I don't enjoy hurting the innocent, and normally I'd love to keep mortals out of fae affairs, but...well, I don't have much choice. I'm as much a pawn as you are."

"I highly doubt that," I snapped. "And you have Gideon. This is his affair, not mine. Not Kit's."

He lifted three fingers off his forearm and waggled them. "See, that's just it. Gideon says he's sorry. He hopes you'll understand. That you'll realize Kit will be safe, just so long as you do what I ask." He huffed out a weary breath. "At least, that's what he was yelling at me by the time I broke five of his fingers. I left the thumbs alone so he could at least wipe his ass. I'm not a monster." He cocked his head the other way in an almost charming way, seeing if I would catch the inference.

"You're lying," I said. "Gideon wouldn't just give her up over a couple of broken bones."

Stone blinked innocently. "You say that but..."

"Fuck you."

"Again with that mouth." He leaned in. "Ava," he crooned, and something in my body went all limp at the way he said my name. "I don't want to threaten your sister. I know this isn't fair, but I promise...it won't be that bad. Just one hit and it's over. Your sister need never know she's being used as leverage in fae politics and you can go on with your normal, everyday, kick-monster ass ways after it's over until you breathe your last."

I raked my hand over my ponytail, pulling it over my shoulder. "One hit? And you'll leave Kit alone?"

He nodded and lifted two fingers, Boy-scout style. "I would promise it's the truth, except fae don't like to make vows."

"Meaning you won't promise at all," I said and kicked the engine into gear.

His hand fell on mine again, and by the time I met his gaze, he had broken into a disarming smile. "I will vow, Ava, if it helps. But you must understand, we take our vows very seriously. Deadly serious."

CHAPTER 12

I WAS NO STRANGER to death, so a vow that presented a seriousness of that level was nothing new. Violence, though, that was something I reserved for the bad guys. Monsters. Demons. I didn't discriminate. Vampires like Fayed lived because he had not, to my knowledge, hurt a living person in my lifetime. Should that change, even the bartender in the Rot Gut Tavern would fall under my wrath. But killing a creature that didn't deserve it was a line I couldn't cross.

With a scuff of boots, I slid from the seat and kicked the stand down to prop up my cycle. I paced the sidewalk, letting Stone stand there while I thought through all the knots and tangles this sort of thing would tie my stomach into. I might stall him, tell him what he wanted to hear, and then what? Try once more to convince my sister I cared enough to save her life when she wouldn't even take my calls? She'd slam the door in my face if I showed up at her apartment. Have security throw me out of her work.

But those were small things. I could put up with those, even wedge my way into some small hole far enough that I'd gain a few seconds of her life. But convincing her she needed to leave without revealing to her all the horrible truths of the supernatural world seething right beneath her feet unknown would take time. Time she didn't have if I could believe Stone.

I pivoted sharply, decision made, only to see Stone standing by my bike, rubbing the mirror with his sleeve. His leather sleeve.

"Hey," I called out, more to get him to stop doing that than anything else. "I get final say on the weapons."

As I'd hoped, he paused to look at me. My mirror was safe. For the time being, at least.

"You've agreed?" he said, pulling his arm away and shoving his hand into his pocket. I noticed where he'd touched the mirror, it was streaked with something glittery, smeared in a diagonal line from corner to corner.

"I've agreed," I said. "Just don't touch my bike. And like I said: I want to choose the weapons I take."

"I'm not sure that I can do that," he said.

I regarded Stone steadily. There was one more thing I needed. Another bargaining chip to accompany that gambit of choosing weapons, openers that would get me the heart of what was most important. Kit's life.

"I want you to remove the threat of that damn hellhound from finding me again," I said, thinking life would be easier if I didn't have to worry about a hell hound showing up somewhere down the line just when I was in the middle of a hunt.

He shifted his weight from one foot to the other, the only evidence that he didn't like what I was asking. "Not sure I can do that either," he said.

My eyelids shuttered enough that he became a blur of black. "OK, then. I need you to swear right here that my sister is safe."

He cocked his head at me, a crafty trickster thinking he'd played me already. "Didn't I already do that?"

I shook my head. "You threatened her, is what you did. You inferred you'd kill her unless I did what you asked."

His hand came out from his pocket to waffle in the air in front of his block of chest. "Same thing."

I closed the distance between us, not happy I had to tilt my head back so far to look at him. "It's not the same thing. On the one hand, she lives, and on the other, she dies. I don't know much about the Fae Mafia. Hell, I don't know much about Fae, but I do know the difference between a threat and a promise. I want you to swear that no harm will come to my sister by your hand. Ever."

A muscle moved in his jaw beneath the brush of stubble. That same flare moved through his eyes, replaced quickly with a smoldering heat that might have made me blush under different circumstances.

"Shall I offer you my pinkie?" he asked, a hopeful look on his face. "Or is it blood you're after?"

My spine stiffened as I did my best to ignore the way it tried to melt under that heated gaze.

"Just say it," I said. "Gideon seems to think you're good as your word."

A long, lingering look on my throat and the pulse hammering away there as he said in a dry voice, "Does he now?"

"Never mind," I said and pulled away from Stone's reach. "I've got contacts. Some money saved. And if I'm the perfect person to kill a man, I'm the perfect person to keep my sister safe."

It was a risk. A huge one. But I committed to it with a toss of my ponytail over my shoulder. I strode to the bike, tried to ignore the way my heart was hammering in my ears.

"Fae don't make promises or threats lightly," Stone said from behind me, making me pause before I could throw my leg over the seat.

I looked at him over my shoulder. "Is that another threat?" My fingers tightened around the handles.

He shrugged noncommittally. "What that was," Stone said, "was an explanation. The language of a vow is very precise. We follow such things to the letter."

His gaze ran over my ponytail, as though he was admitting something he wanted kept secret and couldn't keep my eye. With that in mind, I thought better of getting on my bike. Instead, I strolled to where Stone was standing watching me. Only when the fae planted his hands on either side of his hips, did I get close enough to rasp out my demands.

"You will say out loud, right here, that if I take this job, my sister will be safe from fae interference or violence."

I hoped he didn't hear my omission of the condition that I complete the job. Just that I would take it. If they upheld their vows to the letter, it might protect Kit if something went wrong.

Before I could move, his hands snaked out to grip me by the elbows. At his touch, I stiffened, alarm bells clanging away behind my ears.

His face ducked down closer to mine as he used the leverage of his position and his grip on me to arch me backward, softly, almost sexually. My throat ached as energy pulsed around us, drawing us even closer together.

"Ava Ashe," he intoned, "friend of Gideon, sister of Kit Ashe, I vow that any harm that comes to your sister once you agree to take the job of assassinating a mark of my choosing, will be the result of a hand other than mine."

Energy, hot and liquid, ran down my spine and puddled into the ground at my feet. I sucked in a breath. "That is so not what I said," I murmured through a tight throat.

He pulled me close, running his nose along my throat. I thought I felt the prick of two small teeth. "It is the best I can do," he said against my throat, just audible enough for me to hear. Then he eased away to stare into my eyes. A bloom of red stained his teeth. I could have sworn I'd felt a nip on my neck, but it was gone. A thing of imagination.

"I've taken your word from your blood."

My palm flew to my neck, brushing against the scar there before it found my carotid.

"Like hell," I growled. "What I said and what you promised were two completely different things. You can't take my word if I didn't agree."

He shrugged. "And yet I have. Now. What will you have of me to seal my end of the bargain?" A wicked smile played about his mouth as he leaned his head to the side, exposing a vein that ran with what looked so purple it had to be an illusion.

I pulled away, disgusted with myself for letting him man-handle me into a tricked promise.

"I won't be sealing the deal with that, if you mean what I think you mean."

My fingers came away from my throat sticky, and I rubbed my thumb over them. Yup. Blood. I swiped my hand over Gideon's sweatshirt, smearing the blood onto the fabric. I could almost hear Gideon's protest that it would never come clean.

The fae looked me over, a suggestion in his eyes. "So, what will you seal the bargain with then, lovely Ava?"

My fingers itched their way down my leg to my karambit. Before he could smirk at me one more time, I had it out of its sheath. One leisurely swipe sideways, as though I wanted to brush my hair back, and the blade was biting into the pants he wore, nicking into flesh.

He sucked in a sharp gasp of surprise.

"I don't know if you Fae bleed," I said. "But I'm happy to seal your traitorous bargain with pain."

I stepped back, swiping my blade over my stomach, ridding the blood on it by smearing it across Gideon's sweatshirt.

I narrowed one eye at the fae in front of me. "Is it done?"

He nodded.

"So, then," I said. "Who exactly is my target?"

He smiled and in the expression, there wasn't a stitch of humor or pleasure. "The Iron King. The most powerful of us all."

CHAPTER 13

I'D GONE FROM MONSTER hunter to killer of innocents in seconds. I didn't know much about the Fae. Gideon had schooled me on them, of course, but I'd never met one face to face. Too busy hunting monsters, I supposed.

The breath went out of me as I realized what I'd just signed on for. I let my head hang for a long moment, the tension in the air shivering over the back of my neck. Gone was the worry about Kit, the ache in my chest at the sound of her hanging up on me.

All there was now was a sense of purpose. Clean. Clear of emotion. Just a task that needed to be done with a hundred little steps to get there. Plans needed to be made. Backups, intel gathered. A whole load of things I wasn't remotely ready for in the moment.

"I'm exhausted," I said, my shoulders slumping with a tiredness I didn't need to fake. "Now that I've promised the farm, do you think I could hit the hay?" I slid my karambit back into its sheath and leaned against my bike, just enough to feel its solid weight against my hips. I checked my watch. "It's six am," I said. "I've been up all night."

Stone ran his hand over his hair. "We best get moving, then." He jerked his chin toward the sheath on my thigh, the empty one that had held the spelled blade. "Was that something you needed?"

My fingers trailed to the empty sheath mindlessly. "Nothing that matters now," I said. Discharged and lost to the witch's lair, it would be useful as any normal blade, and no great danger to anyone who found it.

"Then let's move," he said. "I want to be in Fae before nightfall." I lifted an eyebrow in the direction of the horizon that bled a suggestion of the night's death in face of the dawn's birth. "You missed that window by at least twelve hours."

His smirk was only overshadowed by the roll of his eyes. "You mentioned something about cursed objects?"

"Did I?" I asked, knowing I'd not said it loud enough for him to hear.

He leaned against the wall, one ankle crossed over the other. "You did. And there's the whole issue of the Raiment. I'm going to want that back. For you, of course."

My jaw ticked sideways as I ran through the idea of going back to the witch's property, and for the first time, realized that the ambush and meeting Stone at Gideon's was not a coincidence.

"I dumped it," I said, not lying. "I'm not sure I can find it again."

A muscle clenched in his jaw, but I didn't care. I stood my ground, saying nothing, waiting for him to give in.

He didn't. "So, you want all of Fae to recognize the Iron King's assassin?" he asked mildly.

I shrugged. "Doesn't matter what I want, the hell hound probably tore it to shreds because I dumped the corset to get the beast off my trail." I scratched my ribs at the thought of pulling that damn thing on again.

"And even if the raiment can disguise you and keep you from dismemberment and death afterward?" he said. "You'd still not be able to find it?"

"What part of 'don't know where it is' do you not understand?" I asked, feeling more than annoyed that he kept pressing.

"Maybe the part that knows the raiment is in no danger from the hellhound of being destroyed."

I dropped my head back, defeated. It didn't seem likely he'd give up until I at least retrieved that corset, and I had the feeling I wouldn't be sleeping anytime soon unless I gave in. The only good thing to come from that might be the chance to scoop the pouch of dark objects from the seed bin and get them somewhere safe. Like with Gideon.

"Fine," I said with a huff of a frustrated sigh. "I'll go look for it." I scanned him with a thoughtful eye. "You think you can control that hell hound if it's still lurking about?"

"Some beasts can't be controlled," he said with a twist to his mouth, "but I have a feeling that one will listen."

A secretive smile played at the corner of his mouth, and damn me if my mind didn't reel with images of that mouth descending to mine and letting my tongue tease that same corner.

Ridiculous, traitorous body. I was a bit gruffer than I intended when I shouldered my way past him. "Well, we best crack on. And if you try one damn thing I don't expect, I'll kill you."

He followed me to the bike, dogging my heels so closely, I could hardly breathe. The feel of him behind me made my skin itch in a way that did nothing but make me antsy. Fuck. How long had it been since I'd got laid that I'd be so hot for someone who'd just declared my sister as leverage for a job I didn't want to do?

"It will take at least twenty minutes to get back to the witch's property, and that's before the traffic starts to hump the streets for the morning commute, so you best stick close."

"Follow you?" he said, and his breath puffed out around me in the morning air. "And what, by chance, am I to follow you in?"

I pivoted sharply. "I presume whatever the hell you followed me in."

He lifted his foot, angling it in the dying streetlamp light so that I caught sight of well-worn but well-made leather shoes. I raised an eyebrow. "You didn't walk here."

He waffled his hand in front of his chest. "I'm pretty fast and you gave me plenty of time to catch you when you stopped to enjoy a bit of spite-filled vengeance on those human thugs."

Both of my hands went behind my neck, clamping down under my occipital bone. I didn't believe him for one second. "And Gideon's? The tavern? Surely you can hop into what ever brought you there."

"You mean a cab?" he said with his arms crossed over his chest.

"Oh, sweet Jesus." I slapped the side of my leg in disbelief. "You're telling me you hired a taxi to bring you to a hit?" A bark of laughter escaped me. "And you just bullied me into doing a job for you but haven't got a set of wheels to your name?"

He lifted his shoulders. "I don't come to the human world often. I have enough to keep me busy in my own realm without busying myself in yours. Plus, I didn't say taxi. I said cab. A hansom cab."

I pinched the bridge of my nose. "You're shitting me."

"Afraid not." He shouldered past me toward my bike, and I realized with horror that he was going to hop onto the seat.

I jumped into action, terrified he'd grab the handles before I could stop him. I slid between him and my seat so fast even I was impressed with how quickly I'd been able to move. I grabbed the grips.

"Hold on there, partner," I said. "My ride."

I looked him over as he stared down at me, those aqua-marine eyes flashing with irritation. "What?" I asked. "You sure as hell didn't think you were going to take my bike and let me walk?"

"What I thought," he said, "was that we would share. And the longer we argue, the less time we have to re-trieve the raiment and those objects."

My fingers curled around the grips. "First of all, I did not say I would give you those objects. Just the raiment. And second: maybe you should have negotiated better," I said. "Because this isn't a senior's Gold Wing, buddy. It doesn't ride two."

He looked askance at the tiny little seat on the back of my Honda Rebel, gesturing at it. "There's space for you right there."

A cough of indignation throttled through me. "You're not suggesting you'll be the little spoon, leaving me to hang onto you from the back." I snorted.

"You make it sound like maneuvering this little tricycle is a difficult thing."

I threw a leg over the seat with a sigh. I'd selected the Rebel, not because it was a good beginner bike, but because it had a good engine and was small enough to tuck into tight places. It performed well at high speeds, and it handled great on dirt roads. Perfectly flexible for the kind of work I did. But it had a tiny passenger seat. Another perfect reason for selecting such a vehicle when the owner preferred her own company.

"Riding two-up isn't for newbies," I said, taking in the height of him. "You want to ride, you get on the back."

Surprisingly, he gave in, which made me think he'd been all bluster before.

"You know what to do as a second on a motorcycle?" I asked. "Because you could get us both killed if you don't."

"One of us," he said. "It will take more than a little spill off a tricycle in the human realm to kill a fae of my order."

I wanted to ask what exactly that order was, but he straddled the bike behind me, slipping in close, and the feel of his hips against my butt sent all sorts of images flashing through my mind. Bastard probably knew exactly what he was doing. To distract myself and foil his obvious intention to fluster me, I pulled the choke and started the engine.

The little bike purred for me, the engine's vibration sending a nice hum through my body. It took a few moments to school him on how to ride double, and I wasn't sure he completely got it, but I gunned the engine just the same. If it felt like the bike would dump, I'd elbow him into the gravel.

I pulled out into the street and zipped through a more direct route than I'd taken to get to Gideon's. The buildings quickly began clustering closer together, then changed to duplexes, then to apartment complexes as I rushed past. To his credit, Stone leaned when he should and stayed flexible and fluid when I sped up.

The witch's house was close to the park but on the fringes, giving her lots of space for the stately mansion that she preferred the world to see as a bungalow. Yet when we arrived, and I pulled up to the curb where I'd stashed my bike earlier in the night, it was clear the glamor was no longer needed even if she was dead.

"They torched the place," I said, peeling off my helmet after I cut the engine.

Stone had already disembarked and was standing facing the outer garden I'd run through on my escape from the ambush.

"Looks like it," he said in a pensive voice.

What stretched out before us was the remnants of a massive fire too hot and too accelerated to have started by any mortal means. The fae had razed it by magic, certainly. There was the faint smell of ozone in the air mixed with something so sticky-sweet it couldn't be gas or naphtha. I scanned the asphalt for remains of my shirt and bra but came up empty. I sighed. It was my favorite bra. Probably gone now to the tight spaces between a hell hound's teeth. Looking up past the tree line, the garden stretched out into long furrows that lead to a quarter acre of scorched rubble and ash. Several cement pillars stretched upward, part of a sweeping staircase that must have gone up three floors. Twisted metal suggested the frames of appliances.

I hooked the helmet over the handlebars and strode to where Stone crouched and had begun running his hand over the grass.

"What's up?" I asked, recognizing the smell of magic.

"We're not alone," he said.

At that moment, I felt eyes on my back.

"Tell it to go away," I said, the delectable tingle of fear and excitement coiling at the base of my spine, a warning that would have had me crouching low with him if I'd not realized already that it was too late to hide. "We don't have time to convince him to eat doggie biscuits instead of my ass."

"It's not the hound," he said and twisted on his feet as he spun and rose to stand, facing the backyard.

The look on his face had me reaching for my karambit.

Chapter 14

I was ready to kill in an instant. By the time Stone stood, the karambit had slid into my grip with the ease of sliding on a well-worn glove. I expected worse than the hound to be waiting nearby, judging by the way Stone went rigid.

It was a cat. A black thing with a long tail that twitched back and forth as it eyed us, yellow eyes blazing.

I slid the blade back into its sheath. "The witch's familiar," I said. "Lucky kitty."

He shooed it, hissing at it the way an alley cat might at an intruder to its territory. Watching him, I thought he might have a hate-on for the feline genus.

I strode toward the creature, rubbing my hands over my legs as I went to build up a bit of static. "Relax," I said. While I didn't hate cats, I was wary of a witch's familiar hanging about. And with good reason. They were known to harbor part of the witch's essence, a watchful eye that connected the witch's spirit to the dark magic she spun. Fed by the witch's own blood, a creature like that should be given a wide berth at the best of times. And this certainly wasn't the best of times.

There was no telling what sort of magic was still built up in its body, the residue of black powers that would need to discharge the way my spelled blade had to. I preferred that discharge happen far away from me when it happened, and away from any innocent victims it might take with it.

"What are you doing?" he asked as I crouched in front of the creature.

I reached out slowly. "Gonna trap it," I said. "Maybe leave it in the shed with some food. Just till the magic wears off."

The cat's eye remained on me until I was close enough to touch it. I had the feeling it was measuring me, and I almost thought it would swat at me and run. But it braced itself. I could see the stiffening of its spine, and even then, I kept reaching for it. Before I could scoop it up, it jammed its nose against my finger and a zap of electric shock sparked between us. Reflex yanked my hand back. It yowled, jerked sideways, and then beat it off into the garden and out of sight.

I straightened up. "Shit. Now we have to catch it," I said, rubbing my hand beneath my armpit to ease the zing.

"Like hell," Stone said, growling at me. "Why did you do that? Shock it like that?"

I wasn't about to tell him I was testing the thing for magic because I didn't want him to know I could feel the pull of magic's energy. Some things were best left un-said between enemies. What I did do, was give him an owl-eyed look. "What do you mean, like hell?" I asked. "We can't leave it out in the open. No telling what it will do if some kid finds it before the magic discharges."

"If the magic discharges, the cat will die," he said flatly. "It should be dead already. We have things to do. We are not chasing a cat around the city."

He spun on his heel toward the garden and beyond. "Now, where did you put the Raiment?" he asked. "The sun has been up for ten minutes already."

I trailed behind him, watching his back move beneath his shirt and realizing I wanted to trace the lines of his shoulders. "You would leave that poor animal to fend for itself?"

"It will be fine. Cats are always fine." This said with an air of disdain, not awe. Yes. Definitely more of a dog lover.

"Well, you might not care what happens to it, but I do."

I scanned the tree line, hoping to see the faint outline of a cat about to dart into the woods and away from some neighbor's back door.

He crossed his arms over his chest. "Just show me where you stashed the Raiment."

I surveyed the landscape, scorched and ashen, trying to bring to mind the layout as I'd left it, but it had been dark and without landmarks, it was difficult. It took a while before I recognized the plastic seed bin where the seeds had been stored, the place I'd stuffed the dark objects. From there, it wasn't too long before I traced a line to the garden where I'd ditched the corset.

"There," I said, pointing to where a glob of material lay discarded on a fringe of lavender as fresh as if it had just been rained upon.

He groaned. "Fae fire might have damaged the magic."

"I thought you said it was impenetrable," I said, but secretly, I rejoiced. The thought that the fae magic could overpower and neutralize the dark objects along with the raiment might be the first stroke of luck all night.

"It'll increase your problems if that raiment is ruined," he said, striding through the scorched herbs, plants crunching beneath his boots.

I said nothing as I trailed him, catching occasional wafts of that magic with each step until we stood in front of the shed. I signaled for him to keep going and collect the raiment himself, but he paused, as though he'd heard something, and swung his gaze toward the plastic bin. Strangely untouched by the fire. He reached out and I laid my hand on his.

No doubt the black magic of those objects within protected the bin itself from melting, and no doubt he now knew exactly where they were stashed. When he exerted pressure to open the lid, I tightened my grip.

"Finders keepers," I said.

He stepped aside, spreading his arm over the space to indicate I was more than welcome to do the honors of opening the bin.

Suspicious, but not willing to let him abscond with the pouch, I peeled open the latch and peered inside. Seeds. Inches deep. Unscorched and fragrant as stored grain. I considered trying to pretend the pouch wasn't buried beneath, but I was pretty sure he smelled the magic the same as I did. It was what drew him to the seed bin. So, I dug in the sunflower seeds and cracked corn until the gilded cords of the sack showed through the black hulls.

He muttered something from beside me as I reached in to grasp the gold corded ties of the pouch, my fingers moving through the rubble of the top-layer of seeds.

"That's not a very big bag," he said off-handedly, and I peered sideways at him. He brandished the hateful corset at me and my lips pursed, remembering the way it had felt on my skin. No wonder he'd been silent as I dug. He wasn't anywhere near me at all but had gone silently to collect the raiment and returned so fast, I'd not known he'd left. The fact that he was able to do that left me feeling uneasy.

I started to tuck the pouch into an outside pocket as I eyed him. "I always thought it wasn't the size of the package that counted but how it was used."

He rolled his eyes. "Says only a male with nothing but a set of marbles between his legs. Here," he said, holding his hand out. "I'll take that for you. You take this."

I couldn't help a chuckle at the comment. Bemused that I might find that funny, he held out the corset and gave it a little shake.

A bark of laughter escaped me. "I like how things are now with me holding the pouch and you taking the corset," I said, hoisting the pouch high as I spun on my heel to head toward where I'd parked my bike. Sleep was dogging my eyelids like a hound finding a warren of rabbits, and now that I knew no innocent kid had found the relics, exhaustion threatened to pull the shutters down like a shop window after five.

I didn't wait for him to follow, and was surprised to see him already standing next to my bike when I got there. Disconcerted at his speed, I fiddled with my saddlebags, intending to dump the sack of artifacts into the belly of it beneath a wad of dirty underwear. I sighed as I beheld it. The intention of carrying extra in the bags was so I'd have something clean to pull on when I needed it, but I was always forgetting the drawers inside.

His massive hand dropped down onto the seat, catching my eye. "Try it on," he said, holding the corset out to me.

My eyes narrowed at him. "I'm not wearing that thing."

He leaned closer, near enough that I could see the bunching up of his muscles in his shoulders. A warm sensation pooled in my belly at the sight. The man was huge, built like a brick shit house, as my father had been fond of saying.

"We need to make sure the Raiment still holds its magic," he said. "Better to find that out now than when you kill the Iron King and need to run for the hills."

"Then you try it on," I said. "The damn thing itches. I'm not in the mood to be scratching at my skin all damn day."

He put his hand on my shoulder, covering the entirety of its cuff. "I said put it on."

This time, the bunching of his muscles gave me an entirely different feeling. I squinted up at him, more than a little pissed that he would try to strong arm me.

"You're taking a helluva risk touching me that way," I said in as equally a threatening tone as his. I held his gaze, nasty as it was, until he stepped back again, seeming to rethink his tactics.

"The raiment won't work on me," he said.

My right eyebrow arched in surprise. "Is that so? Or is it that you're afraid of what will happen if the fire did something to it?"

"Fear isn't something I feel often," he said in a low voice.

I shrugged. "Alright then," I said. "So much for fae magic."

"All magic has its limitations, Ava," he said. "Even for High Fae. If you're going to wear it, we need to know it works."

With a grunt, I nodded, noting the information to mull over later. If there was an edge I could use, that certainly sounded like it. Even so, something was off in his entire posture. He wasn't looking at me but at the corset as though he was sure it would catch fire in his hands.

I snatched it from him. "Fine," I said in a tight voice because I knew, in the end, he was right. I'd rather know now if it worked than end up with witnesses to my true identity later.

"Turn around," I said, remembering I'd worn it naked before and it seemed to have worked. I didn't relish taking the chance of it not working now.

"I wouldn't take you for the shy type."

The zipper on my duster coat razored its noise into the air as I worked its lever.

"What I am is choosey," I said. "Boobs as spectacular as mine don't come with a free peek."

He grunted at that but pivoted to face the other direction just the same. I peeled off the jacket and sweater, dropping them to the ground before I shook out the corset. So much lace. I swore it had to have been sewn together by a bridal seamstress. The thing felt just as itchy as it had before, and I sighed as I dropped my clothes onto the bike's seat.

Once I'd slipped it on and tightened the front laces, I took a breath. "OK. You can look now."

His feet shuffled on the scorched turf as he turned, lifting a plume of fine ash. I smelled burned grass and rosemary, inhaling deeply at the scent as I waited for his response.

His jaw seesawed back and forth for a second. "It's working," he said curtly.

My eyebrows climbed to my hairline. "Oh? And what do you see?" I asked.

He shook his head. "Doesn't matter. You can take it off."

With a spin, he turned around again, showing me his back and leaving me to fumble for the laces again in the haste to rid my skin of the itchy material.

I stuffed it back into the saddlebag, then yanked on a filthy sports bra I'd found in the saddlebags. Sweater afterwards, cold from the air, then the coat. I only felt like I could breathe again when the leather settled around my shoulders. Just for kicks, I ran my palm over the coat, searching for the vape.

"So, what now?" I asked, indicating he could turn around again. "How exactly do we get to the Fae realm?"

Turning, he breathed in a slow and deliberate breath, as though he didn't want to answer. "Now, we go to a portal."

"And where will we find one of those?"

A muscle moved beneath his ear. "I know a fae male who lives in the mortal world. He has one of the few gates in the city that we can access right now."

"Let's move, then," I said and ignored the completely miserable look on his face as I straddled the bike and waited for him to get astride it.

The ride took us into the knot of the city, to a ritzy, five-storey stone condominium with arched windows. Traffic was in full swing. Horns blared. Fumes wafted along the asphalt like mustard gas.

By the time I'd relinquished the bike to an underground parking lot a block away at his suggestion, I'd used up the entire wad of bills I kept in my saddlebag for emergencies just to pay the attendant. It was enough to buy my bike a month's worth of time, and I reasoned that it was a small price to keep Kit safe.

I hauled the saddlebag with the corset and cursed items, then followed Stone up the broad steps to the building.

"Do you think he'll let us use the portal?" I asked as I followed him inside. "I'm about ready to collapse."

He took a moment to pause in the foyer and run his hand over the security panel. "What Blade decides on a daily basis is a mystery to every fae who meets him. But yes, I think he'll let us use it. You'll have time to sleep at the tavern once we arrive," he said and proceeded to climb the ancient looking wooden steps without looking back to see if I would follow.

My legs felt heavier with each step, reminding me I hadn't slept in far too many hours. Blinking was like rubbing my eyeballs with sandpaper. I found myself praying the male lived on the second floor as I trailed along behind him. I hoisted the saddlebag higher up my shoulder as we passed the third floor and continued on up to the top.

By the time we reached the penthouse, I was winded and ready to curl into a ball. Stone rapped on the door and stood back. Seeing that, I did too. But it seemed the precaution was for nothing as the moments dragged on. The much needed wake-the-hell-up stretch that was arching my spine nearly cracked it when the door opened and I caught sight of the man standing there in its maw.

He was taller than Stone. His hair was wet and so black it caught the light from behind him in a way that rimmed him in halo. Eyes so green they looked like the bottoms of old-fashioned 7-up bottles except where they were rimmed in a bright light of silver. High arched eyebrows hooded that gaze and a smirk stretched his full mouth. A white towel swathed his hips, wrapped and bunched into a knot at the side. One thumb was hitched into the knot as he leaned against the door. Each fingernail in sight sported black nail polish, all except for one the pinky. That was crimson.

Despite the feminine coloring to his nails, he gave off alpha male vibes with each breath he took. Where Stone was built solid and thick, this one was corded with lean muscle from his chest and biceps right down to the hard V line that disappeared beneath the towel.

It took me five whole seconds to drag my gaze back up to his face, tracking along each raised bit of scars that ribboned his form in what looked very much like brands. A flash of image ran through my mind, of car headlights and the shadows of a tavern's alley with a neon light beckoning me inside. With a start, I realized he was the man who'd been lurking outside the Rot Gut. I'd mistaken him then for a vampire, but while I'd been wrong about that, I was not wrong about the energy he gave off. Predator, my mind whispered. No matter how gorgeous, no matter how broad and powerfully cut that body, he was a predator.

Something more like Stone than a vampire, I realized. Judging by the perfection of those features, I was willing to bet he was fae. And yet, he didn't acknowledge meeting me. Didn't mention to Stone that he had ever seen me before. And that made me doubt just how well Stone knew this Blade and what we might expect from him.

But the spark of recognition did move in those eyes as his gaze flicked from Stone's face to mine, maybe flaring to a coppery red for an instant before his eyes roamed my body as though he had already mapped out every curve and freckle on my skin and was revisiting them.

It was an effort to hold his gaze, an even greater one to stand still when his eye halted on my neck. I felt the brush of his eyes over the faint scar that circled my throat, a remnant of the rope the drug dealer from my youth had used to string me up. I lifted my chin, giving him a better look. Yes, my eyes said. Yes, I nearly died, but just try me and see how long it takes for me to cut your throat if you cross me.

All that rang through my mind in those seconds, and yet, even as my confidence flared, as my defiance rose to its tippy toes, I felt the weight of that old truth bow my shoulders. Few understood the significance of that scar. Fewer still knew the origins of it. Gideon would know it. Kit too. But neither fully grasped the strength of the grip it still held on me all these years later.

And so, even though I typically refused to surrender to the weight of that old shame, habitually choosing to deflect and ignore whenever confronted, right then, I shrank beneath the leaden sensation of memory. I'd never felt so naked as I did beneath that penetrating study that felt for all the world like he was tracing it with the tip of his thumb and sending shivers down the back of my neck.

Finally, his eyelids shuttered. Nostrils flared as though he smelled my shame and that it excited him. Once more, the warning flag flapped in my mind's eye, red and insistent. Predator. Monster. Danger.

A moment later, he shifted his attention to Stone, and the mercy of relief sagged my spine.

"You brought me a gift," he said in a voice that was both deep and smokey, inflecting each syllable with a hint of sensual promise even as he somehow managed to look annoyed at the fae who stood at his door. Were he a man, I might have shivered with delight at the sound of that voice. But the fact that he wasn't showed itself as clearly as the intense gaze he shot my way, surveying me in a breath the way a lion eyes up a hare.

He ran his fingertips down along his ribs as he studied me and I rankled beneath that scrutiny. By the time his hips thrust subtly in my direction, he finished his assessment.

"Pretty as she is, Stone, she's what the humans call a tweaker." He tucked his thumb into the towel, and for a second, I had the feeling he was going to peel it away. My eyes flicked downward despite myself.

"Take her back where you took her from," he said. "I can't use her. Too risky."

I slid my hand into my pocket as he slid his gaze along my throat to the pulse I knew hammered there. It took an effort to stand there, feeling for the vape almost absently while his ruthless gaze took in what it liked. But I did it for Kit. Even so, the bald assessment came off like too close a bikini shave with a dull razor.

"First of all," I interjected. "No one *took* me, and the man who thinks he can do that will discover he's lost the ability to breathe. Secondly: I run on caffeine far more than I'd like, and while I might be severely under drugged right now, I wouldn't call myself a tweaker. Just an exhausted chick hoping this ordeal is going to be over real soon."

His nostrils flared as he drew in a long, deliberate breath. "Sure, Ponytail," he said in a mocking voice. "You might fool Stone here with that line, but I know a thing or two about addicts." He inhaled again, holding my gaze. "They have a certain pheromone." He tilted his head. "Maybe it's something else you crave. Sex perhaps?" His eye drew a line from my face to my breast. "If so, maybe I can use you after all." His grin flashed with a line of white teeth, two of which were a bit more pointed than Stone's. "I'd need to sample the vintage, though. Make sure the cork's not cracked or the wine oxidized. Too often retailers try to schill old merchandise."

He seemed to be waiting for me to rise to the bait, testing me in some way. Under different circumstances I might have sharpened my pencil and dotted his body with my response, letting him know exactly what sort of woman he was testing, but this wasn't about me. My ego didn't matter. Gathering my composure, I pressed my lips together so hard it hurt, and I waited for him to invite us in.

But in the back of my mind, I tucked away the thought that this Blade was a bastard. A gorgeous, thrilling sort of monster, sure, but a monster none the less, and eventually he would be on the other end of my ire. So when Stone slipped a protective arm around my waist, I gave it a glance but let it remain there, hot against my skin, because it served me to let him seem like he was in control.

"She's not a gift for you or anyone else."

It was odd, that protective tone, the way his fingers curled against the curve of my back. Another woman might have felt appreciated and protected, might have kissed him for the thoughtful defense.

I wasn't most women. Gideon thought I was cold-hearted. He was wrong. I'd just learned to wrap a plastic shield around my emotions because feeling anything in this sort of world was asking for trouble.

So despite my urge to squirm out of his touch, I stayed still, even enjoyed the sense of warmth because that too was useful. I discovered I'd started to tremble somewhere inside my core every time I thought of Kit and it was getting difficult to keep the plastic wrap intact. It seemed that my lack of movement drew the bastard's attention.

His eyes had narrowed with barely suppressed emotion, the lingering gaze on my throat intense enough that an ache started in the small of my back right where Stone's hand rested. Possession. That's what I saw there. Regardless of my own sense of agency, or Stone's declaration, it seemed Blade had already decided that the 'gift' being offered was already his, and addict or not, he didn't like that I was out of reach.

"If you're not here to bring this woman for indenture," he growled, "then what the hell do you want?"

Tension hummed between them in a way that curled my fingers into fists. But Blade flicked his gaze back to me, then, noting the balled up hands, and a slow smile rode his features. There was that predilection for violence peeking out from the facade, seething right below the surface. I felt like I'd won some argument.

"I need the portal," Stone said curtly.

Blade gave the door enough headroom to reveal through the broadened gap, a willowy blonde reclining on a black sofa in the middle of the living room. Her shapely legs, bare beneath a silken sarong that fell so far from her thighs that I could see she was naked beneath it, flexed and let go as she watched his back.

"My portal?" he asked, running a hand through his hair and tousling it mercilessly. "I'm not sure your friend has what it takes to pay the price."

Again, that shuttered glance, smokey and inviting and so very infuriating that I nudged Stone's arm and jerked my chin pointedly toward the woman inside. "Maybe we can come back later."

Said woman brazenly spread her legs and slipped her hand beneath the fabric as I spoke. Shocked, I pulled my gaze away so quick I didn't realize it had landed on the fae standing in the door again until he spoke.

"I'm busy." His voice was a lazy drawl, full of amusement. "But for you? I could be persuaded." His thumb dipped lower into the towel slung dangerously low on his hips, like he knew exactly where my eyes would go. He jerked his chin at me, smirking. "Unless you'd rather just stand there and stare, Ponytail. I don't mind the attention."

I wasn't sure what infuriated me more, being lowered to the status of a hot chick or the sexual tone behind the way he said ponytail.

"Fuck you," I said.

One of his eyebrows lifted. "Are you offering or thinking out loud?"

The way Stone put his hand on my arm, I realized I'd given in to the strong urge to send my fist into Blade's throat. I fought back a groan of frustration as he pinned it at my side.

"Blade," he said in an exasperated voice. "We need the portal. We'll be in and out long before your prostitute can fake an orgasm."

Blade straightened up from the door long enough to lean on the frame, propping himself with his forearm. "Is that what your lovers have to resort to, Stone?" He sighed theatrically as he looked me over yet again and a smirk played over his mouth. "Maybe you should stay and watch. Learn a thing or two."

"I'm not doing this with you today, Blade," Stone said in a tight voice. "We need the portal."

"Use the one in the Shadow Bazaar like every other fae."

"The Blood Gate and all the others in and out of the bazaar are down. Maddox is dead and now it's the wild west over there. I barely made it through with any of my powers intact. That damn bazaar will not let me back through without taking the rest of my magic just to keep itself running."

That news surprised Blade enough to make him drop his arm from the door jam. His voice went from brooding and arrogant to thoughtful and concerned. His tone shifted so quickly that I realized whatever the Shadow Bazaar was, it meant something important to these two. "That bad, huh?"

"Yes. That bad," Stone said. "Some other fae might risk it, but I can't. You know I can't."

Blade's lips pressed into a tight line, but he gave a short nod and stepped aside. "You'll end up in the Velvet Boar," he said. "You realize that, right?"

Stone nodded, and Blade let him stride past the woman on the sofa. She blinked owlishly, and I realized she wasn't quite present. Drugs, I thought. Or magic. And most assuredly high on one or the other.

"I thought you weren't into addicts," I said, unable to stop the taunt from rising to my lips.

"I said I couldn't use a tweaker," Blade quipped without a beat of hesitation. "I didn't say I wouldn't fuck one."

Stone eyeballed the woman with a look of distaste, and I followed him inside. Before I'd even caught the waft of sulfur and cinnamon that pervaded the apartment, I'd already decided to pay Blade a visit when this was all over. A late night raid on silent, thief-soft feet, karambit in hand. A full-blown ambush with Gideon, perhaps. Maybe I'd send Vicki Graves and her boy-toys to salvage the poor blonde's soul from this bastard's clutch. Whatever I decided, however it went down, this male need to go. Permanently.

Stone gestured me ahead of him, breaking into the hunter's monologue running along at top speed in my mind. "I don't care if it's the Velvet Boar or the stable outside it," he said to Blade. "Just so long as we arrive in one piece."

I strode in carefully, heeding every sound and marking everything from the ticking of a clock to the hum of a fridge as non-threatening. And yet, the heady, brooding sense of tension clung to the air as Blade's voice rose in response to Stone's comment. Within seconds, one had pulled the other off to the side, near the kitchen peninsula, where they argued beneath their breath.

I let them go and halted in front of the woman reclined on the sofa. "Are you alright?" I asked her.

Eyes that were two big pupils and not much more looked back at me. "I'm groovy."

Groovy. I rolled my eyes at the outdated term. Drugged she might be, but she was consenting at least. I briefly wondered at her age, since the term was as old as a rotary phone, but decided if she was indeed consenting, it didn't matter. Even if she wasn't underage, something was off about her. It took the startling sound of my own name in a voice both commanding and sharp to tear my gaze from hers and back to the men beside me.

Both Blade and Stone were watching me. Blade's expression was unreadable at first, but then his lips parted slightly, his gaze sharpening with something almost indulgent. It was the kind of look that made me certain the woman behind me had resumed stroking between her thighs—putting on a show just for him. And from the way his attention flicked past me, I had no doubt he was enjoying it.

"What?" I said, distracted by the bald lust on his face.

Blade nudged Stone with his elbow. "I don't think your date wants to ride the portal, Stone. I think she wants to stay here with me. Maybe ride something more exciting."

"If she does," Stone retorted. "It's because she plans to gut you while you sleep."

I almost choked on my own spit at the accurate response. I might have considered kissing the fae after all, and certainly once a look of renewed interest played over Blade's features. He hadn't expected that of me. There wasn't time to revel in the surprise, since Stone took me by the elbow and guided me past Blade and into the apartment proper. Blades' gaze was like lit cigarette ends sizzling tiny brands into my back. Feeling the weight of them, I strode purposefully alongside Stone through the lushly decorated apartment. A statue of some Roman emperor held court over a bank of books that looked older than the empire itself. By the time we reached what looked like a bedroom suite door based on the pair of panties dropped on the floor in front. Sarong chick's underwear, I was guessing.

My lips curled back as Stone guided me toward the door. "You first," he said, pushing open the door and stepping over the underwear as though they weren't there.

Blade called out from the living room. "Don't mess with the toys, Stone. I have them arranged just the way I want them."

I wasn't sure what he meant until I entered the room to see a massive bed with black silk sheets and a mattress covered in all sorts of sex toys. Some of them made my cheeks flare with heat, and I was no shy violet. I spun on my heel, panicked for a second that I was in the middle of some human trafficking operation and had been tricked into getting myself abducted.

Stone barred my way, and I almost clocked him until I saw the blush on his face. He averted his gaze and I knew sex trafficking wasn't on his mind. I almost pitied him for the embarrassment that bowed his shoulders.

"That would be the portal," he said, pointing toward a sex swing hanging in the corner. There was a resignation in his tone that suggested he expected no less from Blade and felt more than a bit put-out that he had to show such a thing to me.

I stared at it as it swung gently on the air currents. "You've got to be kidding."

He released a long and irritable sigh and opened his mouth to speak, but it was Blade who answered, cutting him off.

"My portal. My choice," he said.

The horror must have shown on my face because he grinned in a wicked way. "You don't have to use it."

My lips twitched in a tic that gave away exactly how I felt, and noticing it, Stone sighed heavily. "It doesn't thrill me either, Ava, but here we are. It's our only way through. I won't let anything happen to you that you don't want. Now, hold out your arm."

My gaze narrowed at him. "And why am I doing that?"

"I need your blood."

Chapter 15

I WAS NOT GOING to let him cut me. If he thought I was going to just bleed for him when he was extorting me to kill a king, he could pound sand. Lots of it.

I crossed my arms over my chest. "No way. If you need blood to get this damn thing going, use your own."

He was nonplussed by my resistance. "Would you rather I take it from your throat?" He flashed a set of tiny fangs, not the size of a vampire's, certainly, but enough to make my fingers trail to my neck, running over the feathery scar I'd had since my teens. Another time, another circumstance, and I might fantasize about those teeth coming down on my skin, but never on my throat. And certainly not now with that dictatorial tone.

I shook my head. "Nothing doing. Use your own."

Stone gripped my elbow. "I'd love to," he said. "But this is Blade's portal. I have to play by his rules. It needs to be human blood, and it needs to be voluntary."

"I didn't volunteer for any of this," I said, flashing him a glare. "In case you haven't noticed, I'm not exactly a team player. Maybe you should have checked with Gideon about that before you decided to switch weapons."

"You're going to be difficult?" he said. "Now, of all times? Over a drop of blood?"

I stepped back. "It's not too late to rethink your strategy," I said, hoping the look of doubt on his face meant he might be rethinking his choice to take me over Gideon.

"You've got a lot to learn about human women," said a voice from behind us.

Blade. Great. Like I didn't have enough Fae testosterone to deal with.

Stone swiveled to face him. "This coming from someone who drugs his dates with magic," he said and cursed beneath his breath when his gaze fell on the man in the doorway. "And put some clothes on, will you?"

At the comment, I peered from beneath veiled lashes to where Blade leaned with his shoulder against the door, one ankle over the other, arms crossed. He was naked now, the towel discarded on the floor in the room behind him.

I mean. He was gorgeous, sure. There was no denying that. With his attention on Stone, I had a nice long look, and if I was honest, I didn't think I'd ever seen as well-cut a body as his. Even the placement of the scars and branding gave him an entirely aesthetic appeal, as though the hand that marred it had an artist's soul.

But I knew men like him. He would be a selfish lover, taking what he wanted with brutality. No regrets. No apologies. Someone like me, using another body for relief as much as lust. Not that I was looking for a relationship, but Stone would be my choice if I had one. Stone looked solid. Like he'd want to give pleasure and wouldn't mind a woman taking it, taking him. But there would be a different danger with Stone. Stone was the kind who wanted more than a body. He would want intimacy.

By the time Blade's gaze turned to me, I was sure he knew exactly where my mind had gone galloping. I was even more sure when his voice took a dive in pitch and his gaze dipped along with his head, as though he was trying to see into my face. I let my ponytail fall forward to hide the most of it. I wasn't scared of him, but I didn't relish the idea of him seeing the heat in my cheeks and mistaking it for interest in him. I might be an unlovable wretch, but I still had my decencies.

"It's my apartment, Stone," Blade said after a moment. "I dress or don't dress however I like. Or what the ladies like." He smiled wide, flashing white teeth that, like Stone, had sharp points on the canines.

I edged sideways, trying to get out of his way as his long strides swallowed up all the space between him and me as he headed for Stone without a stitch of embarrassment.

When he stopped in front of me, I decided to look him full in the face because I'd be damned if I'd let my gaze drop further and let him see an ounce of discomfort show in them.

"If you think I'm bothered to see you naked," I said, gathering a bravado I didn't feel. "You've got me all wrong. I've seen the insides of a werewolf's bowels." I dropped my gaze to his hips. "A bit of skin and a tiny ball sack doesn't exactly scare me."

"Ouch," he said with a grin. "Kitten has claws." He towered over me, peering down as if he expected me to wince or avert my gaze. It was a dare, I knew. A test of some sort.

How I met it was to let my gaze travel his body slowly, taking him in the way he had me, as though I had all the world to assess what I saw and decide if it was worthy. He knew he was magnificent, from the brandings all over his skin to the thick cords in his shoulders and neck, but he was nothing to me, and I let him see it in my face.

He huffed a dissatisfied sigh and reached for a shirt from the top of the bureau. But he didn't put it on, merely bunched the fabric into his hands and let the sleeves trail down strategically over his hips.

"You win, Ponytail," he said in a heartbreakingly soft voice, and I almost smiled until Stone stepped between us.

"Back off, Blade," he said. "Ava isn't here as a trinket for the tavern." He hooked the swing rope with one finger and let it go. The swing rocked forward and back. "It's just like you to program the portal to take mortal female blood," he said, his voice thick with barely concealed ire.

Blade reached out to stop the movement of the swing. Another challenge, I thought, as his eyebrows rose in feigned innocence when he regarded Stone.

"I happen to like mortal females," he said as he held the swing in his grip. "Is it my fault they find me irresistible?"

I did my best to keep from rolling my eyes as he shrugged in a helpless sort of gesture before he slid his gaze over me like a pour of hot oil on a griddle.

"Your problem, Stone," he said, putting an inflection on the name that suggested an insult of some sort. "Is that you don't understand human women." His palm ran up and down his stomach beneath the material of the shirt in leisurely strokes. "You think you have to drag them kicking and screaming into Fae, when there are other, far more inventive ways to get them to comply."

The brushing of his palm against his skin halted, and he propped his arm against his chest, balancing the opposite elbow on his forearm. "Ever think of just asking?"

Stone's fists clenched at his sides, an echo of my own posture. "Don't imagine he's some champion for mortal women's rights, Ava," he said through gritted teeth, ignoring the insinuation. "He is not kind to your kind."

For a moment, Blade's expression yielded nothing to Stone's comment, but his voice was dark and threatening when he spoke—not to Stone, but to me. "Ask him why he's really using my portal, Ponytail, and you'll find out just how kind he is." This time his expression hardened as it landed on Stone, and inside that gaze, a serpent of copper coiled around the green of his irises, replacing the silvery light there as easily as a lick of flame.

"I don't drug them with magic and trick them into blood-sharing," Stone countered. "Making nice neat compliant packages for delivery. "

Blade's face all but blanched as he stepped up to Stone, looming over him. "It's my job, is it not?" he said in a tight voice.

"You like your job too much," Stone said. "Now open the gate." He inclined his head toward the living room, where the blonde had started to rub her temples. "Better hurry. The magic is making her sick."

With a sigh, Blade beckoned her over. "Come here, Sigrid," he said in such a husky voice, I almost felt my own legs moving. She smiled brightly, taking her fingers away from her head.

"Is it time?" she asked.

I noticed her pupils were a bit smaller than when we'd first arrived. She wavered on her bare feet and Blade reached for her almost tenderly, the hand with the polka dotted nail flashing out quickly to catch her before she fell sideways.

"I'm sorry," she said. "I don't know what's wrong with me."

Blade shushed her while Stone's steely gaze raked over them. "You remember how to get it to work, baby?" he said, his voice all throaty and filled with a dark lusty note. She nodded, all owl-eyed and pouty.

"Are you coming with me this time?"

He shook his head. "Neither of us are going, babe. I just need you to activate the lock."

Stone muttered something about the ludicrousness of having a gate that needed a human lock, and Blade silenced him with a look.

"I can travel any time I want," he said, then nodded in my direction. "But if you're taking her with you, you need some sort of mortal consent. It's only fair, isn't it?" His voice was a demand, a dare, for Stone to argue.

He turned back to the girl, but he reached out to me. "You have a knife, I take it?"

I stiffened. "I'm not handing over my weapon, and certainly not so you can cut another woman."

His eye roamed my face with interest. "You want to travel?" he said in as equally a throaty voice as the one he'd used on Sigrid. "You have to pay the fare. It's your blood or hers."

A test, I knew. Although I wasn't sure what kind or what the correct answer was. I just let my attention drift to the woman's arms. She had a dozen or more scars crisscrossing over her skin, and yet she was holding out her wrists as though she were a kid waiting for candy. I stepped back, nausea biting the back of my mouth. Any other time and I'd be trying to rescue this woman.

"I'll do it," I said, distaste filling my cheeks as I eyed him, knowing he'd subjected her to this same atrocity many times before we'd even arrived. Not this time, I told myself. I might not be able to save her at this moment, but I wouldn't forget her, and I wouldn't let her bleed one more time for my sake.

I pulled my karambit from its sheath with all eyes watching me, ran the tip over the back of my hand. A bubble of blood rose to the surface, and I winced at the sting. I watched the pool gain in diameter, waiting for some indication that it would be enough.

When no one said anything, I held out my hand in query toward Blade. "Is this enough?" I asked in a tone that was more accusation than question.

His hand lashed out so quickly to grab my wrist, I barely saw him move. His fingers splayed over my skin in a vise-like grip that had me recoiling, my lizard brain screaming at me to react, to run, to fight. It took an effort to stand there, letting blood, my blood, dribble over his fingers as he inspected the cut. Part of me braced itself, long hours of responding to attacks from Gideon to make my defenses automatic, but I managed to hold back as his lips pressed together thoughtfully. He drew a line through the streak of blood with his index finger, lifted his gaze to mine.

I watched him with hooded eyes, waiting to see what he'd do, fully aware that my other hand tapped the sheath where my karambit rested. Blade blinked once, a thin rim of red rose and disappeared around his irises. A breath. Two. Beside me, Stone began to shuffle. I was aware that he'd closed the few feet between us, ready. Just in case.

Then, as swiftly as he'd taken it, Blade let go my hand and stepped away. He walked backwards several steps until his hand met Sigrid's waist, and then, without taking his eyes from mine, he ushered her toward the living room. I couldn't be sure, but I thought I saw him slip his bloodied finger into his mouth before he turned to follow her, leaving Stone and I to stare after him.

The back of my neck prickled with unease. From beside me, Stone released a soft breath that might have been relief, but sounded more like nerves, and I wondered what sort of Fae Blade might be that he brought out such a reaction in the hardened mafia soldier.

It took a moment for me to realize blood was still trickling down my wrist and onto the floor. Droplets puddled into circles, with miniature spikes crowning the perimeter. Tiny flowers with pointed petals. As if in a daze, I lifted my hand toward the ceiling, squeezing the wound to stop the flow. While my chest was no longer tight, my heart was racing.

I'd been measured in those moments as surely as I'd ever been. I didn't dare wonder what sort of scrutiny had been going on behind that gaze, what it had seen or decided on, but I was glad it was over.

Neither Stone nor I said anything as we waited, but his shoulders were a knot. His hands were wound into balls of white knuckle. Without thinking about it, I moved into a fighting stance.

When Blade returned, a pair of track pants was pulled over his legs and hips. He waved the towel toward the swing like a white flag. Beyond him, standing in front of the wall of smoked windows, Sigrid stretched like a cat as she looked out at the city.

"Hop on, Beautiful," Blade purred as he tossed the towel over his shoulder so casually he might have been inviting us to take a seat at a restaurant table, not a sex swing that—to be honest—looked like it had a fair bit of use.

I eyed it with some trepidation. God only knew what sorts of fluids were soaked into the material. I wondered if I could get cooties through my pants.

"Well," he urged. "What are you waiting for? Climb aboard."

I shot him a hateful look that he facetiously ignored, then gripped the velvet ropes to hoist my bottom onto the seat. It was higher than I'd thought, and despite my decent height, I had to get on my tiptoes to hop onto the seat.

"Let's get this over with, then," I said as I fiddled with the footholds hanging down at either side of the seat. I waved Stone forward, doing my best to scoot awkwardly to the side so he could fit in, but all I managed was to set the damn thing to twirling slowly in a counterclockwise motion that turned the room into a blur.

Blade's laughter cut through the air. "Seriously," he said in a voice filled with amused annoyance. "It's like neither of you have seen one of these before."

He grabbed one of the footholds in order to still the motion of the apparatus, and I immediately stopped twirling. I faced him head on, my legs spread eagled, him standing between them. My breath caught in my throat. My mind sent up bright red flares to my body. My skin prickled with urgency such as I'd only ever felt when confronting a monster.

By the time he turned that emerald gaze, filled with amusement, to mine, I was already climbing out, my whole body tingling with outrage as I tangled in the various ropes.

"I think I'd rather take the Blood Gate," I said, peeling the last of the rope from around my midriff. I didn't care where the portal was or what it would take to get through it, but I'd rather just about anything so long as I was out of range of this particular fae's face. Because someone was going to die if I didn't.

"I told you," Stone said as he shouldered the ropes of the swing aside so I could duck completely out of the way. "I nearly didn't make it through, and I doubt you'd even be able to step over the threshold before it chewed you up." He shook his head. "We can't go that way." He sighed heavily as he looked me over. "We have to take this portal."

In his voice was all the dread I felt at the truth of the statement. So, at least we both felt the same way.

My jaw clenched as I took in Blade's smug expression. "Fine," I said. "But the first man who dares touch me is going to lose a testicle and half his junk."

Blade's eyebrows rose. "But if no one touches you, Pony-tail, then no one travels. Blood is just the key. If you want to turn the lock, you have to *swing*." He said this last with a deliberate intonation that gave the word swing a sexual connotation.

My chest went tight and hot all at the same time. I didn't care if he was joking or if he really was just being a misogy-nistic prick. I didn't wait to see Stone's reaction to allow the karambit to seat itself in my fist, although by the time I was scrambling from the seat, it was angled and ready, and he was already boiling toward Blade.

The latter fae stepped neatly out of the way of a round-house punch, delivered with all the rage I felt train-wreck-ing through my chest. He chuckled beneath his breath as he slid out of range like oil on a hot griddle. Stone pivoted with the grace of a dancer, partnering Blade's moves as though they'd danced the tune a good number of times already. Both of them looked beautiful in their movements, warriors both, no matter how much Blade protested to be a mere businessman.

I stood back, watching, studying. There might be a time, I knew, when I'd have to come up against Stone and I was curious what sort of fighter he was. But the fight didn't last long. When the next fist landed solidly on Blade's jaw, and the smack of knuckles against bone caught Sigrid's attention from the other room, she turned around. Blade waved her back casually, as though the strike had been a moth's kiss.

I had the feeling he'd let Stone land that first punch. Like a test or a taunt. Likely the latter, and I was stunned to think maybe he was doing the same thing I was...ferreting out the fae's skills and power.

"Sweet Jesus," he drawled as he cracked his neck, snapping any residual tightness in his muscles from the blow with an audible pop. "If I didn't know better, I'd think you're sweet on the girl, Stone."

He cocked his head at me, suggestion in eyes and in the quirk of his half-smile. "He's never bothered with mortal women before, Ponytail. You must be quite something, to get him all hot and bothered like that...even if you don't know how to work a swing."

I blinked, stunned by the rawness of his assessment, knowing I shouldn't react, that it was exactly what he was looking for. I went rigid at the insult, not sure whether it was the insinuation of Stone's interest in me or that the bastard had mocked me that made me so hotly furious. The innuendo took the last of my resolve to remain cool and collected. I waved the karambit toward him, letting it twitch in a motion that suggested I planned to razor straight up from his sack to his stomach if he so much as approached me.

His hands flew up in mock surrender. Stone took a step sideways. My head went down, a bull's glower as I faced them.

"I might have to be here," I said, "but I don't have to take shit from either of you."

The words came out through a throat so tight every word hurt. I slid the karambit out past my hand, letting them see the curve of the blade. "If either of you touches me, you'll find yourself searching for your dick in the morning and wondering why you're pissing through a hole where your junk should be."

Stone held out his hands, trying to calm me down. He needn't bother. I was calm. Deadly calm.

Blade sucked the back of his teeth. "Quite sure you'd be dead before you could use that butter knife of yours, Pony-tail."

"I have a name," I ground out.

Blade ran his palm up his stomach to his chest and that green gaze captured mine, flared copper for an instant, then went decidedly calculating. Almost intentionally so. "Your name doesn't matter, Ponytail," he said in a voice that raised the hairs on the back of my neck. Yes. Predator, I thought. "As far as anyone in Fae is concerned, you only have a few uses, and no one needs to know your name for you to do them."

Blood boiled behind my brow. Before I knew what I was doing, the karambit sliced out all on its own, my reflexes doing most of the work. I didn't really expect to connect, so, when the blade's edge fetched into flesh, tearing along as it completed its arc, spraying blood back at me, I kept swinging because that was what I'd been trained to do. Act. Don't think. Swing. Don't stop.

Even when the spray struck me in the face and misted over my chest, I recoiled to swing again. When his blood, sickly sweet and tasting of cinnamon and cloves, like Christmas candy and peppermint, I kept moving, striking. There was no thought. Only action and reaction.

Blondie screamed from the other room.

Stone latched onto my elbow. He yanked. Hard. I fell against him, and then righted myself, my fist still sweeping out in a slashing arc as I spun out of reach. Blade had danced away already. Blood streaked his chest, running over at least three silver brandings, symbols of narrow bits of skin that caught the blood and let it pool before sliding down to the next.

"Stop, Ava," Stone yelled.

My chest heaved with emotion. Like Hell I'd stop. This bastard thought he could toy with me? I stabbed out again when Blade grinned at me, taunting me, goading me. Stone had to yank so hard to dislodge me from my planted stance that I nearly fell when I whirled on him, furious.

"Back off," I snarled.

My karambit slashed again. Once more. Both times, it met a breeze of empty air.

In the next instant, Blade had me.

It happened so fast, he moved so fast, that I didn't know I was pinned until I tried once more to stab outward and pain razored across my shoulder blades. My elbows locked behind my back as he held me in his powerful grip. The karambit clattered to the floor.

In that instant, I realized he'd been deliberately baiting me, not Stone. He wanted my reaction. I'd not scored his skin by any sort of skill or happenstance. He'd let me cut him.

His breath moved the tendrils of hair that escaped the elastic and clung to my temples and neck.

"Gods above, you're like a wildcat," he said against my ear. "And I've bedded a few in my day, so I'd know. Are you as wild in the sack as you are in a fight?"

I was still spitting over a retort when he released me, tossing me toward Stone. It was a gentle push, not violent, but I staggered back at the sudden freedom long before I impacted with Stone's chest. I stood there with my own impotent rage, rubbing the ache in my shoulders and decided I didn't need him to steady me. I shouldered myself away from him to stand between the two of them with my fists at my sides. Air whistled in through my nose as I fought for control.

"You've got skills; it seems," Blade said, cradling his midriff where a smear of blood marred a gouge in his skin. "Good to know you won't just be another damsel in distress in the land of Fae. There are too many there already." He sent Stone a meaningful look.

I blinked, the fire of adrenaline tampering down into ashes in a grate under the command of several long exhales. Each flare took one more dose of self-restraint. My fists curled and uncurled at the effort. Some part of me weaseled past the anger to whisper a warning in my ear. It took several seconds before I realized what I'd just done. Kit. What if I'd just failed some test that would put her life in danger. Again.

"I'm sorry," I said to Stone through gritted teeth. "But it *is* what you hired me for."

Blade raked his hand over his hair, tousling the pitch-black ends behind his ears as he scoured me with a heated gaze. "You hired her to come into my home and attack me? I always knew you were a coward, Stone, but never this weak."

I expected anger from Stone at the comment, but a quick glance showed he was grinning ear to ear. Apparently, slicing into this bastard gained me points, not lost them. I had a mind to swipe a few bonus marks while I was at it, but Stone bent to retrieve my karambit from the floor where it had fallen, leaving me standing over him, looking down at the top of his head.

When he straightened up, he caught my eye and his blue eyes danced. I shot him a tentative smile. Maybe he didn't have to be an enemy. Maybe he could be an ally in all this. If I played it right. If I was careful.

"When I come for you, Blade," he said in a low voice as he passed me the blade, handle first. "You'll know it's me."

I took the knife with a nod and sheathed it along my thigh, silently watching the interplay between the two males, marking, recording each flicker of gaze and clench of fist.

Except it was Stone who seemed most affected, not Blade. His hands were the ones making and unmaking fists, his gaze seeking Blade's and being met with complete disinterest. I had the feeling that he wanted Blade to argue with him, but Blade's casual lack of acknowledgement and choice to inspect the wound on his stomach instead bothered Stone enough that he had to prod it, like a man with a sore tooth.

Stone crossed his arms over his chest. "Ava is a killer, not an asset for the court," he said, a tidbit of information that seemed unnecessary in light of the reaction between the two of them.

Blade looked up from his wound, a thin slice of his skin that bled a sort of silvery crimson. Like those eyes, rimmed with light. Intrigue lit his gaze as he studied me anew.

"A killer," he said and loosed a thoughtful sound from deep in his throat, but I had the feeling he wasn't the least bit surprised no matter how much feigned thought he put into the sound. "You might have warned me."

A long moment of silent communication moved between them, and I had the feeling that Blade didn't need a warning at all. Not for me. Not for anyone. And both he and Stone knew it. I'd been a bit of putty in his hands, being warmed and flattened, a sort of kiln test of my limits. To see where I'd crack. If I'd got in a strike, it wasn't by luck at all. It was because he let me get it in.

He held the edges of his wound together with the fingers of his right hand, the black fingernails turning red with his blood. The polka dots on the pinkie finger completely disappeared beneath the fluid and as I watched, the wound stitched itself tight, healing into a raised worm of flesh bigger than the other brands.

"You can go now," Blade said to Stone as he looked up. With a gesture at a small closet on the side of the room with a carved wooden latch, he said. "I've turned the key for you. No need to thank me. Just get the hell out."

Stone furrowed his brow in confusion. "You said the swing was the portal."

Blade rolled his eyes when Stone huffed in annoyance. "You think I'd turn a toy that gets so much use into a gateway to the Fae realm?" He snorted. "Rookies," he snapped the word out like a popped wad of bubblegum. "Go before I change my mind and nullify the magic."

He dismissed us with a flick of his wrist.

I took the lead, brushing past him and letting my shoulder butt into his as I went by. It felt like I was slamming into granite and he didn't move an inch even though I was sure I'd bruised my shoulder on contact.

"Bastard," I muttered, the adrenaline still running riot through my muscles.

"I prefer prick," he said with a half-grin as he turned to catch my eye. "Suits me better. Now run along. You have a very important date with mediocrity." He glanced meaningfully at Stone.

My steps were wooden as I headed to the closet. I had my fingers curled around the latch, Stone close on my heels, when the thought struck me. I swung around, finding Blade exactly where I'd left him, watching us.

"If you needed your blood to activate the portal, then why didn't you just cut yourself instead of egging me on to do it?"

Blade shrugged. "Where would the fun have been in that?"

Stone's hand laid itself on my shoulder. It felt warm and comforting, and I didn't brush it off. Ally, I told myself. If all fae were this powerful, this fast, I'd need one.

"Don't bother trying to make sense of anything he does," he said. "Blade delights in torture."

Not for the first time, I found myself wondering how well the two knew each other. So I took a bracing breath and waited for Stone to enter the closet with me, for Blade's blood to engage whatever magic would take me to the Fae realm.

I had time to see Blade's eyes turn a coppery red and for him to poke deeper into the wound, coating his fingers with his blood. He drew shapes in the air. A buzzing moved behind my ears. A buzzing, a whisper. Nothing more.

I wasn't sure what I expected. Safe, quiet passage. Whirls of color. A long rabbit hole like Alice fell down. It was none of those things.

It turned out to be a long bit of piercing agony.

CHAPTER 16

WE BROKE THROUGH TO the Fae realm in a bathroom stall. I was still catching my wind and gritting my teeth against the pain when Stone cursed out loud, distracting me from the razoring sensation of having my insides sliced through.

"Figures that the gate would drop us in the ladies' bathroom," he said as he swung the wooden door open. "The man's a pervert."

I rubbed my solar plexus, wondering at the suction feeling still making it ache as the pain subsided. "Thank God for that," I said. "Because that ride made my bladder ache."

I shoved at his shoulders to push him from the stall. "Get out."

He spun on his heel and backed out, his eye on mine. "Someone could have been in here," he said with a twitch of his eyes toward the toilet.

I shrugged and started unzipping my jeans. "At the moment, I couldn't care less if he's a perv so long as you leave me alone in here." I kicked at him as I yanked down the back of my jeans and hovered over the seat, my bladder unwilling to wait for him to leave. "But since you're still here, you might as well enjoy the show." I eyed him pointedly.

He shook himself and hastened out of the stall, closing the door behind him. Not a moment too soon, either, because my bladder let go as soon as the door clicked shut. I sighed in relief, my thigh muscles quivering.

"Seems to me you'd have known where we'd end up," I said, lifting my chin so I could aim my voice over the door.

I heard him lean against his side, a shuffle of material catching on splinters in the wooden door. The constant trickle of water into the bowl didn't seem to faze him one bit as he remained there, the shadow of his form casting a smoky look to the oiled floorboards of the room.

"I haven't used his portal in decades," he said absently, maybe to cover up the sound of water streaming into the bowl. "Blade changes it up from time to time. Last time, he dropped me into the pigsty." This with a sour bite to the words as his shadow finally moved and the sound of a tap turning on came through the door.

I was pretty sure I heard him muttering about Blade being a bastard, and I smiled to myself. At least we agreed on that.

"I thought you said you knew we would portal to the tavern." I pulled up my jeans and buttoned them. "He implied you wouldn't like it."

"Would you like not knowing where you're going to be dumped into a building?"

I thought about that as I stepped from the stall. I supposed there were worse places to land than a bathroom stall or a pigsty. I closed the door behind me, noting he leaned against a grand porcelain sink. The mirror behind him showcased the back of his head with its chestnut hair and a cowlick right at the back. His broad, well-muscled shoulders took up most of the mirror. He was beautifully built, but I had the feeling he would exude power no matter how massive his shoulders and neck were. Several muscles bunched and let go as he crossed his arms over his chest. I blinked. Swallowed reflexively.

A glimpse into that mirror also revealed exactly how I looked in comparison, which was a bit of a shock.

Blood spray turned my ponytail gummy and wet looking in spots. Usually, my skin was clear with a pallor Gideon always said made me look like a milkmaid, but now my face had a sweep of dried and crackled blood from one cheek to the other, crossing my nose and half my mouth. My expression looked both surprised and pissed. And I looked very, very small compared to him.

It wouldn't take much of a shift in his expression to make a woman feel uneasy, a sudden twist to his full mouth into a hard smile, the crinkle of a predatory squint along the planes of his temples. But for now, that expression showed a careful mask, as though he was reining in every reaction that wanted to play over his features.

I ran my hand over the curve of my cheek, tracing the path of blood that had sprayed on me when I'd cut Blade. Where it wasn't dry, it smeared onto my fingers. "What a mess," I murmured to myself.

Stone hopped off the sink. "He marked you."

"What's that now?" I asked as I clomped over to the faucet and turned it on with a squeal.

Water ran frigid, then too hot in mere seconds. Yanking my hand back until I could adjust the temperature, I raised my eyebrows at him, waiting for his explanation.

"He marked you," he said again. "It's why he goaded you into cutting him."

I didn't know what that meant, but it didn't sound pleasant. "And as obvious as that was, you just let him?"

He passed me a soft towel from the shelf beside the sink. "I tried, Ava. You're very...independent."

"Meaning difficult," I said, flipping the towel over my shoulder and testing the water stream again with tentative fingers. "I get it. I can be a handful sometimes. But whatever it means, if it's like a tomcat pissing on its territory, he can forget it. I don't present my ass to just anyone who gives it a sniff."

I thought I heard him choke and wasn't sure if he was holding back laughter or shock. I smiled, pleased enough at his reaction that I stored it away. If things got too dreary, it might prove an interesting pastime, trying to shock him.

"Blade's natal magics are unique," he said. "With his blood on you, he can track you wherever you go."

The thought of being traceable made me want to puke. "And why would he do that?" I asked, staring into the mirror to watch his face as he angled to look at me.

He loosed a long-suffering sigh. "Who knows why he does anything?"

The water finally grew tepid enough for me to scoop out handfuls of it and splash it over my face.

"Well," I said, water running down my chin. "Let him try to find me once his blood is all gone down to the sewer. I'd love to see him portal into a shit hole to get me."

I scrubbed as he chuckled, and again, I found a strange sort of pleasure in his laugh. It made me feel less like ants were crawling beneath my skin, and more like my insides were being basted with warm butter.

With a glance upward, I noticed there was still red in my ear. I ran my wet finger around, then poked the towel's corner in to mop up the liquid. I wiped my face and hands and angled my boots in Stone's direction.

"Done," I said with the final inspection. "What now? A bit of food and warm milk and tuck me into bed, I hope." I splayed my shoulder blades with a stretch backward. "Man, am I beat."

Stone took the towel from me and tossed it into a bin. "Traveling any of the portals takes getting used to, but Blade's portal isn't like any other, which is why I prefer to use any but his." His thumb came down on my jaw before I realized he'd moved and swept along the curve. I stiffened beneath his touch, afraid to move because I wasn't sure what I would do when I did.

"Missed some," he said and showed me the pad of his thumb before he held it beneath the stream of water before shutting off the taps.

"What makes his so unique from any other portal?" I asked, my voice coming out in a thready tone that suggested I was in big trouble if I didn't push away from him. Like. Now.

His answer was vague and mysterious and laced with an undercurrent of disgust. "His portal requires a blood share. You saw him taste you?"

My head angled sideways. The comment was far too sexual to actually mean what I thought. "He tasted me?"

"Yes. When he cut you. You saw him put his finger in his mouth, I'm sure." He shook his head, confused. "Usually, the mortal woman also has to taste his blood in order to initiate the magic. It's his little kink, I suppose, or maybe he just does it to infuriate me."

I thought about how his blood had caught me in the mouth, the sweet taste of it, not acrid and coppery like human blood, and I sighed.

"I did swallow some," I said, mulling over the whole ordeal and deciding I would never have willingly let that happen even if I'd known what it would do. It was vexing to think he'd goaded me into drawing his blood rather than just telling me it had to be done, but it was more interesting to hear that Stone assumed he'd done it to spite him.

"You hate each other long?" I asked.

"As long as I can remember," he said with a strange look on his face, a mixed expression of regret and distaste. I guessed fae lives were long enough that eventually everyone had a hate-on for another, no matter who they were. Like humans, they'd find little ways to twist a knife they'd placed in a secret, strategic spot in order to cause continual discomfort.

Whatever was between them, it didn't matter to me. I had a job to do. Get in. Get done. Get out. Trying to work out the relationship between two males would just be a distraction. And I had enough of a distraction in Stone. I peered over at him and caught him looking. I couldn't help grinning at the look I saw on his face. Hell, he was gorgeous. Even knowing I should hate him didn't detract from his looks. Bullish, but somehow elegant at the same time.

Stone's body was very different from Gideon's, who was built of a wiry sort of muscle. I was tempted to ask if all fae were as beautiful as he and Blade, and even that nasty bastard who ambushed me at the witch's house, but I decided I'd find out soon enough and there was no sense letting him know I found him beautiful. No good could come from that. None at all.

He leaned in and swept his finger over my hair, and my neck tingled at his touch all the way down to the base of my spine.

"You missed some," he murmured in a raspy voice. "You might want to try washing with some soap." His gaze roamed my face and my throat clogged up like a stupid schoolgirl.

To mask my reaction, I turned away from him and, as I did, his hand left my hair like a trail of beads through a curtain.

"I should see if I can arrange a couple of rooms," he said, clearing his throat. "We still have a long ride and there's no sense setting out until we've rested." He ran his fingers under the tap and looked at me sideways.

"No need to wait," I said. "You drive. I'll sleep."

"When I say it's a long ride, I do mean ride. Fae hate human technology. It's why only the rare few flee to your realm."

"Flee?" I said, catching the most important word.

His lips pressed together as though he'd said too much. "We'll need horses," he said, electing to ignore my question. "Can you ride?"

It was my time to snort. "If it's a Dark Horse, then hell yes."

He canted his head at me. "I take it by the gleam in your eye and the tone of your voice that's some sort of human conveyance and not a creature with four legs."

I sighed. "And I'm taking your ignorance of a classic motorcycle to mean I'll be sitting on a real horse." I rolled my gaze to the ceiling. "Can't we just portal to where we're going?"

A woman with long pink hair pushed through the door, and catching sight of us narrowed her gaze, checked the signage and when she realized she was in the right bathroom, started to reprimand Stone with a haughty look. He shut her down with a glower befitting a mafia man, and she hastened back out. The door thumped shut behind her.

He turned to me, scrubbing a hand over the back of his neck. "Portals bridge worlds. They don't transport you within one."

"Magic?" I said, waving my hand as though he could whisk us away with a gesture. "Can't we go that way?"

He shook his head. "Some Fae have the power to teleport, but I don't. I'm just wickedly fast on my feet."

At that point, I grabbed his arm and ran my hand along his back. "No wings?"

He caught my hand and held it, the heat of his palm sending all sorts of writhing sensations through my belly. "I'll explain the Fae orders as I need to, but no, I don't have wings. I'm not in an order that possesses them."

His thumb stroked the back of my hand and I only then realized I hadn't pulled my hand from his.

"We keep some of our natal magics and aspects secret, Ava, except to those we trust. Some are powerful enough that it doesn't matter. Like the Iron King. His power is legendary because his natal magics span several orders."

He flipped my hand over, continuing that constant stroking, this time over my palm and I had to fight not to close my eyes and enjoy it all, the mesmerizing tone of his voice, the sensual feel of the callouses on his fingers scraping over my skin.

"Most Fae of any power keep just how much they have to themselves. The Shadow Court is filled with fae whose powers might rival the Iron King's."

My throat went inexplicably tight. Every piece of information I could glean would be useful later. In all my work with Gideon, he'd never provided information on the Fae beyond the basics, and despite all the creatures I'd fought and killed, I'd never considered them to be more than a myth. I was hungry for more, but I didn't dare prod too much.

Even so, I felt Gideon knew more than he was letting on if he'd gotten himself Adam's apple deep in a mess with the Shadow Court.

CHAPTER 17

IF I HAD TO act as an assassin in a world I didn't understand, then I was glad Stone was trying to make it easier. The method he'd chosen to force this task upon me had been brutal and callous. But I knew the way of soldiers and warriors. They took the orders given them and followed them until they were done. Personal feelings got shoved to the bottom of a deep and musty trunk where they could molder and rot till they were forgotten.

But after spending time with him, I began to think differently. He wasn't just some callous mafiosi with no empathy. Just how far he'd go for his family, I wasn't sure, but I had the feeling he was coming to think more of me than just a weapon.

That could be helpful if I played my cards right. And if I kept my own feelings buried in one of those moldy trunks.

But something kept tumbling around in there like a dust bunny under a bed. All I knew was that it had to do with why the Shadow Court would reach out to a human killer if the Iron King was so powerful. Wouldn't they need an assassin with equal magics?

I decided to let the problem sit and gather dust in the hopes it would also pull out a little glitter, and when I lifted my eyes to his while the niggle tickled my psyche, he held my gaze over my hand for a long moment. Something in my chest grew warm. Unexpectedly so.

Those jewel-bright eyes sparked with something equally sexual as his touch on my palm before he pulled his hand away and shoved it into his pants pocket. The tension coiled into the base of my spine and stayed there. I could barely catch my breath.

He cleared his throat roughly, then pivoted on his heel.

"Finish cleaning up," he said. "I'll go get those rooms and meet you at the bar."

I watched him leave, telling myself the entire time that I was not attracted to a made-fae of the Shadow Court who was forcing me to kill a king whose power in the realm was legendary. Nope. Not jonesing for that body whatsoever. Because feeling that way seemed like so much more a betrayal to Kit than all the things I'd done to her in my miserable life.

So, to push those unwanted fantasies out of my mind, I tucked out from the duster jacket and tossed it over the vanity shelf. Then I ran my hand under the soap dispenser and rubbed it through my hair, rinsed and repeated until the water ran clear. Once I felt more human, I pulled my jacket back on, letting my ponytail hang over the back so it would soak the leather and not my sweater.

I headed to the exit, my hand close to the unbuttoned panel of the jacket, within reach of my karambit.

I paused at the door and scanned the room, looking for Stone. The tavern played before me like a scene from *The Witcher* or *Game of Thrones*. It could easily have been 1800s Earth, just with creatures that reminded me more of *The Hobbit*.

Candles lit the gloom of a space with few windows. A broad fireplace snapped cheerily on one wall while a rough-hewn timber bar dominated the other. The tables were make-shift in places, with barely planed boards of oak lumber, and in others polished and stained wood.

The main door to and from the tavern was massive, far larger than needed to be to allow entry by men of an average stature. Its intricately carved surface depicted creatures I recognized as nymphs cavorting with naked women, its edge embossed with crude looking phallic symbols. The unmistakable sound of horses beyond the wooden door magnified the off-balance feel of time travel.

I spied several men hanging around the bar, hunched over in their grimy leathers and boots. Only a few of them looked to be better dressed. Those wore clean linen tunics with belts or sashes and some wore very mortal looking suits. One or two of them wore twenty-first century shirts and jeans. One scan of the room proved that not all Fae were beautiful.

It was the women, however, who caught my eye. Each of them was completely naked and painted with lively colors that swirled on their skin like clouds moving across a stormy sky.

Tavern would be a loose term for where I stood, I realized. If this was Blade's establishment, then Blade was a pimp, and this was his brothel.

It was only during this study that I noticed not all Fae ears were pointed, something I'd assumed as I'd scanned Stone and Blade's appearances. Along with the slightly pointed canine teeth, I expected each fae to have them. Not so as I looked over the patrons of the Velvet Boar.

Firstly, many of them were stout and almost ugly, without the magnificent pallor of near glitter to their skin that Stone and Blade possessed. Hair sprouted from the edges of some ears and trailed down the backs of some necks in a line that looked more like a trail to a heavy pelt than a brush of hair.

Nowhere did I see wings or anything that remotely resembled wings, but I did see several short, ordinary looking men with six fingers or ears big enough to droop over at the top. Some of the patrons possessed an aura, and where they did, the auras were lined in different colors. Some yellow, some blue, some black. I had a lot to learn, it seemed, if I was going to blend in enough to assassinate a king without going unnoticed.

For now, I trailed through the crowds of seated patrons and women flaunting themselves to the men. Careful study showed that all the women were human. Not a pointed ear among them. Five regular fingers. Smooth, ordinary skin. There was a flatness lining the edges of their bodies, as though they'd been Photoshopped in to the realm and not carefully blended.

Rage seethed in my chest at the man who had probably abducted them and sent them through his blasted portal. I wondered if Joy Sharpe knew Blade was funneling human women into the Fae realm as prostitutes, and if she did, why hadn't she and the others done something about it?

Pondering that and how I might rid the world of Blade and his revolting tavern, I settled onto a seat at the bar far away from any of the patrons. I waved at the barkeep, a round man with a large black mustache. When he saw me, the tiniest set of wings unfolded above his neck and fluttered.

He might as well have been Tinkerbell's father, except he reminded me of a bee when he flitted over to me quicker than a man of his size should have been able to.

"You must be the mortal woman Stone wants to bed," he said.

"I beg your pardon? What's that now?"

He canted his head at me. "You must be the woman—"

"I heard that part," I said, cutting him off. "He isn't looking to bed me." Even as I said it, I hesitated, rethinking my choice of words because I was pretty sure he did want to bed me. And I was feeling pretty much the same way. But that wasn't the point.

The man lowered his chin, making a pooch of flesh wrap up around his jaw. "He isn't?" He made a sound that was half chuff and half laughter. "Don't you want a bed, lass?"

"Not because I'm a prostitute," I countered.

His amiable grin disappeared. "No one here is a prostitute." He said this as though I'd insulted him.

I waved my hand in dismissal. "Whatever," I said. If he wanted to pretend, what was it to me? "Stone was looking for rooms. Did he ask you?"

He smiled, and his whole face lit up. "Indeed. It's what I was trying to tell you, lass. We have the best room set aside for you. No one will accost you."

He said it like getting accosted was a common enough thing that he felt it should be mentioned. Nonetheless, I sagged on the stool. I had a feeling I wasn't going to sleep well with my adrenaline checking in every few minutes no matter how exhausted I was.

I looked around, scanning for the large man with the thickly muscled neck and broad shoulders. "Where is he?" I asked. "If he secured rooms, then why isn't he meeting me at the bar?"

"Room," the bartender corrected. "He secured one room. The others are all booked." He rolled his eyes upward to indicate where said chambers would be located. "And he's gone to acquire horses." He shook his head as though that task would be far harder. "Good luck with that."

So, I might be here a while, might as well have a nightcap to help me sleep.

I tapped the bar with my fingernail. "What do you recommend for a mortal woman who needs to get a bit of shut-eye without losing all her wits?"

He lifted a bushy black eyebrow as though he thought the answer should be self-evident. "Water, lass."

I crossed one ankle over the other and leaned on the bar with my forearm. I was going to tell him to forget it when someone slipped onto the stool next to me. She slid a glass of water across to me. "He's not kidding," she said with a shy smile.

I took in the gaunt face covered in freckles that looked like constellations all over her cheeks. Auburn hair with a glint of gold so bright it couldn't be tarnished in the gloom of the tavern. She could have been a farm girl from corn country. The bright green eyes, so fresh and open, the easy smile. But for the swirling paint all over her naked body, I'd presume she was just offering me a cup of tea and a slice of apple pie.

She nudged it closer to me. "It's OK to drink," she said when I didn't pick up the glass right away. "It really is water and not some magical potion set to drug you into oblivion." She tittered as though that happened all the time.

The bartender watched me pull the glass toward me. "I wasn't worried about drinking it," I said. "I just wasn't happy about the contents."

I tried to smile, but I had the feeling it looked more like a grimace. To cover it up, I raised the lip of the glass to my mouth and watched her over the rim.

She leaned closer to me, her shoulder touching mine, saving me from having to take a sip.

"You really should be careful about drinking when you don't know where or who it comes from," she whispered, and the bartender shot her a nasty look.

She waved him away. "Don't worry about me divulging any secrets to the wrong people," she said to him. "I'm guessing if you gave her water, then she's not marked for transit."

He pressed his mouth into a tight line before reaching under the bar and depositing a vial of some purplish liquid onto the top. "If I'd met you before you got hold of this, I'd have given you water, too, Jasmine."

Whatever the purple liquid was, it obviously had been the catalyst for her jump into Fae. Maybe it was responsible for her trip long before she even made it here. I eyeballed the bartender, searching his face for signs of malice and found none.

"Seamus here served me my first glass of purple fairy," she said, watching the direction of my gaze. "He was working one of the fairy bars in the mundane realm."

"We have fairy bars?" I asked, my mind working at recalling each bar I'd visited and coming up short of any that might fit the bill.

She nodded. "Not many, but one or two. It's how they lure us." Her shrug was so offhand. I imagined she had been in Fae a long time already and had probably begun to accept her fate, whatever that was.

I didn't have the heart to pump her for her particular circumstance. It didn't take too keen an intellect to figure out what the mortal women were used for, judging by her state of complete undress.

But the information did find a nice dark cranny to hide in for when this was all over. I was sure Gideon and Joy would send out the troops to roust those bars from the world of mortals like they torched vampire dens when they found them.

"Surely the bars don't traffic in every woman who enters those bars," I said, thinking of some bar flies I'd met in my day who were a little long in the tooth.

She trailed a finger along a wet spot on the bar, drawing out shapes that pooled back into one puddle the moment she moved her finger to another spot. "You're right," she said. "Most women come and go without a single incident. They have no idea who or what owns the bar. But if they come back frequently, or they catch someone's eye, Seamus here tells them someone bought them a drink."

"Let me guess," I intoned, tapping the back of my nail against her glass. "The gentleman who does that is Fae and, of course, he's gorgeous. So how could she resist?"

She touched a finger to her nose. "In my case, he was the most magnificent man I'd ever met. I took one look at him across the room and I didn't just take the drink, I sashayed over to thank him, offering him a quickie in the bathroom."

I hemmed to myself. So, she'd sold her soul to the devil for a glass of booze. Two guesses as to just who that devil was. I was pretty sure I'd ridden his nasty portal into a bathroom stall in this very tavern.

"Jasmine," I said, tilting my chin toward the vial that sat on the bar in front of her. "That's a pretty exotic name."

She picked up the glass of liquid and stared at it. "You mean for a plain ole down home girl like me?" Her toothy grin was a little too reminiscent of Marie Osmond to not keep imagining the farm and cows and fresh, warm milk. "No one gives their real names in Fae. Names are power. I picked it because I loved Disney's *Aladdin*." She sighed heavily and downed the draft.

Immediately, the down home look transformed to sultry siren.

Chestnut hair cascaded around her shoulders. The green of her gaze became so intense, she could have turned a light on inside her skull. The creamy complexion smoothed out even more, but filled in with color in just the right places. The jaw line widened to give her a fuller mouth.

I found myself gawking at her.

Her shoulders sagged as she dropped the empty vial onto the bar. "I was pretty at home," she said. "But here, because of this, I'm more." She pushed the glass back at the bartender with an elegant nail. "I wanted to be an actress."

She sighed and took a long look around the room. "I guess my wish was granted."

She straightened up and threw her shoulders back. The smile she gave me was authentic looking enough that someone who didn't understand addiction the way I did would have believed her.

"Take care of yourself," I said. I didn't know what her circumstances were, but she'd been kind. If I could, I'd find a way to get her home again.

She ran a hand over her hair. "I've got a patron to do that," she said. "Otherwise, I'd be in the Kennel. He owns my life."

It was a strange way to speak about a debt, but before I could ask her more, gentle fingers touched down on my arm and she slid from the stool.

"Be careful here," she said. "One wrong move, and you'll wish you were dead."

CHAPTER 18

I HAD NO IDEA what would be worse than death to a girl like Jasmine, but if I thought it was something as simple as being forced to be a fresh-faced country girl again instead of the sex siren she became after drinking the potion from the bartender, he disavowed me of that notion pretty quickly.

"She's a sad one," Seamus said, watching her saunter away from the bar and engage a rather thick looking male in a greasy shirt in conversation. "Spent two years at the Kennel."

"You mean she wasn't trafficked here?" I blurted out, and he glared at me.

"Trafficked is a human word. And it applies more to The Kennel than here."

His tone was gruff enough that I found myself apologizing, even though I wasn't sorry.

"So, this Kennel," I said. "I take it that's an entirely different level of servitude."

He plucked Jasmine's glass from the bar and slid it beneath the counter. "There's not much coming back from the sort of stuff that goes on there."

I propped my elbows on the bar. "You say that like you know."

He tossed a towel over his shoulder. "Worked the Kennel," he said. "I've seen a whole host of human women indentured to that place. It isn't pretty."

"You're saying they have a better life here?" I couldn't help the sarcasm. Seeing all the human women all but serving themselves up to the men in the place made me lose most of the empathy I might manage to drum up. "We all make choices that aren't good for us."

He took the glass from me, his expression souring. "Choices like you've made, perhaps? That got you here with the likes of Stone? Let's hope you don't end up in a position you can't get out of because of some foolish favor."

My eyelids shuttered suspiciously. "You sound like you made some pretty foolish moves yourself."

A sigh fled his lungs in a rush that deflated his barrel chest. "I'm demi-Fae," he said. "We all want to be more than we are."

He jerked his chin in the direction Jasmine had gone and who was now sitting on a man's lap, his hand between her legs. "If that's the worst that happens to that girl here, she'll be far and beyond what she would have suffered in the Kennel. Trust me on that."

With a slap on the counter that startled me, he said, "Now. Enough jibber-jabbing. You have a bed waiting and you look like you're going to collapse right where you sit."

A yawn slipped free at the mention of a bed. "Does this room have a bathroom?"

He shook his head. "The shared one at the back of the bar is all we have. There's a dry sink, though, and a washbasin. A chamber pot under the bed."

"Not a very handy set up for a brothel," I said with a raised brow.

"Keeps the girls from staying too long in the rooms, and forces the males back out into the bar where we can serve them more ale. Gotta get them back on the floor as quick as possible or no money goes in the coffers."

So. A method to the madness. I didn't want to ask how many trips the room I was going to stay in might have had over the last few hours. It probably wouldn't matter; I'd be out by the time my body hit the mattress. God, I hoped it had a mattress.

I stretched and decided to make a quick run to the toilet before hitting the hay.

I was on my way to the bathroom, passing by Jasmine and her gentleman, when I heard her yelp of pain as he yanked on her hair.

It took seconds for me to pull my blade and slip it against his thigh. Jasmine had long vacated his lap and was hunched over, doing her best to extricate herself from his grip. Her hair was stretched out like a clothesline between them, and she was trying to wrestle it from his hold.

He let go when I pressed the blade just a bit deeper into his leg.

"I suggest you let the girl go," I said.

He eyed the blade, then ran his gaze up to my face. "Do you know who I am?"

"You could be the transgender queen of Piccadilly Lane," I said. "Or a rat glamored to look like a man. Either way, I don't give a flying hell-fuck who you are."

That was when a cluster of men knotted themselves around me. I eyeballed each one of them before dragging my eye back to Jasmine's gentleman.

"Do you know who *I* am?" I asked him.

Jasmine started shaking her head at me, those lovely green eyes wide as the moon. "Don't," she said. "I'm not worth it. Just. Don't."

I didn't look at her, but kept my eye on the Fae around me as I spoke. "You are worth it," I said. "Trust me on that."

There was no warning. One second I was pressing my blade tip into the revolting prick's leg and the next, someone's fists came down on the backs of my shoulders.

My lungs evacuated their air. I coughed. Spluttered. Someone pushed me out of the way.

I nearly fell to my knees, but long hours of training with Gideon and hundreds of logged hours of fighting kicked in and I pin-wheeled, using the motion and thrust of my arms to lift me enough to offer time to regain my balance.

Instinct took over, then. Fat boy came at me, aiming a wickedly long blade of his own. I side-stepped. Neat. Fast. Avoided his slicing arc. The sharp edge of his knife slammed into a table, scattering the women.

He pulled the blade free, but not before I managed to deliver a swift kick to his kneecap. He buckled backwards. The knife clattered to the floor.

I launched myself at him, then, and only narrowly missed having a tankard strike me in the head by some eager low-life. The ale sloshed over my clothes and splashed onto the floor, punctuating the sound of the heavy tankard striking wood.

I slid into the foam, pausing for just a second to survey my assailants and their positions.

A flicker of candlelight suggested someone had moved behind me. I dodged, sliding my entire body sideways to make the smallest target possible.

When the whoosh of a body breezed past me, I dove for the first opponent. Blade out. Fully planning to drive it into his chest.

Before I could score a piece of flesh from his cheek, the diminutive fae who had leaped for me summoned a gust of air. It blasted toward me. Scorching heat sailed over my shoulder.

The force of it tossed me off my feet. I had to roll under a table to avoid any further attack. Booted feet shuffled around the room, angling for attack or getting out of the way.

The table above me flew away as my attacker stuck it with another blast of wind. I was on my knees in seconds, jabbing out with the karambit and striking into flesh.

He screamed. I was silent.

But that was it. Beefy looking bouncers, Fae all, with knuckles the size of trolls, grabbed at each of us, peeling us away from each other.

"No magic allowed at the Velvet Boar," the bartender said, stepping into the ring of bare floor his bouncers had created. "And a demerit to those who brought violence to the tavern."

I shrugged. I couldn't care less about demerits. I didn't plan to come back here. Ever. But fat-boy glowered, his head slung low, peering up at me with hatred brimming in his eyes.

Seamus made a quick motion with his hand, and for a second, everything froze in the pub. Fae, mortal, and movement of every sort stood still. If I blinked, I wasn't aware.

When things moved again, a large, block-faced letter V stood out on the fat fae's forehead. My gaze traveled from his face to the faces of the others. The same letter stood out against their skin.

I ran my fingers over my forehead, but I felt nothing.

"The brand remains until the allotted time of penalty is over," the bartender said. "And only then will you be able to buy drink or pleasure. In the meantime, all magic you own belongs to the tavern to use at our whim."

I almost smirked because none of that applied to me, but then the bartender swung his gaze at me. "Humans are subject to a fine or a hex."

Jasmine caught my eye and made a gesture that indicated money. I figured she knew best, but I didn't have a penny to my name. "Erm," I began. "What sort of fine?"

He held out his palm, where two gold coins appeared. I craned closer to see they were stamped with images. One was a bust of a man wearing a short, corded crown. The other looked like a dragon. "A full crown and a dragon," he said.

Jasmine sucked the back of her teeth with a sharp hiss. The fae who had assaulted her smirked at me.

"Fat lot of chance of finding a dragon." He chortled and slapped the back of one of his cronies. "Almost worth losing my magic for an hour." He grabbed for Jasmine's hand but the bartender peeled her away from him.

"No pleasure," came his flat statement. Jasmine looked most relieved.

I turned to the barkeep. "I'm sure Stone will pay," I said, shoving my hands into my pockets to see if I could use anything at all to trade instead of gold coins. All I had was the vape. "At least let me clean up while I wait for him?"

The barkeeper's jaw ticked back and forth. "If you can't pay, I'd choose the hex," he said. "Forfeiture of remuneration is subject to the offender becoming a painted lady."

My hand ran over my vulnerable belly as if on its own. He noticed and a sort of soft light surrounded him. Sympathy, I realized. Without a word, he shot me a quick nod. I fled to the bathroom with the adrenaline still soaking my body like a fine mist. By the time I sagged against the door from the inside and took a breath, I was breathing so shallowly the edges of my vision was going black. I took long breaths, driving oxygen into my lungs with purpose.

Fight or flight cared for no one's skill. The dump of epinephrine also flushed all extraneous liquid into my bladder. I had to go and go now.

With a shove of the nearest door, I flung myself onto the seat, just barely getting my jeans unzipped in time. Too late, I noticed the door had no lock and had to hold it closed with my boot, my leg outstretched awkwardly as I let the stream go.

I dropped my head back in relief, and was closing my eyes from sheer exhaustion and release when I heard the door open and soft, almost padding footsteps move across the room. I finished up and stood, buttoning my pants.

There were two stalls in the bathroom, so I didn't rush. But then the outer door creaked open again and a familiar masculine voice drifted over the top of the stall and I froze.

"What did you need?" Blade asked, his voice so sensitive I doubted it was him until I peered through the crack in the door and caught sight of a thickly muscled arm with raised symbols banding his wrist.

I muttered a curse beneath my breath. Never mind that I couldn't believe he cared what I might need. I was not in the mood for his false interest in my welfare.

Just when I was about to tell him to piss off, someone else spoke. A woman. I bit down on the response that came to my lips because I realized he'd been talking to her and not to me.

"Money," she said. Jasmine's voice, I thought. "I need money."

It took a long time for him to respond, and while I considered barging out into the bathroom so they would know I was there, something made me wait. Instead, I peered through the crack as his boots shuffled closer to her bare feet. He'd moved close enough to her that he could cradle her chin in his fingers and thumb. She lifted up onto her bare toes and kissed him on the nose. He barely moved at her touch, but I saw the hand hanging by his side curl its fingers.

"You don't need to do this for a bit of money, Jasmine," he said in a gruff voice, thickened by lust.

"It's OK," she said. "I want to." She wound her arms around his neck and pulled him down to her. "He's always that way. I can handle him, but..."

If Blade planned to move away, he didn't have a chance before she hopped up onto his waist as though she had springs in her legs. She wound those shapely thighs around his waist and hooked her ankles together.

"It's been a while," she murmured. "You look wound up tight as a spring." The magical paint flared brightly, sending up a glow to her face that intensified how incredible she looked.

"You're too damned sensitive," he growled. "It's going to end up killing you."

There was a long moment where I could have exited the stall, one where his entire body tensed, but then he dragged in a gust of air and spun her around. His hands went to her backside, and he pivoted around to prop her up onto the sink.

By then, it was too late. I realized in that instant the true horror of what was happening out there.

His head lowered to hers and a growl escaped him, one that sent a strange, thready flutter through my belly. My breath caught in my throat, making it ache in a way it hadn't in a very long time.

I was paralyzed, terrified to move and get caught and dreading what I knew I couldn't turn my gaze from if I wanted to.

When he claimed her mouth, it was with a bruising force, and yet she mewled like a kitten beneath him. Her embrace pulled her closer to him. She tightened her legs around him and he let her go long enough to scrabble for the front of his pants. I felt the tip of my finger against my lips before I realized I'd lifted my hand from the handle of the door.

I had to back up. I couldn't go out there now.

I was about to find a way to drop my ass down onto the toilet seat and pull up my legs as quietly as I could when the door to the bathroom swept open and two of the women strolled into the room, both in deep enough conversation with each other they didn't realize what they'd walked into.

This was my chance. A quick dash. That's all I needed.

Blade lifted his head from Jasmine's neck and angled his head in their direction.

"Get out," he said in a quiet, threatening tone.

The girls back-tracked so fast I didn't have time to push the door open to take the opportunity. I dropped my head back, frustrated at missing my chance.

"It doesn't matter," Jasmine said, working her hands from around his neck to his hips, eliciting a moan from him that seemed to come from a hollow space so dark he'd forgotten it was there. "They've seen worse."

I didn't need much imagination to know what she was doing with those hands. The way Blade's ass cheeks clenched all of a sudden was clear enough indication.

He let loose one, snarling and dragged-from-the-pit-of-his-lungs groan, and then grabbed her hands with both massive paws of his. He slammed her wrists against the mirror, holding them high enough that the position presented both of her heavy breasts to him.

His gaze flicked up to the mirror, and my entire body seized up like it had been struck by an arctic blast, one that burned its cool trail all the way down my spine. It took forever, it seemed, for him to pull his eyes away and to drop his head to those breasts.

Freed as suddenly as I'd been frozen, I didn't wait one more second to sit down on the seat, lid up and my butt hanging down into the bowl as I pulled first one foot, then the other up out of sight.

I waited, doing my best to drown out the sound of flesh mating, of moans smothered by mouths, of release to reveal itself in a stifled cry.

By the time it was over, I had my head propped on my forearms, my arms on the insides of my shins as my crossed legs held me up from the bowl. I was shaking, and breathless, and if I was honest with myself, just a little wet.

"Take this," he said above the rustling of fabric being readjusted. His clothes, obviously, because she was naked but for the paint that shifted on her body, giving her the impression of wearing something even if it was the skyline and clouds or a mossy woods.

She laughed with a pleasant, tinkling sound. "That's more than I need."

"You earned it," he said. "But it's not all money. Look again."

A long pause where I tried desperately to see what he was passing her. All I could make out was a flash of gold and silver.

"It just looks like money," he said in a low voice. "But it isn't. It does something much more interesting than buy things off the black market."

"It's not for the black market," she said in a soft voice, and I couldn't help leaning closer to the door. I wanted desperately to hear what the item did.

Through the small gap, I could see his head lower to hers as he whispered into her ear. A rustle of clothes and movement came next. But all I got was her response, a strange little sound filled with wonder and confusion.

"So, that's what it does," she said. "I didn't know such a thing was even possible." She straightened up suddenly, her voice growing clearer. "But I can't take this. Someone might need it."

"You might need it," he said, an unmistakable command in his voice. "I have plenty."

The chatter of coins went silent. Where she put the money, I didn't want to think. It wasn't any of my business. I just wanted them to leave.

As if she'd heard my silent prayer, her feet padded across the tiles toward the door. I heard the groan of the hinges and the slam of the door, and only then did I consider dropping my feet onto the floor.

Except I'd only heard one set of footsteps. Hers. So, I kept them raised even if my legs were starting to cramp.

The next time I heard a voice, it was his.

"I know you're there," he said, and damn if my heart didn't jump at the sound...so much closer than it should have been.

The door to the stall flew open and there he stood. His shirt was wide open, exposing all of that glorious and scarred torso. Branding, I realized from the puckers of raised skin. Someone had taken a hot brand to his flesh over and over and the sight of it made my throat hurt.

He leaned against the door, his shoulders filling the space.

"How did you enjoy the show?" he asked.

CHAPTER 19

I'D BEEN CAUGHT WATCHING Blade's peep show through the crack in the bathroom door, and I knew it. But there was no way I was going to let that fact put me off my game, no matter how leisurely his eye trailed down my body. I'd hold up to the scrutiny no matter how long it lasted. Even if it made my neck flush with heat and sweat bead on my temples.

Marshaling what dignity I could, I sighed. "I've seen better," I said in a bored tone, and felt a grim satisfaction in the way one of his eyebrows lifted an inch, the insulted quirk to his lips.

He crossed one ankle over the other as he leaned against the frame of the stall. "If that was true, you wouldn't be so flushed," he said.

I unfolded my legs and stood, surprised to find them just a bit quaky.

"Please. I have chick-lit books with more spice than that."

He stuffed a hand into the waistband of his pants, letting the thumb hang over it. "Careful, Ponytail, I might consider that a challenge."

"Take the chance to prove something to me and lose a much-prized part of your anatomy." I let my gaze travel purposefully down the gap in his open shirt to his waistband. I let it linger there suggestively, expecting him to fidget or flinch.

He did neither. Instead, his thumb slid the button of his pants through its hole and he started to unzip. A dare. Challenge. My God, he was going to force my hand, and I was so not ready for his reaction that a chirp of protest escaped me. Before he could unzip those pants further, I shouldered my way past him.

If I expected him to resist, I was further surprised. He turned sideways to let me by, chuckling beneath his breath.

"Just as I thought," he said to my back as I crossed the room to the sink and turned on the tap. "All mouth and no action. Or did you get an eyeful after all and realized I was too much for you?"

My lips pressed together in a determined effort not to take the bait. I soaped up slowly at the sink, lathering my hands purposefully. I took my time smoothing the bubbles over each finger, avoiding the mirror and keeping my eye pinned to the workings of my hands.

There was no way I would flee the restroom. I was a damn hunter, for Pete's sake, not some shy, wilting flower.

His boots scuffed across the floor until I knew he stood right behind me. I felt his breath move over my hair. The heated scent of cinnamon enveloped me. The spot right between my shoulder blades tingled.

But he said nothing as he stood there. Not. One. Thing.

With my neck growing ever hotter, I rinsed off and shut off the taps. If he thought he was flustering me, he could damn well stand there and see just how much he wasn't affecting me. As I reached for a towel, his fingers met mine.

I pulled my hand back. My gaze flew to his in the mirror.

"Too hot to touch, I guess," he said with a chuckle. "I get that a lot."

I spun to face him, my hands dripping with water. I refused to answer. Instead, I ran my hands over his shirt, wiping them dry as I held his eye as steadily as I could, taking my time drying my hands. The passage of my fingers left large swaths of wet fabric in their wake.

When I finished, I forced my face into an inscrutable mask. "What you are is cocky."

He leaned closer, his chest exerting pressure on my palms. "I get that a lot, too."

I considered blackening his eye, but hitting him would just prove he had bothered me. I wouldn't give him the satisfaction. I pivoted sharply and headed for the door.

The feel of his gaze following me was like a hot brand. I was a foot away from the exit when the door swung open again, nearly catching me in the head. I flinched, leaping backward to avoid getting struck. I expected Jasmine again, or one of the girls who had come in earlier and been chased off by Blade.

But it was Stone who stood there, a smile beginning to worm across his face as he spied me...right until he caught sight of Blade by the sink.

Immediately, his eyes narrowed, and a grim line of fury replaced it. One filled with suspicion and hurt. I didn't need to look behind me to know what he saw. Blade, with his shirt still unbuttoned, my wet palm prints all over his front. It shouldn't have bothered me, what he thought, but it did.

I tried to catch his arm, drag him outside where we'd be out of range of Blade's irritatingly arrogant grin. He avoided me, ducking sideways and planting his feet the way a boxer would as he faced Blade.

I looked back to see the other fae coming towards us, his treads careful and deliberate. He paused, as though moving caused him some discomfort, then he arched back in a stretch that creaked out a few pops in his spine.

Sweet Jesus. He wanted Stone to think we'd been going at it like rabbits. Just the way Stone was probably already imagining. Fuck him. I tried to shove my way past Stone, but he was as immovable as a boulder.

"What are you doing here, Blade?" he demanded.

Yup. He thought exactly what I thought he would and exactly what Blade inseminated with that ridiculous posturing.

I gave some thought to explaining, more to cut the drama short so I could go to bed, but then to save face because if I had bared my backside and bent over a sink for the bastard, it would be my business. Except I wouldn't. He was not my type on any given day.

"It's nothing," I said, scraping my palms over my head and smoothing my ponytail along my neck. "Just ignore him."

"What am I doing here?" Blade asked, his voice smooth as oil. "I own the place, remember?"

Hot realization seared my solar plexus. He was the one forcing all these mortal women to cavort around the place with nothing but a bit of paint to hide their unmentionables. I grit my teeth together to keep from spinning on my heel and punching him round on the jaw.

Stone stepped between us. "You don't own anything," he said to Blade in a tight voice. "You're just the lackey that runs the place."

Blade stepped closer, angling his body toward mine as he began buttoning up his shirt with a leisurely air.

"You know why I named the place The Velvet Boar, Stone?" he asked. "It's because when I took it from you, I thought it should retain some suggestion of its original proprietor."

His shoulder slammed into Stone's, who went rigid with fury. Even the edges of his mouth went white.

"You're soft, Stone," Blade said in a soft voice. "And you're boring."

"And you're a violent, uncontrollable bastard," Stone said.

"Oh, come on," I said, rolling my eyes. "Just measure your dicks already and let's be done with it. It's getting late."

Blade waggled his eyebrows before he flashed a look my way. "Careful, Ponytail. You might end up seeing more than you bargain for."

My fists clenched at my sides. "I'm not taking the bait, Blade."

He grinned. "It's not bait. Just a warning. If you throw in with Stone, here, you best learn to act; otherwise, you might end up painting clouds for a living." He shot Stone a meaningful glance.

It was such an obvious reference to the magical paint the women in the brothel wore that my hand went to my karambit. "That doesn't sound like a warning to me," I said. "It sounds like a threat and I don't react well to bullying."

His gaze followed my hand. "You expected something different from a violent bastard?" he said, but he pushed past Stone. He had his hand on the knob when he turned to look at me over his shoulder, that green gaze flashing. "No need to worry about your fine. I paid it for you." He pulled on the door and swept out with a secretive grin that had my fingers itching to strike out at something.

The door closed quietly behind him. Stone hadn't moved. Neither had I. We both stared at it for a long moment, my chest heaving with coiled energy.

"Fuck," I said, finally, because after all, I was completely exhausted but wired as tight as a nun's truss. The fight. The peep show. The unspent fury at Blade. It had my adrenaline so ramped up I'd have to hit myself with a hammer to fall asleep.

"What's this about a fine?" Stone asked in a tight voice.

I shook my head. "Nothing. now. Just tell me where the room is," I said through gritted teeth. "The sooner all this is over, the better."

"It's the last one on the left," he said, but he still didn't move. The muscles of his jaw were so clenched, the words came out sounding as though they'd been screwed together under pressure.

Without a word, I strode across the tavern, avoiding making eye contact with anyone else. The last thing I wanted to do was see what was going on as the mortal women—women just like me—exploited themselves for survival. No good could come from me spying any of that right then. I was too tired to cash any checks my mouth decided to write.

So, I kept my attention forward, heading for the stairs at the side of the bar. The barkeep tried to stop me as I brushed by, but I jerked away. I was done. I needed to sleep. I needed to kill the King. I needed to go home where I could fight monsters I understood. He dogged me all the way to the stairs, informing me in a hushed voice that my fine was paid. That he'd send up some bread and cheese. I gave him a tight smile and declined the food. I was too tired to eat. If I wondered how Stone had managed to settle up, I figured it was because of his damnable speed and ascended the wooden stairs, my feet clomping loudly out of sheer exhaustion.

The sounds of sex permeated the hall upstairs as I climbed, magnifying the sensation of free-floating that had taken up some space behind my ears as I tried to shut it out. A curling, unfurling sensation flooded my lower belly as I passed the doorways that led to my room.

I was vaguely aware that Stone had followed me, and he trailed along behind me quietly, no doubt lost in his thoughts and anger. By the time I reached the door, my feet could barely move. He was right behind me, his breathing not the least bit labored but with a strange hitch at every inhalation that suggested he was still pissed.

I paused with my hand on the doorknob and twisted to see him. "I just need eight hours horizontal," I said. "I can't do anything right now. Not even think."

"Agreed." He nodded.

A sort of tension fired between us. Confused, I waved my fingers at him. "This is my room, right? I'm going to bed."

He canted his head at me. No hint of guile anywhere in it. He was probably too exhausted as well.

"It's our room." He brushed his arm past me to twist the knob.

Even if I wanted to protest, I didn't have it in me, and I was still staring at him when the door swung open to reveal a massive four-poster bed with black velvet curtains and luxurious silk pillows in all shapes and sizes. A fireplace crackled cheerily on one side. A stacking of milk crates formed a quaint bookcase on the other.

I stepped inside, too enthralled with the complete shift in decor from the tavern downstairs to register the fact that we had to share the room.

As a hunter, I'd stayed in some pretty shabby places. I'd slept in a stairwell outside an abandoned brownstone, pelted by rain. I'd curled up in the corner of a crypt with just my coat for a blanket.

I'd seen it all. The worst and the awful. But I'd never seen the magnificence of this room, and it was so startling that I might have let a low-throated moan of desire slide free. I peeled off my duster coat and dropped it onto the wingback chair as I strode to the bed. I thought I heard the clunk of the vape as it struck the wood of the armrest.

I knew before I even landed ass-first on the mattress that it was just the right firmness. I felt like Goldilocks.

"Oh my God, it's just right."

The honey-colored rafters above me supported several wrought blacksteel candlesticks circled by lit candles. Wax didn't drip from a single one, and yet, I knew they were wax and not plastic. As I eyed them, they dimmed, casting a mellow glow over the room.

I spied a boar's head hanging over the mantle of the fireplace, its fierce looking teeth protruding from a wide-open mouth, frozen in a bellow at its prey.

My palms ran over the bedspread, moving against the pile of the material. "The Velvet Boar," I murmured as I peered at the trophy. "And Blade wanted us to believe he'd named it after you.

"Don't remind me," Stone said wearily as he strode to an armoire and dropped the pouch of cursed items inside. "We just narrowly avoided a fight and magic here is forbidden."

He sighed as he heeled off one of his boots and followed it with the other before kicking them toward the wall. "This room is the reason for the tavern's name, actually, and he well knows it."

Stone closed the door of the closet. "I've arranged for eggs poached with salmon and a hearty sauce at first light to get us going."

He gestured to a wall to the right, where a set of curtains matching the bedspread stretched across nearly the entire wall. "It will be the most quiet here over the next few hours before the tavern starts to accept the bulk of its patrons. We'll use that time to rest before our small dinner. We can break our fast properly in the morning as the sun comes up."

At his comment, I pushed myself from the bed and strode to the wall. A jerk of the curtains flooded the room with slanted sunlight through double French doors. Since I'd been up all night, we'd traveled in the morning, so I presumed it was at least past midday. The black velvet had acted as blackout curtains, giving the entire space a nighttime feel.

I twisted the knobs and took a step onto the balcony as the door pushed open. Potted plants and herbs gave the space a woodsy feel, and the fragrance of flowers and rosemary moved on the afternoon breeze. I inhaled sharply, taking it all in. Calming myself to flatten the bristles of adrenaline that still pumped through me.

The world beyond the tavern was laid out with rolling hills and a countryside that suggested it would be at least a day's ride to the Iron Court. Stone fences kept cattle and sheep restrained on the horizon, and the road leading from the tavern was mucky from a recent rain with ruts and holes that reminded me this wasn't anywhere near a mortal city.

I propped my elbows on the railing and leaned over to see below. The tavern itself was two storeys, but shaped in a letter L with a second wing off to the right.

The room where I stood was situated over the main entrance, where a hitching post and cobblestones bedded the building. Dogs scampered about with some strange creatures that looked like griffins. Several horses were tied up to the hitching post, two of them with tacking nearby.

Stone came up behind me, and I could sense him there so acutely, the hairs on my arms stood on end. My body was still dealing with the multiple hits of adrenaline. The peep show with Blade didn't help matters. Neither did the sounds of rutting coming from the window next to us.

"I'm too amped up to sleep," I said and sagged into one of the chairs.

He took the other one across from me. "Maybe you just need a full belly," he said. "And a tankard of wine or ale." His blue eyes all but sizzled as they looked at me and my breath caught in my throat at the expression on his face.

I gestured toward the horses below. "I'm guessing yonder lies our ride to the court."

"You don't miss a trick," he said, but it wasn't sarcastic.

"I've never ridden a horse," I said.

"Then it's going to severely suck being you in the morning."

I shifted in the chair, letting my leg stretch beneath the table. My foot butted up to his. I swallowed a hard lump of desire, an unfortunate residual of adrenaline dogged by exhaustion.

"You could be a bit more sympathetic."

He laid his hand on the table, palm down, and leaned back, his eye falling on the scar around my throat. "I don't expect you expected much sympathy at all," he said. "You don't look the type to want it."

My jaw ticked at the assessment even as my fingers rose absently to the scar. "Pity is dangerous," I said. "Both giving it and getting."

He leaned forward, capturing my eyes with his, and again my stomach did a flip-flop at the bare desire it saw there. "That sounds terribly bitter."

I snorted. "Trust me. I'm a bitter pill to swallow. Always have been."

For a moment, I thought of Kit, slightly overweight Kit with her green eyes and mouse-gray hair that forever got into her eyes. She always looked haggard and worn. Worry lines had creased her forehead before she turned 23, and all that had been from worrying too much about me.

Taking up with Gideon, though, that had been the last straw. When I threatened to move in with him, she let me go, telling me to never come back, and I knew right then she'd lost all interest in me, in saving me, in loving me.

My throat ached at the memory, and I looked away from Stone because I didn't want him to see the sadness in my face. I let the rolling hills have all my attention for a moment until he laid his hand on top of mine, drawing me back to him.

"Has anyone ever tried to sweeten you?" he asked in a voice thick with what I knew was the same amount of lust as I felt right then. "Surely, not that weak excuse for a hunter you ran to. He doesn't have the stones to try."

"Freudian slip?" I quipped, but my eye flicked down to where our fingers had begun to tangle together. I didn't need love. I didn't need acceptance. I was enough for myself. Hunting filled me like a lover.

But there were times, like right then, when all the energy, pent up and boiling like water on a hard fire, needed to be spent. I wasn't shy about what I wanted. Never had been. But I was always careful to approach only those who showed interest. I'd chased Gideon long enough unrequited that I never wanted to put myself in that position again.

But this made-fae...he would do. He wouldn't refuse me, I knew. I'd known it since we'd met that he wanted to bed me. Violent men would see the violence in me and respond. Maybe there was something about the excitement of trying to dominate a reckless woman, or maybe it was the boiling rage he felt for Blade frothing over the sides of his kettle.

Whatever it was, I would take it. I would use it. I would toss it in the trash and enjoy the hot burn of it.

And then...then maybe I would sleep.

"Do you think you have the stones to try?" I asked.

In answer, he pushed back from his chair and yanked me out of mine. I came up hard against his chest and those battle-hardened hands ran up the back of my sweater, burrowing beneath the material. The callouses skimmed my skin in delicious ways.

"I think I'm just the stone to try," he said in a rough voice that reminded me of sand paper smoothing down a burled piece of wood, and then his mouth came down on mine in a growl.

For some reason, Jasmine and Blade came to mind, her hands held captive over his head, his merciless thrusts into her, and I used the leverage of my hands on Stone's shoulders to leap onto his waist when that image fueled the pent-up adrenaline.

I straddled him, hooking my ankles the way she had around Blade's waist. I pistoned myself higher, taking his kiss like a starving woman.

He angled us toward the doors and shoved through, pushing them open with the force of our weight. His long legs ate up the distance to the bed. With the doors laid open and the air wafting in over us, I let him peel me away long enough to drop me onto the mattress.

My hands went for the hem of my sweater, and I was pulling it up over my head as his hands worked at my jeans. I kicked along with him, trying to wrestle myself out of them. They sailed through the air as I flung them away.

The heavy clunk of the karambit hitting the floor beneath my pants sounded very much like a knock at the door, and I breathed the order to ignore it against his neck.

He fell to his knees between my bare legs. The sight of his face upturned toward mine sent a flush over my skin that went all the way to the back of my throat. The sound of my breath, coming faster now, drowned out his ragged breathing as he regarded me.

I blinked, recognizing the one moment I could change my mind, stop the progression of this insanity, but I didn't want to stop. I needed release. So did he. His need was already coating the air with pheromones so strong I felt as though the room was an oven baking a thick, custardy crème brulé.

When I reached for the band of my underwear, I felt his gaze blazing the same trail, and his breath hitched.

"Let me," he said, plucking my fingers from the waistband.

I swallowed nervously, remembering suddenly, the image of myself purchasing the pair from a shop that specialized in women's athletic undergarments.

To me, they were hunter's underwear. No lace. Not even cotton. Just industrial, worker-bee bamboo material that wicked away moisture and moved freely.

But the shop specialized in adding little touches, and that was why I frequented the place. Expensive, but an indulgence I never regretted.

Every inch of material in the shop, from its bras to its yoga pants was of such fine material, and so finely sewn, with little embellishments that beckoned the feminine in the most hardened of women.

A bit of lace overtop a panel of black cotton just where the hairline dipped in. A tiny, threaded logo. Scalloped legs.

Mine were crimson, high-cut, and probably frayed at the edges from so much wear.

"You're beautiful," he said, and at the sound of the huskiness in his voice, my throat swelled with an ache I couldn't swallow down.

I knew my body, knew it tended to curvaceous despite the muscle that shadowed it like an underpainting. Without all the scars and bruises and nicks, it might indeed be beautiful.

But the skin was marred, and because of that, few of my lovers got to see me completely naked. Gideon knew every inch of me, and could mark each scar, but I wasn't a leisurely lover, and I didn't let him linger.

Stone's touch was different. At once commanding and insistent, the electricity of his fingers as they moved across my flesh held me frozen with something different from mere lust. I wanted more in that instant than to rut and release.

For an instant, I didn't want to be Ava the hunter. I wanted to be Ava the woman. I wanted to be seen as beautiful. I wanted to be seen.

The scars. The bruises. I wanted them to be approached as the war wounds they were, markings to be touched and whispered over, revered for the purely magnificent things they were because I had labored for each one. Countless would-be victims could never know the beauty of the violence I'd done on their behalf.

So in those moments when his thumb slid beneath the waistband of my panties and eased the material away from my flesh, I wanted to be beautiful so badly I shivered with the need of it.

My breath caught in my throat as the gooseflesh rose along my spine.

"You're trembling, Ava," he whispered. "Are you afraid?"

"No," I said, laying my palm on the top of his head. "Maybe."

Even so, I let him peel away the material, slowly, as though he was an archaeologist brushing away the dust of eons from a priceless artifact. I felt each satiny movement of fabric whisper along my flesh in such acute anticipation that I couldn't help dropping my head back, losing myself in the terror of being examined so closely.

A soft moan escaped him as he freed the material from my hips and peeled them down my leg. The sound of it drew my other hand to his head, both of them planted along his temples, a small pressure pulling him toward me. Straining for his mouth.

"Your skin is like elven cashmere," he said, his mouth against the tender swell of my inner thigh. His breath was both feather and fur on my skin as he sighed. "Like the belly of a kitten."

The last material clinging to the arch of my foot let go and, freed, my legs spread apart so smoothly I might have been melting.

"Do you taste as divine as you smell, Ava?" he whispered.

I couldn't answer. My throat was so tight, the only thing that would loosen it would be a groan of climax.

I was ready...so ready. I let his words, lies all no doubt, whisper over me with the most delicious abandon. They lit the coals of heat low in my belly to a flaming roar that must devour or be devoured by itself.

Never a romantic, never one to respond to words of kindness in any form, I didn't know how to react, so I growled, low in my throat, demanding he take me.

He rose, climbing over me, pressing me backward onto the mattress, and I laid back, open, ready.

Then a hard rap sounded on the door. He froze. I froze.

"I'm busy," he snarled over his shoulder.

"Whatever it is keeping you so occupied, you'd best wrap it up," came the voice, one I now recognized easily as Blade's. "Because I'm coming in."

CHAPTER 20

THE WORDS HIT LIKE an icy shower, but before I had time to peel myself out from beneath Stone's considerable weight, the door flew open and Blade stormed in.

I had time to catch sight of him as he took in what was going on. At first, Blade's eyebrows climbed to his hairline at the sight of us on the bed. Then he rolled his eyes back as though he'd caught Stone far too many times at exactly what he was doing with me and was sick of it.

"You ever knock?" Stone demanded.

"The King's Guard is here," he growled and pointed at the floor as though to indicate precisely where they stood underneath him.

Stone reacted by waving at Blade to leave. "Take care of it," he said. "I told you I was busy."

I cringed beneath his body, trying to make myself small enough that Blade couldn't see the plentiful bit of skin on display.

Blade set his feet apart, his boots scuffing the wooden floor as he portioned himself against the door. His shoulders knotted as he planted his arms over his chest, that inscrutable expression of his riding his features so hard I blushed.

Or was that the embarrassment? Because I was mortified. My mind started reeling through the last few minutes to remember just what I might have said to Stone—specifically whether I'd been talking dirty or just moaning, because I was pretty sure in the heat of the moment I'd been doing one of those things. Maybe both, and I did not relish Blade hearing any of that.

Instead of turning tail and doing as he was bid; namely, taking care of the guard, Blade whistled loud and shrill. "He's up here, boys," he said at a pitch that had to travel down the stairs.

"What in the hell?" Stone reared back and jumped from the bed faster than a man of his size should have been able to. "Are you trying to get me arrested?"

I used the opportunity to scrabble off the bed like some guilty cheating housewife and grabbed for my sweater. All the while, Blade's gaze burned into the base of my spine with the heat of a hundred suns, and I was painfully aware of how much of my body was in plain view. My pants. My pants. Where in the hell were my pants?

"I'm trying to inform you that the king's own guard is here. You don't seem to care."

"Of course I care," Stone grumbled as he buttoned his trousers. Evidently, he was used to being found with his trousers off and wasn't the least bit embarrassed. He did, however, look antsy, even if he wasn't in a significant rush to haul up his trousers. His subtle but pointed glances around the room gave him away. And when he rushed to grab for his boots and held them in one hand instead of cramming them on, I knew he was eager to hide.

I pointed out the door to the closet as a good hiding spot. His glare indicated he did not find my help funny.

I didn't either, to be honest. I was just deciding I might dash into the space myself when footfalls on the stairs had him breezing past me toward the balcony. The curtains flew back with a noisy rattle as their wrought blacksteel rings jangled against the rod.

The strangely whooshing sound of the door closing behind his back was the only sound in the room for a moment as he disappeared through the velvet.

Blade watched him go with a half curve to his mouth before he turned that hot gaze on mine, letting it travel my legs with leisure.

"I know you might be trying to tempt me, Ponytail, but I have other things to do, and I'm sure you don't want the guard to find you like that." His head angled in the direction of the doorway, listening.

There was more than one set of boots on those stairs, I realized.

I tugged the sweater down to my hips. My hand itched for the karambit, which, of course, was sheathed somewhere beneath my jeans. And God knew where that article of clothing had gone. I'd yet to spy them on the floor where they should have landed after I'd kicked them off.

Holding down the hem of the sweater, I scoured the floor for the rest of my clothes.

"Best hurry," he drawled. "They won't care if you're dressed or not when they arrest you."

A glimpse of blue caught my eye from the side. My jeans. Hanging from one of the bookshelves, hooked by a rather garish bookend.

I lunged and grabbed for them. "I haven't done anything," I said. "Why would they arrest me?"

He ran his hand over the back of his neck. "Interesting," he said. "I wonder if Stone would appreciate your assessment of his prowess."

He strode across the room to the French doors, where he paused with his hands on the knob.

With his back to me, he flung open the doors and stepped outside. I didn't waste a second, and tugged my pants on over my legs without bothering to look for my underwear.

If he was going out onto that balcony to taunt or talk to Stone, I was using the chance to do a little yakking of my own. Namely, to the guards. If they were truly the king's guard, then I might just salvage this fiasco after all and be home in a couple of hours.

I had just enough time to zip up my jeans and pull my t-shirt up to my chest before the door to the room burst open, showing a crowded hallway stuffed with men who looked more like trolls than a regal guard.

Each of them held a short sword on one side of their tunics, belted around their waist over the top a thin, iridescent mesh that changed color as they moved. On their right sides, they had a black leather pouch tied off with a rather feminine ribbon.

A crest in the shape of a shield took up a palm sized space on their left. That was divided into three, but I didn't bother looking closer at the symbols. I didn't have that kind of time.

"Gentlemen," I said too loudly as I ambled forward to the arm of the man closest to me, the biggest of them, with black leathers and a head of shaggy red hair. "I think you have mistaken me for a prostitute." I tried on an indignant tone in case Blade and Stone were listening, which, of course they were. "Perhaps I should complain to management."

He started to argue, but I put my finger to my lips and leaned closer, smelling the hot oil of his perspiration and boiled leathers. "I have information for the King," I rasped out. "Information I can't discuss here." I held his eye as I said, much louder. "I demand you leave my room at once."

The captain, as I presumed by his thrown out chest, a fae male with eyebrows three shades brighter than his hair and a scar splitting his nose into two continents, nodded and lifted his hand to gesture toward the others. "We have word two violent criminals are hiding in here."

"In my room?" I said in a high-pitched tone that somehow managed to sound both breathless and assertive at the same time. "I just got here. If there are criminals hiding in this tavern, they are not in my room. Now get out," I shoved him with admittedly very little resistance toward the door.

"You think you can order the king's guard around?" he said in a bad acting voice that made me cringe. "Mortal women have no power here."

One of his nostrils was larger than the other, and it flared when he peered down at me. I got a sudden, horrible sense that if I moved too fast, he'd strike like a cobra, and I'd have to drop my shirt to defend myself. I hoped to avoid that if I could.

Thankfully, however, he flicked his wrist at his comrades and they eddied away like flotsam on the tide. Their entries into the other rooms were less abrasive, I noticed, and several girlish squeals rose above a lot angrier male voices.

When he turned back to me, my spine tingled with threat even though he kept smiling and leaning toward me conspiratorially, as though he was totally and completely in sync with me. He wanted me to think he was on my side. I wasn't fooled.

I backed up, releasing his arm and running my palm down my leg, searching for my karambit out of habit. His eyes followed the progress of my hand like a rabid dog.

Of course, neither sheath nor karambit was there.

Two things raced through my mind in the seconds it took for him to pivot toward me.

The first was that I could and should deliver a sweeping roundhouse kick and take the bastard down before he did something I would regret.

The second was that if I just gave him the information, he'd see it for the critical bit of intel that it was and gather up his soldiers and be gone, taking me along with them to the King. Out of reach of the Fae Mafia with an excuse that might keep Kit alive.

Instinct bade me take the first option. Reason made me take the last.

But it wasn't reason that failed me. It was that moment of hesitation, created by second-guessing the instinct that had kept me alive for years of hunting. It left open the time the guard needed to wrestle my arms behind my back. The shirt fluttered to the floor at my feet.

I kicked, but too late, and the troll of a man lifted me high into the air, my back against his chest, my arms yanked backwards. Both of my shoulders wrenched painfully as I fought for freedom, thrashing and rolling like a gator, but he had too good a hold, and was far stronger than I expected.

I'd hunted down an ogre once. At over seven feet, with shaggy hair and corded muscles that moved beneath coarse skin, it had taken strategy and speed to beat him. Luckily, the ogre had bad eyesight and relied on brute strength to fight, so I was able to use that to my advantage.

This troll-like fae was similar, except he was well-trained in formal battle. Bad news for me.

It wasn't like me to give in to the typical female response, that ingrained and hopeful part of an untrained female lizard brain that expected sympathy from a male instead of violence, but I'd second guessed myself and paid the price.

I felt stupid and ridiculous and that made me angry as a bear with a sore ass.

"Listen, you fool," I said into my shoulder as he boiled toward the bed with me kicking at the air like an overturned beetle, unable to get the purchase, or the thrust I needed to throw him off me. "I'm not joking. I have important information. You have to listen to me."

"Oh, I'll listen," he said in a gruff voice as he pinned me to the mattress, my face down. "I'll listen to every moan, screech, and shriek you make as I take what I want from you. You can even call me every sort of bastard you want," he said. "I like my bitches with a little fire in their veins."

The words lanced me with horror. He wasn't just planning to arrest me; he planned to do what soldiers throughout time had done to women they considered spoils of war.

Nausea welled up in my belly as his mouth nuzzled against my ear. The stink of fish wafted over me, making the spinning of my stomach even worse.

I had to swallow down the revulsion that rose to my cheeks as I thought of Stone and me just moments earlier. I would not let this moment distort the memory of that one. I would not think about how badly I'd wanted him, not allow these two moments to get tangled together.

Instead, I'd think only of the scents wafting up from the mattress, the wonderful, enticingly comfortable mattress, and how it smelled of soap, and good, innocent sleep sweat.

A deadly calm moved over me. I clung to the fragrance, wholesome as it was, and reminded myself that fear would only whet his appetite. It was critical to act as though this was nothing to me, a trip to the dentist or the hairdresser.

"You're quiet for a wench who has such important information," he said. "Could it be you have nothing to say and just wanted some time alone with the Captain of the Guard?"

"I'm just quiet because your fat stomach is cutting off my air," I said.

At that, he bit my earlobe, sending a jolt of pain into my scalp. "You're not fighting, wench," he said. "Have you no idea what's about to happen to you, or are you looking forward to it?"

Because he wanted me to struggle, I went completely still, laying my cheek against the bedspread, determined to rob him of the satisfaction that he had all the control, that he could do whatever he wanted with me.

There was nothing so hateful as stealing that sort of victory away from a bastard. I would not feel shame. I would not feel powerless. No matter what happened.

I took deep breaths where I could. One of his hands burrowed between the mattress and my chest, finding and pinching my nipple. I had to bite back the urge to swear.

Keep calm. This wasn't over yet. I'd offer him what he was really after, deliver the information clearly. Because that was the real issue. That was what I needed in the end. To get Kit in the clear.

And if he didn't get the hell off of me then, well—

"You're here for the Shadow Court male, right?" I asked in a quiet voice, craning to look at him over my shoulder. "That's what brought you to the tavern? What if I said I know where he is? What if I said I know he and his organization have your king marked for assassination?"

He grunted at that, and I half expected things to shift with the information, for him to let me go, ask me for more details. But he didn't loosen his grip. Not one bit.

Instead, he let all his weight fall on top of me, squeezing the air from my lungs in a whoosh. My face planted into the soft rasp of velvet, my mouth open. I tasted soap and a hint of lavender.

The hand between us pushed down further as he reached for the waistband of his breeks. I realized with horror that I'd lost any opportunity to fight back.

"Message delivered," he said. "Now if you don't mind, I'm going to rut into you like a bitch until I'm done. I expect you to fight. I want you thrashing beneath me, not lying there like a dead cod."

He said the words soft and as calmly as I'd delivered the news of his king's imminent death. There was no way anyone but the two of us heard what he said. And yet...

They were the last words I heard him utter before his weight was peeled from my back.

A brush of fresh air moved across the nape of my neck, lifting the sweat of adrenaline from my skin but doing nothing to cool me down.

It took a full second for me to realize I was free and that the curses I was spitting into the velvet bedspread were no longer just a smothered raft of syllables. And then, I rolled to the floor so swiftly, it made me dizzy. I sprang to my feet and fell into a fighting stance.

Knife or no knife, I would tear the man's balls off and shove them up his ass.

But there was no one to fight. A sweep of the room with a wide-eyed gaze showed the captain of the guard lying on the floor, spread-eagle, his hand still on the waistband of his breeks as though he'd had not a second of warning before he'd been yanked from me.

Blood leaked from his ear and was pooling into the mat of his bushy red hair. I was sure I caught sight of a long slash across his cheek in the same direction as the scar on his nose.

The crest on his tunic took all my attention and my gaze seemed to lock onto it for an eternity, long enough, certainly to separate all the three sections into their individual panels. A pair of golden wings with delicate silver cloth of silver filigree at the top. The middle with its crown adorned with different color embroidery meant to suggest precious gems. The sword on the bottom striking up into the heart of the crest, separating the other two sections.

It took forever, it seemed, for my eye to trail to the boots of the man standing over him. I don't know why I expected it to be Stone, but it was Blade watching me, looking as fresh as the moment he'd entered the room except for a splatter of blood dotting his face. Beyond him, the velvet curtains danced on the breeze.

I lifted my gaze to his. A flash of copper moved through his eyes as he flicked them toward me.

One blink and it was gone.

I knew I should say something, but the words were stuck in my throat. With horror, I realized my cheeks were wet and that my eyes stung. I dropped my gaze to the captain, taking in every bullish feature, the blood on the floor, and realized it wasn't enough.

I brought my foot down on his face, my lips curled back from my teeth with the force of the blow.

His nose crunched beneath my heel, and he bucked upward in reflex. A hollow sound of pain escaped his lips.

It still wasn't enough. My lips trembled with exertion as I pulled my foot back and rammed my heel with a donkey kick to his ribs. My teeth chattered at the impact.

I kicked again and again, and when hands fell to my shoulders, yanking me clear of the captain, I reeled on the owner of those hands too, ready to kill. With my teeth if I had to.

My left fist jabbed forward even as my right brought up a strong upper cut an instant later because I wanted those hands off me. I wanted to be left alone. I wanted to feel nothing. The hollow space of pain needed to numb everything into a tiny pinprick of emotion I could stuff into a corner of my mind and never think about again.

Blade met both swings with cupped hands that resisted my swings like a heavy bag, and the blows were softened without hurting my knuckles.

"Get the fuck off me," I said, and I danced a step backward, just enough to prepare for a roundhouse kick. He watched me, eyelids hooded, waiting for me to strike without doing a single thing to prevent it.

Except. I didn't. I halted. I pulled it back and let my foot just drop to the floor as I stood there, staring at him, my chest heaving.

"I didn't need you," I said.

He pursed his lips thoughtfully. "I know," he said. "But I thought I'd expedite the whole process, seeing as how the others are on their way back."

He looked over his shoulder toward the door. "Best pull on the Raiment," he said. "They'll be here in about thirty seconds."

He reached down for the corset as it lay on the chair and tossed it at me. He gestured for me to hurry, and so without a single bit of compunction, I peeled out of my shirt and shoved my arms through the corset.

I was lacing it up when the contingent of guard filled the doorway again. They looked from me to Blade to the captain and, without a word, surrounded us so quickly, I didn't have time to blink.

"I hope for your sake that the captain of the king's Guard is still alive," said one, a short man with a long mustache that reached his chin on both sides. "Because the penalty for his death is yours."

CHAPTER 21

I KNEW I WAS going to be executed for killing the Captain of the Guard, and I didn't care. The bastard deserved it, and even if I hadn't delivered the killing blow, given the chance, I'd have done it in a heartbeat.

But just as the little guard reached into the leather pouch hanging from the side of his belt and pulled out a pair of handcuffs that were no more than purple light sizzling with blue trails, a long, keening moan came from the space on the floor where the captain lay.

Impossible. Worse than that, hateful. The man should be dead. I wanted to drop to a crouch beside him and slam his head into the floor, this time hard enough to stop the sounds coming from his mouth. I wanted to lay my hand on his mouth and press down until I saw the light go out of his eyes.

I must have moved, because Blade's fingers circled my elbow. A gentle, but insistent pressure held me back.

"Just a misunderstanding," he said to the guard. "See?" He gestured to where the captain had begun to moan. "The captain is perfectly fine physically." His brow furrowed. "As for his emotional well-being, I'll leave that to those who can accept a man's brutal treatment of a poor innocent pixie."

He looked askance at me in a look that suggested I should hold my tongue, when I shot him a bewildered look.

A breathy sort of cursing rose from the lump of troll on the floor and several of the guard rushed to their captain's aid. The soldier watching us didn't budge. Instead, he shook out the light cuffs and held them out.

"Accosting a Captain of the Guard warrants arrest," he said quietly but with enough firmness that I didn't doubt he'd use force if he had to. "If you come along peacefully, we will not have to resort to magic."

I cocked my hip. "Go ahead," I said, my mouth finally getting tired of being on the sidelines. "They punish those who use magic here."

Blade sent me a shriveling look, and the little guard laughed.

"Everything in this part of the realm is subject to the King's rule first," the guard said. "Whatever other rules they have in place are for the rest of the rabble. It doesn't apply to us."

Meaning they could do whatever they damn well pleased, and Blade knew it. What sort of magic they possessed that might cow him into accepting arrest, I wasn't sure. I just knew I needed to take his place if I was to get out from under this devil's bargain.

So, I stuck out my wrists in the guard's direction. "Arrest me then," I said.

He took one look at my hands and laughed aloud. "Are you saying you're the one who knocked the captain senseless?" His lifted eyebrows suggested he thought the idea was ludicrous. "You? A poor innocent pixie?"

"That's exactly what I'm saying," I told him and jerked my wrists toward him again. "Now arrest me."

He laughed again and shook the cuffs out so that a long trail of light dangled between them. "I'm no fool," he said with a shake of his head. "I know what's going on here. Your pimp here decided to shake down the Captain of the Guard and you're supposed to take the hit for him, so he stays out of jail while you suffer the torments of the cells."

He glared at Blade. "You lot are despicable, using the innocent goodness of a pixie to seal your own hedonistic ends. You should be ashamed."

"Oh, I am ashamed," Blade said with a twinkle in that green gaze as he held out his wrists. "But you have no idea the kind of coin a man can get for a pixie when she's as fiery as this one."

He ran his eye down my throat, and I could swear he watched my pulse racing with fury. "The trouble is the men who want to steal their innocence are often cowards who hide in the shadows at the first sign of trouble."

I knew he was talking about Stone, who was hiding on the balcony, and who probably overheard the whole assessment. The thought of him out there, with his ear to the door, waiting for the guard to disappear, made the sense of urgency that much more potent.

Because if I let Blade get arrested instead of me, I'd be right where I started.

If there was any chance of me salvaging all this and keeping Kit safe, I couldn't let that happen. I had to act. Now.

I made a dash for the captain, who was already getting shakily to his feet with the aid of two other guards. His face upturned at my movement, a dazed and confused look on his face. Concussion, probably.

Whatever Blade had struck him with, it had to be solid enough to make those pupils remain wide and black. I doubted he really saw me when he caught my eye, but I let fly with a roundhouse swing, anyway.

There was time for the captain's eye to flick over my shoulder. I braced my spine for impact by shuffling some distance between my feet, letting my hips swivel with the thrust to use as much kinetic energy as I could.

The moment before it landed, someone grabbed my arm, holding me back. I swung on that someone, furious. Blade's cool gaze met mine.

"You don't want to do that," he said. "Trust me."

While I stood there, gawking, the rest of the guards brushed me aside, shoving me against the bed as the little guard snapped the cuffs down around Blade's wrists. A crackle of electricity tore through the air as the cuff locks met each other in a final embrace, one so loud and so powerful I felt it in my core.

Blade gave them a shake, maybe testing the fit. He pursed his lips thoughtfully and made a pensive sound in the back of his throat. Was he awe-struck or simply intrigued? Who could know?

Not to be deterred, I dove for the little guard, but he was ready for me after my attempt on his still dazed captain. He stopped me with a blast of magic that exploded from his palm and struck me in the chest. He was still shaking his hands as though the magic had hurt him when he said, "Someone get control of that pixie."

I staggered back, dazed and suffering a race of tremors that turned my muscles to gelatin. I had to lean against the bed just to keep from sliding down to the floor. I watched them with as dazed an eye as the captain's.

Pixie. I had no idea what a pixie was, but I had shades of memory from cartoons, and they were tiny little things. They didn't realize I was human. The corset was some piece of work if it could make a full grown woman look like Tinkerbell.

I blinked stupidly at the lot of them as they shouldered Blade to the doorway and shoved him into the hall. The little guard turned to study me for a moment, then with a grunt of satisfaction, pushed Blade through the door, following him without another look back.

They all left the room without a single look back. All except the captain. He turned all the way around to peer over his companions' shoulders to scan the room with a confused eye. Looking for something. Or someone.

When his gaze landed on me again, it narrowed suspiciously. No doubt he was looking for the mortal woman he'd tried to assault, wondering where she'd gone to, and although some part of him must have realized I wore a glamor, he just couldn't see through it. Or maybe he was still too dazed to think clearly.

The magic that held me like a drunk pup let me go the moment they all crossed the threshold.

Running in a stooping form that collected my karambit and sheath from beneath the bed as I raced by, I tore into the hallway behind them. They were already halfway to the stairs.

"Wait," I said, holding the blade behind my back. "You don't understand."

They ignored me, of course, marching down the stairs with a strangely subdued Blade in tow. Frustrated, I trailed along until I noticed Jasmine threading her way toward them. As the soldiers filed through the chairs and tables toward the exit, she weaved between the guards who didn't bother to give her any room, instead barreling along as though she didn't exist.

I took the steps two at a time, knowing that in moments they'd be out the door and out of my reach.

"Stop," I said loud enough that the soldiers at the back, at least, would hear me. The last thing I wanted to do was alert Stone of my attempts to pass on the information of the coming assassination, but I also couldn't just let them leave without finding a way to get pulled along with them.

I was several treads from the bottom, and they were on their way out. "You can't just leave."

For a second, I thought the contingent would halt. Every action in the tavern certainly did. Eyes turned to me curiously. Several stares narrowed as though they were trying to work out what sort of woman would try to command the king's Guard. And a pixie at that.

Those holding Blade paused, though, thankfully. When he lifted his eyes to mine, his long gaze made my neck tingle. The corset moved over my breasts, catching on the nipples in a way that made them itch again.

"It wasn't him," I said, trying the same line again.

The captain looked back at me over his shoulder. The vigor had returned to his face, and he wasn't leaning quite so heavily on his comrades. Revolted by his attention but encouraged that I'd not completely lost the opportunity, I sped the rest of the way down the stairs.

By the time I made it to the bottom step, Jasmine had made it as far as Blade. Cuffed, Blade's hands snaked out from in front of him and grabbed hold of her wrist. A snap sounded that made her flinch, and a burst of light snaked its way up her arm. She sagged against the railing.

Blade's captors swung around, drawn to the reaction of the cuffs. But while Jasmine looked pained, Blade showed no signs of hurt. Instead, he leaned closer to her as his captors fired off another jolt. An eddy of power pulsed up the chains to the cuffs. He shrugged the magic off and whispered in her ear.

I watched, gaze narrowed as she turned her face to him, held his gaze so intimately the entire tavern had to feel the heat. Then she nodded and looked up at me. Her eyes widened in surprise. Me. He'd said something about me.

Gaze shuttered, I watched her, fully expecting her to climb to the top based on the hard stare she was giving me. I lifted an eyebrow, daring her to come up. Sure, my gaze said, I'd love to hear what Blade said about me to you. But then Blade nudged her attention back to him. He jerked his chin toward the activity swelling behind her. The captain and his aids, swaggering now, with his cloak blooming out behind him.

I could swear I saw her pull in a long breath before she launched herself in his direction. The captain caught sight of her and a disgusting smile slid over his face like ten-year-old brake grease leaking out a caliper.

He hooked her as she went by, but only because she stuck her elbow out just enough to make it an easy catch. Then his meaty hand circled her neck, pulling her even closer. She stumbled at the suddenness of his strike, a cobra's speed in that thick arm.

One more second and he had pulled his cloak over her, blanketing her from view except for her head.

She got dragged along with the contingent then. Blade's attention returned to his progress toward the door, as though nothing was going on behind him. Dread climbed my spine as I realized what the captain planned for her if she stayed in his hold.

"Bastard," I said, realizing with horror that Blade had just ordered Jasmine to throw herself at that revolting prick.

Still wearing the pixie glamoring corset, I raced down the rest of the stairs. And across the tavern floor, tailing the soldiers as fast as I could. By the time I reached them, Jasmine was already wrapped up in the captain's cloak tight enough that it was tucked around her waist.

"Hey," I said. "Hey, she can't leave here." I whirled around, looking for the barkeep. "Stop him," I said to no one and everyone at once. "Somebody has to stop him."

What met my scan were a dozen eyes too afraid to do more than stare at a crazy pixie begging to save a mortal woman from the guard. Ludicrous. Who would even bother? Seamus had already come out from behind the bar and was hovering near the door, his hands wringing together, but he was doing no more than giving me a strange look.

"Do something," I said, gesturing madly at Jasmine. As a pixie I wouldn't be able to do any more than that, but by God I was going to have to do something if the girl so much as pressed a toe into the grass beyond the door.

He shrugged, implying he had no idea what to do.

Well, damn and hell. Maybe he wasn't going to do anything to save one of his waitresses, but nothing was going to stop me from interfering. There was no telling what would happen to a mortal woman past these doors, if what happened within them was any indication.

I stomped toward the contingent, shouldering my way through the throng of them. They gave me evil eyes but otherwise paid me no mind.

Blade was up front, held by three soldiers, one on each side and one behind, effectively pinning him in. He looked over his shoulder at me, eyelids at half-mast, his brow furrowed as though he was peering at some bomb about to explode. The analogy wasn't too far off.

"You," I said to the captain with all the sternness of a hunter who had spent a decade trolling through nasty beasts. "Let her go. You can't take her out of here."

He halted. Of course he did. I had a damn commanding voice, pixie glamor notwithstanding. There was also the small matter of the karambit hanging from my grip beside my leg.

And yet, with one gesture, he bid the rest of the soldiers to keep going and managed to corral Jasmine even tighter to his side.

Her disgust for him was clear as she eyed him, but even so, she shook her head at me. I shook mine right back.

I planted my feet, toes finding some balance against the wooden floor. "Release her."

He chuckled without turning around. "She's wanted by the King," he said without deigning to look my way as he spoke. "Now leave the guard to its business."

Jasmine glared at me over his shoulder. Blade was already outside. The sun was striking his black hair and catching copper highlights. He stood alone with his hands submissively in front of his hips while his captors peeled a long snake of light out from their saddlebags and were joining it to his chains.

I dragged my gaze from them to the captain, who had grabbed a large tankard from a table by the door and was downing the contents. My chest ached with the desire to run the karambit over his Achilles tendon, but for the sake of those in the tavern, I would do this the right way. With my words.

I took my time, leisurely strapping the sheath to my thigh, holding his gaze. "You," I said, projecting my voice toward him. "I told you to leave her be."

It took a long time for his gaze to move from the tankard he placed ever so carefully back onto the table and then to me. Before he could get a full view, Jasmine stepped between us, pulling free of his hold just enough to gather his attention.

Just when I was sure the captain would shove her to the side and come after me, the bartender managed to free his feet from the glue that rooted him to the floor.

"The warrant," he said, rushing forward and shouldering me out of the way and behind several other women with painted bodies and hair piled high enough to block me from view.

The captain winced at the word.

"She's indentured," the bartender said with a shrug as he nudged the captain toward the door amiably.

Jasmine went rigid, her fists clenched at her sides as she watched.

"She's owned," the bartender went on. "If the King has business with her, you best come back with a warrant for her owner." He said this with all the indulgence of a man who knew there was no real business with the king, but was merely offering a way for the captain to save face.

I wanted to ruin that face, but I held my tongue, chest heaving and aching with the desire to pommel the bastard.

The little bartender smiled widely. "It's the King's own edict. An indentured woman may only leave her place of servitude with a special warrant. Surely, as a King's Guard, you know this. Surely you have such a warrant with you if you're planning to take her out of here?"

The captain pressed his lips together and swung his heated gaze to Jasmine. For a second, I thought I might have to cross the line that had been drawn for me, but with a disgusted shove, he let her go.

She stumbled at first, then caught herself on the back of a chair. One of the other women took her by the arm and wrapped her in a comforting embrace. Both women, I noticed, didn't bother to hide their hatred for the soldiers as they stared at them from beneath fringes of their hair with pure hatred.

Beyond the door, the sun had begun to set finally. Blade's back rose higher above most of the guard, his shoulders broader than the rest of them. He seemed to be going along almost amiably.

I watched from the doorway until they'd saddled up and set their horse's hooves onto the road. The bartender stood beside me. The tension in his body was palpable. Only when they'd turned a corner in the road and the trees had swallowed them did he sigh and turn to me.

"Ale," he said simply. He gestured Jasmine and the girls away from the door and crossed the tavern to the bar. At his movement, the patrons went back to their drinks. The chatter grew louder. By the time I followed him across the room, it was as though the guard had never been there.

I sank onto the seat of a stool and leaned on the bar. Something was up. I expected the bartender to fill me in, but I was weary to the marrow and waiting for him, I found my head bobbing on my neck. I tried to count the amount of hours I'd been awake and realized I probably didn't want to know.

Seamus the barkeep came over with a tankard foaming at the top with a heady ale that sprayed its fizz at me like a cola. "Most pixies don't get involved in trouble," he said, laying his finger against his nose. "In fact, most pixies don't come to the tavern at all."

There was something about the way he looked at me, as though he were seeing through me. Just when I was about to ask what was on his mind, he ducked behind the bar, and I lost my chance to question him. I propped myself onto my elbows, trying to crane over the surface to see if I could catch his attention again.

The sensation of another body taking up space beside me took my attention. Jasmine. I peered sideways at her and saw her looking right back. Her expression made me think I had a big mustard stain on my shirt.

"What in the hell is going on?" I demanded.

CHAPTER 22

I was tired. I was cranky. I was about ready to explode if someone didn't tell me what in the heck was going on.

Jasmine's gaze dipped to my cleavage, and I looked down, not sure what had her attention enough to raise her eyebrows. Everything was in place. The corset looked the same, the same lacey sheer material with long laces that tied in the front that I'd pulled on upstairs. My nipples poked out through the fabric and itched enough that it took sheer will not to start scratching them right in front of people.

Even so, I had a feeling I knew exactly what was happening. It came to me as I realized the comment Seamus had made earlier about magic being outlawed in the tavern along with weaponry and violence. My lip twitched at the truth of it.

"The glamor from the corset is gone, isn't it?" I asked.

She gave me a crooked smile. "Not gone, just fading. And if I can barely see it, then I imagine most Fae can see who you are and what you're wearing. They'll recognize a magical garment."

My jaw ticked. "That's not good, is it?" I didn't need to hear about all the ways it would suck for anyone in the realm to have a good eyeful of a mortal woman wearing a holy Fae garment, especially when the King's assassination was already scheduled. Especially when the use of magic in the tavern came with a hefty fine.

"Blade noticed first," she said. "He asked me to distract everyone."

So, that's what that was all about. I didn't want to think about why he would bother to try to let me keep my disguise. He had nothing to gain. In fact, it didn't make sense why he bothered to let himself get arrested. Why he knocked out the captain. None of it made sense.

Right then, Seamus popped back up with a bottle of paint and a large brush. "I did what I could without breaking the rules." He shrugged with just one shoulder.

"Reasoning that if the magic was waning, it couldn't really count as being used. Am I right?"

He gave me a wan smile. "Magic is currency in Fae now. Once it used to be breath," he said. "The Shadow Court wants to control as much as they can, own it like you humans do money. And since the Velvet Boar belongs to them, they fine anyone who uses it here. Keeps the tavern nicely within their control." He scratched at his hair with the end of the brush. "Your raiment is powerful enough to bypass the tolls, but as it wanes, it will register and its magic will halt altogether." The paint brush jabbed in my direction. "I don't think you have much time."

"Slip out of it," Jasmine said, leaning toward me. "Give it to Seamus, and he'll paint you. You'll look like any of the other girls and no one will see your unmentionables." She tried to smile, but something was off in her expression.

I eyed Seamus. This all seemed a pretty convenient way to get hold of a magical relic that could offer quite a bit of protection to the right person.

"I'm not baring my boobs and painting that harlot paint on myself," I said to her. "And I'm not giving him the corset."

Jasmine's hand rested on my forearm, squeezing it. "Corset?" she said with a snicker. "It's a tube top, honey. And don't worry. No one will try to sell your ass in the few moments it takes for you to go back to your room. The fairy paint is just so you aren't completely naked. If you want to blend in, you need to blend in."

"Then give me a coat or a sweater or something. I just need it to climb the stairs." I waggled my fingers at him, a command that he give me his coat.

"That's not blending in," she said and gave me a pointed look, inferring that a human woman with my sort of attitude was doing exactly the opposite of blending in.

Which made me concede that she did actually have a valid point. Knowing what I would be doing in the next few days, I really didn't want anyone to remember me.

"If it makes you feel better, you can have Seamus paint you in a corset." She gave me a cow look that suggested she wasn't the least bit insulted by my comment, suggesting only prostitutes wore the paint. "He'll even make sure it flatters your narrow waist."

With a sigh, I nodded my consent. "But I'm not giving him mine. I'll hold on to it myself till he's done."

She brightened measurably. "Perfect." A glance at my stomach and she let out a little humming sound of worry. "Best hurry, though."

With her help, I peeled off the garment, knowing full well my breasts would be bared and feeling more than a little conspicuous.

"Pants too," she said, holding out her hand in such a way that brooked no argument.

I slid my pants down my legs and dropped them into her hand. The weight of the karambit seemed to surprise her, but she merely folded everything up and laid the pile on the bar.

To his credit, Seamus came around the bar and stood in the way of prying eyes as he swept the brush over my skin. Like a doctor, he angled his head this way and that, checking to see every place was covered. I supposed he had painted his share of boobs and worse, and wasn't the least bit interested in my rack, that, though full and pert, sat atop more than a feminine curve of muscle.

"Nice abs," he said as he drew the lines downward. "Most Fae like their mortal women to have a bit of fat on their bellies, but yours is nice and hard. Takes the paint better."

The compliment did less to ease the embarrassment than his tone did. It was professional. An artist choosing a palette or a canvas. A doctor inspecting a sutured wound.

I relaxed under his work, watching Jasmine's expressions change as the painting went on.

The bristles barely touched my skin but where they did, warmth spread into my flesh and then outward like someone was pouring warm oil over me. It wasn't unpleasant. In fact, it was making me pretty damn sleepy.

Drowsy and mesmerized, I sagged on the stool until it was done and he stepped back to admire his work.

"What is it?" I asked. "Tell me it's not a black lace corset."

"It's beautiful," Jasmine breathed out, and Seamus lifted his chin with a haughty sort of pride.

"Fairy paint changes depending on the viewer," he said. "I can tell you I painted a Valkyrie with fiery wings and a golden crown. I can't tell you what others see."

My eyebrows climbed my forehead. "So, I'll probably see a damn black corset if I look in a mirror and not a kick ass chick with razors for wings? Just my luck."

I hopped off the stool and angled my feet toward the stairs. I had to make my way through several throngs of patrons just to get across the room. I grabbed for the pile of clothes, karambit and corset and all and tucked it against my hips with the aim of getting all the way to the staircase without getting accosted and having to punch my way free.

That would most assuredly blow my cover.

It only then occurred to me that Stone might be waiting for me. It was a bit disconcerting that he'd not come down in all the hubbub, and part of me was disappointed that he wouldn't face the guard or investigate the ruckus. I was giving it considerable musing when Jasmine hooked my elbow, halting my progress to the staircase.

"The paint isn't just to get you safely upstairs," she whispered and jerked her head toward a booth made of scorched wood with several candles emitting a warm and inviting glow. "I have things to tell you. Things that will suit us for you to look like one of us."

It was so secretive, my drowsiness evaporated.

"Lead on then," I said and trailed her across the room, shouldering past several patrons who reached out to stroke her ass or thighs as she went by. I caught one of the men's hands and gave it a hard twist as I kept walking. His pained grunt got cut off quickly when his comrades started poking fun at him.

I pushed into the booth across from Jasmine and waited for her to speak, which evidently was giving her some trouble because she kept watching for people walking by. At our first moment alone, she leaned across the table.

"I've put something inside the tube top," she said as she handed it over the top of the worn table. "It will look like a token, the kind you get at the fairs. Except it will be gold."

I let my palm roam the surface of the table. "A golden token? Stuffed in the wad of material of the corset." I eyed her thoughtfully. "And where did it come from?"

She dragged her gaze from mine and settled it on the pile of fabric between us. "You should be asking what it will get you admittance to."

I leaned back, letting my palm remain on the table. "I have a good idea where it will get me."

"Do you?" she asked. "Because it's a pretty big deal. That token is rare."

Crossing my ankles beneath the table, I watched her face closely as I answered her question. "It's going to get me access to the Iron Court."

Her eyebrows climbed to her hairline. "Not just the court," she said. "The Gala Ball."

I tried not to let my feet clomp down on her bare toes at the words because the thought of dancing around in balls and gowns brought images of beasts and tusks and animated teacups with saucers, and the thought of that made all this seem far too surreal.

"Tell me more about the ball."

She blinked. "I only know what I was told to pass on to you. And that someone will come for you."

Stone. This had to be his work. He must have gotten spooked by the guard and slipped away, leaving her to pass on the token so I'd be able to get into this ball. But when would that happen? And how long would I have to wait in the tavern before I could get this distasteful task started. The thought of idling here, impotent and ignorant, made me want to wring his thick, bullish neck.

My gaze darted to the raiment as it lay between us on the gouged wooden table, looking for some glimpse of it. I reached for the material, deciding to poke about until I came away with it right in my hand, lay eyes on it for real. Her hand dropped down over mine.

"Don't," she rasped out in a hiss. "Fae will kill for it. I wouldn't let anyone see it if I were you."

"If you were me, you'd want to be sure no one had already stolen it," I said dryly.

I didn't want to suggest she'd steal it, but if it really was all that, then it could very well buy her a way out of Fae. I'd seen people do far worse for far less.

She leaned back in her chair, her gaze hooded as she regarded me. For a moment, the blank, hypnotic expression disappeared while she assessed me. "You doubt its value," she said. "Seamus told me his own son was murdered for one a hundred years ago."

"So, you've shown it to Seamus?" I leaned forward on my forearms. "Strange thing to do with a valuable relic that could get you killed." My eyes narrowed at her. "Unless you tried to sell it for yourself?"

"You think I'm lying."

"I think if it was so valuable that it's worth killing for, it would be worth stealing."

Part of me wanted her to have taken it. Part of me really wanted to see her slip out from the clutches of Blade and this bar and find her way home again. I'd seen how she was with Blade in the bathroom. Patty Hearst had nothing on this chick.

My heart cracked a little at the thought she'd live her life out here, a painted prostitute with nothing to look forward to except a scrap of attention from the bastard who pimped her out. And so if she hadn't actually stolen it, maybe she should.

"It's there," she insisted. "I'm just not stupid enough to pull it out in plain sight. This isn't some nightclub in the city. This place is dangerous. And that token was paid for by a fae life."

"If it's so valuable, why are you just giving it to me?"

She blinked at me owlishly, her expression devoid of any evidence that she could think behind those eyes.

"Seamus's son was killed for his token by the Shadow Court," she said. "If you've been given one, I'd say you should know who gave it to you. I'm not about to cross him." Her gaze moved across the room as though she needed to deflect from the words. "I was told to give you the thing. I've already said too much."

"So, what makes that token so coveted?"

Her eyes flashed with a strange light, and she shook her head the way a dog does with an earful of water.

"Are you alright, Jasmine?"

She gave me a blank stare. "I'm fine, why? Don't you like your fairy paint?"

She was gone. No doubt that small bit of information had been planted magically, and now that she'd delivered her message, it had evaporated from her memory.

I patted her hand and thanked her. She got up, and without a glance at me, sashayed across the room to allow herself to be scooped onto a wiry-looking fae's lap. She never once looked my way again.

That left me pondering more than what the ticket would gain me entrance to. Stone must have given the ticket to her and suggested she pass it on to me. But why? He could give it to me himself when the time came.

Unless he wasn't in the tavern anymore. I couldn't see him just abandoning me, though. Unless he'd got scooped up along with Blade and arrested, and this was the best he could do to keep me on task.

If that was the case, I was on my own. I stared down at the table, panic trying to worm its way through my chest. On my own, in a realm I knew nothing about. Frustration and exhaustion fought for prominence as I struggled to rein in my mind as it began cavorting with all sorts of doom and gloom scenarios. Someone would come for me, she'd said. I supposed I had nothing to do but wait.

Exhaustion was claiming my faculties. I needed to sleep. A few hours would grant me the acuity of thought and reason that I so desperately needed right then. At least I'd have the room to myself, I thought with a wry twist to my mouth. I was pretty sure Stone wouldn't be waiting for me in the room.

Even so, when I climbed the stairs and opened the door, I was still disappointed to see the balcony curtains spread wide, showing a view of the lit city beyond in the distance, but with no Stone anywhere outside or within. A niggle of thought raised itself like a worm in my mind. The dark objects.

I sped to the armoire where Stone had stuffed the pouch.

"Please, please, please, dear God, please," I muttered as I yanked the doors open.

Nothing inside. Not even a dust mote.

"Damn and double damn," I grumbled.

The corset clenched in my hand got flung aside to the floor. And there, just like Jasmine had said, peeked out a tiny golden corner. She'd spoken true. Against her own best interests, she'd done what had been asked of her and left it with me.

Heaving a sigh, I bent to retrieve it. The thing took up no more than a moth in my palm. Despite it being made of gold—real gold, I realized—it was light. The hexagonal shape had substance but very little weight.

The side facing up possessed a luminescence that had me squinting as I examined it. A delicate embossed pattern traced a line around the edges and converged in the middle where a stag's horns seemed to hold aloft the very stars that surrounded it.

Interested, I flipped it over to see a glimmering faerie ring with an ornate border of intricate symbols. I ran my thumb along the edge and felt more etchings, but none of them regular or even. As though each carving into the gold had been done with the consideration that the etchings should not repeat.

Clenching my fist around it, I sagged onto the leather chair beside the fireplace, feeling strangely betrayed and sick to my stomach. Dropped the bundle of clothes onto the floor beside the chair, and the karambit hidden in the folds fell with a thud that matched the descent of my heart to my stomach.

I didn't think the guard had taken those objects. Stone would never have given any indication they were even there.

That they were missing had to mean he hadn't been arrested at all, but had fled. And he'd taken the pouch with him.

And that left me with nothing but a big problem, because without those objects, all I had was a corset and a token that put a target on my back.

CHAPTER 23

I WOKE TO THE sun shining in my window and a knife at my throat.

Cursing myself for letting my body get so run down that it wouldn't respond to the sound of intrusion, I peered up past the blade resting against my jugular, reasoning that whoever held it would have cut my throat by now if they wanted me dead.

The shock of seeing the fae from the witch's house, plus five of his cronies standing clustered around him was the only thing that kept me from jumping instinctively and accidentally embedding the knife in my skin.

No matter how badly I wanted to swallow, I didn't dare.

"Get up," he said, those eyes swirling with an unsettling and familiar flare.

Instead of doing as he bid, I dropped my gaze pointedly to the blade, and he harrumphed.

"Slowly then," he said, easing the pressure enough for me to rise off the back of the chair a mere inch. My core quivered at the strain.

Be calm, I told myself. Don't piss the nasty fae off. "I don't have them," I said, thinking the hell hound was probably somewhere nearby, having tracked me all the way from the mundane realm to this, all for the cursed objects Stone had taken.

"Someone stole them, so you might want to back off," I said in as polite a voice as I could manage.

Instead of giving me another inch to move off the chair, he slid the knife sideways, so that it was behind my ear, but low enough to snick right across my carotid with a flick of his wrist. I moved slowly, inching in the other direction as I rose from the chair.

Bit by bit, we danced that way until I stood, barefoot and covered in fairy paint that somehow hadn't come off on the chair. He held the blade close, but not against my skin.

It occurred to me that he couldn't possibly recognize me from the witch's house. I'd worn the corset then. He must be here for the token, then. He'd either seen Jasmine pass me the ticket or he'd been sent to my room by someone else. Maybe Seamus. Maybe one of the other prostitutes looking for a way home.

Eying the men behind him, all with drawn swords and blades, and one by god with a mace, I raised my hands slowly over my head. "What do you want?" I said.

He snorted. "What do you think we want?"

I backed away carefully. I knew my karambit was still on the floor somewhere beside the chair in all the layers of clothing.

"I'm not one of the waitresses here," I said, using a euphemism for what the human women did below in the tavern. "I'm just a traveler."

He canted his head at me. "Mortals don't come to Fae except under duress." He peered over my shoulder. "And they certainly can't travel here without fae blood."

I coughed. "That might be," I said. "But that doesn't mean I'm a common harlot."

He sneered. "I think the Indentured would take offense at that description."

I thought of Jasmine and her complete uncommonness and tended to agree.

"That might be true too," I said, reaching behind me for the blade, "but I'm a pretty rare chick myself. If I say I'm not a whore and that I came to Fae as a traveler, then I suggest you believe me."

He let his eye roam my face, falling to my arm. I knew he saw me reaching for the bed. I knew he presumed I had a weapon. I hoped he thought I was reaching for the token and would just let me be out of curiosity until I could grab my blade.

Before I could make my move, the men closed in on me, their expressions cold and determined. He stood back, watching, assessing as though he'd been ordered to study my movement. I had no time to do more than note his position when the first man lunged at me.

I sidestepped, using his momentum against him. With a swift strike to his gut, I knocked the air out of him, momentarily disabling his attack. But the others quickly took his place, circling me like predators closing in on their prey.

I danced between them, wondering why they weren't using magic to subdue me, utilizing my agility and quick reflexes to evade their strikes.

A jab to one man's jaw sent him stumbling backward, while a well-placed kick to another's knee caused him to buckle under the pain.

Seeing I wasn't going down without a fight, they began to coordinate their attacks. A blow landed on my ribs with a sickening crack, sending a jolt of pain through my body.

I gritted my teeth, refusing to let it slow me down. Drawing upon my training, I retaliated with a series of precise strikes and grapples, exploiting what weaknesses I could find and using their own weight against them.

But each punch and kick took its toll, draining my energy, which was already depleted from long hours of staying awake. The only thing keeping me going was knowing that once they subdued me, they'd trash the room and find that token. And without that token, Kit was good as dead.

"You'll have to kill me," I said through gritted teeth, my voice laced with defiance.

The fae smirked, relishing in the challenge. "I might enjoy that," he taunted. "But alas, we have other plans."

Before I could consider what he meant, the blast I'd been expecting finally came. He lifted his hand almost leisurely toward me. A hellish looking purple light gathered in his palm. I almost mentioned that magic was forbidden in the tavern, but I had the feeling he wouldn't care, nor would he stick around long enough to suffer the consequences.

I dodged another blow from one of his men, just enough to give me space to lunge at him.

He smiled, a thin, hateful worm of movement across his face. And then he let the energy fly. It struck me in the solar plexus. Even as I curled inward, shrieking in pain, blows rained down upon me from behind.

CHAPTER 24

THE NEXT TIME I woke, it was in a dark and dankly cliché dungeon.

One sweep of my palm over the floor told me whoever had taken me didn't care much about their prisoner's comfort. Or warmth, for that matter.

The stones were dressed in sweat from my breath. Grime rose in tracks that spoke of decades of dirt, and my lips curled back from my teeth. No telling what sort of filth it comprised.

I ran my gaze over the area from where I lay. I was in a cell of some sort that was no more than eight feet square, a generous size, considering I could stretch out if I wanted.

Symbols were scratched into the stones of the floor and as I eyed them from the spot where my cheek was pressed flat, they reminded me of secret messages my chums and I had penned when we were kids, back in the time when I was still a good, innocent kid. A ghost of a smile played across my mouth as I thought of them. Drawn in letters so long, they could only be read if you peered at them from the edge of the paper, they were fun ways to pass information.

Lying there, I wondered what messages they left for the unfortunate Fae who could read them. I certainly couldn't make sense of the markings. They might as well have been random, childish scrawls from an illiterate prisoner.

Probably, that's all they were. Without the means to understand them, I dismissed them in favor of more pressing things.

Like how in the hell I got there and why, exactly, I was lying on my side, all but naked except for the duster jacket I'd come to Fae with draped over my legs.

And maybe once I figured that out, I'd have time to care why the bars of the cell were covered in lush vines.

I didn't need to reach for them to know each stem sported thorns like razor wire—I could plainly see the inch thick girth of them nestled in the leaves. That didn't bode well. Whoever had dropped me there expected me to try to break out.

Well, that much wasn't a stretch.

I lifted my head and immediately dropped it again, smashing it on the floor because it was entirely too heavy to hold up. The ache behind my eyelids indicated I'd been struck by something hard before I'd passed out.

It took several moments of me lying there in a fetal position, feeling for other wounds, to remember the fight with the fae at the tavern. Six of them were too many for one woman, no matter how well trained she was.

I'd not given up, I remembered that. They'd taken my karambit. One of them, the lanky black-haired one with the pointed teeth, he'd kicked me in the stomach after blasting me with a charge of energy. That alone made me contemplate whether he'd done it to feel the personal and intimate contact of violence or if he'd depleted his magic stores. Hadn't Stone told me all magic took a toll?

Whatever reason that bastard decided to use his boots on me didn't really matter. If he'd done lasting harm, I was in for more hurt than a bit of physical pain.

I felt along my ribcage, my fingers spidering along each intercostal muscle carefully, feeling for telltale pain that might indicate a break or a crack.

Nothing. That was encouraging. I was sore, but not broken. At least so far.

The mere notion of poking fingers into my stomach made me nauseous because I was worried what I might find after such a vicious strike. But I did it anyway.

Again. Nothing. Even more encouraging.

Just my head, then, and even that was clearing. It didn't feel quite so leaden now. The fog of pain had grown fissures around the temples, making room for me to think more clearly.

Confused but grateful, I rolled from my side onto my palms and pushed myself onto my haunches. I got a better look at my prison then. The vines I'd spied were the door to the cell. Beyond them, glowing with an eerie purple illumination, several torches lined a square space with at least three other vine-covered doorways.

Swinging my gaze over my shoulder, I noted one window, completely bare and wide-open. At least a head higher than I would stand, it framed gritty looking cobblestones trod by leather shoes and crystal heels going in both directions.

Strangely enough, no sound leaked through the window to indicate the pedestrians strolling by were anything more real than a television image.

If I craned my head to peer upwards, I could make out several floating orbs of light and crystal buildings side by side with old-fashioned stone and wood ones.

The musky stink of horse dung reached in to the cell with curling fingers. Of course. The sense that would come through in 3D would have to be smell. Any villain worth their salt would make sure no one could hear their victims, but what about the sight? If I could see out, shouldn't they also be able to see in?

And why leave the window open to the air at all?

I pushed myself to my feet so I could test the barrier with a tentative finger. It took some doing to get my legs moving without shaking, but by the time I got to the window, I felt much stronger. Raising my hand over my head, I waggled my fingers toward the window, pushing for the landscape beyond cautiously because going gangbusters into something unknown was a recipe for pain and/or humiliation.

A sizzle of pain flared all the way to my collarbone as I met the boundary.

I sucked in a hiss and rammed the digit into my mouth out of reflex.

I had my answer. Sort of. They didn't worry about covering it over because they wouldn't have to worry about anyone climbing out. I didn't taste any blood on my finger. A quick check of my skin for signs of injury proved I didn't have a single scratch. Painful enough, though, to keep me from testing again.

Crawling through it would take an almost masochistic set of steel nerves. Or a spell that would numb my entire body. Neither of which I possessed.

I craned my neck back. If I had a bed or a crate, I might be able to reach the window to climb out. But then, I imagined that jolt sizzling along my entire body and balked. A last resort, then. If I needed it.

My bare feet ground into the stone floor as I spun to eyeball the wall of my cell that was open to the rest of the dungeon. The vines that barred the way at the door were no doubt enchanted, too.

While I was no coward, I also wasn't keen to test it, but instinct told me that finding a way to hoist myself up to the window and then crawl through it would be a near impossibility even if I could stand the pain it caused.

The doorway seemed more accessible. Providing it didn't inflict worse horrors on me.

I crossed all eight feet of the cell to the door, where the vines seemed to unfurl their leaves as I neared it.

Close examination showed them spreading out over the thorns, hiding them from view within the lush green of the foliage. With a fingernail, I started to pull one of them back.

"Don't touch it," said a female voice.

My hands froze mid-air. I looked up. Past the vines and into another cell opposite me, I could make out the rosy flesh of skin and black hair. A Human face. Familiar.

"I know you," I said, my eyes narrowing to try to see past the mottling of vines and light to the person who spoke to me.

"It's Jasmine."

I squinted through the vines. I couldn't imagine what they wanted with Jasmine to bring her here too. Had they seen her give me the ticket? Did they think she had more? My mind worked feverishly over the information, tilling it into neat furrows as I tried to understand why they even held us at all.

"Are you alright?" I asked.

A quiet sigh came from her cell. "Alright enough," she said.

It was about as adequate an answer as I could expect under the circumstances.

"What's the deal with the vines?"

"They're poison," she said simply. "The fellow over there tried to get through them." She pointed at a cell at the end of the hall. "He died about an hour ago."

She paused, and not just for effect. I had the feeling she was gathering her courage. "It wasn't an easy death."

I did my best to follow the direction she'd indicated, but I couldn't see past the vines. At least, I knew there was room in the dungeon for at least three cells. That, too, was helpful. It gave an indication of size of the place we were being kept in.

"You didn't try to escape?" I asked, and I could almost imagine the shrug in her voice as she answered.

"What would be the point?"

I wondered how long she'd been in the land of Fae if she gave up that easily, but I reasoned that at least she hadn't been foolish enough to try the vines. She'd been here long enough to know better, apparently.

But for her, I might now be suffering the sort of death our prison companion had. I might not be able to see him from where I was, but I didn't need to know the details to know it wasn't pleasant if it horrified Jasmine.

"How long have we been here? Why are we even here? What do they want?" Information. I needed information. I hated being unclear of what was going on. I hated being out of control, with someone else pulling the strings and no motivation in sight.

"A few hours," she said and after a minute added, "There's a tunic in the corner," she said. "In case you're cold. And your jacket." She didn't say in case you don't want to be naked when they came, and of course, she didn't have to.

With a sigh, I looked over at my discarded duster. What did I want to bet they'd divested the pockets of anything useful or dangerous? The corset was gone. So, too, my karambit. What did I want to bet the Bloodmist had been confiscated too?

Cursing beneath my breath, I bent to scoop up the tunic from the corner and pulled it over my head. The jacket would be too bulky if I needed to fight. The linen smelled of lavender and honey, and it was a welcome fragrance. I inhaled deeply, finding gratitude in that small blessing. I'd had visions of it stinking like death. And at least I wasn't naked anymore.

I leaned my shoulder against the wall beside the vines and lifted my head enough toward Jasmine that I could hear her. She stood about a foot away from her door. The mottled shading of her body suggested she was dressed in the same sort of tunic.

"They washed the paint off," she said absently, and it sounded as though of all the things that could bother her, this was the worst.

"It's a mark of servitude anyway," I said. "Better rid."

She huffed out a massive, heartfelt sigh. "It had its own power. At least beneath the paint, I knew I looked how they wanted me to look. Without it, they can see the real me."

I thought about that, and though part of me wanted to tell her that wasn't a bad thing, I couldn't find the words. Instead, I sunk down to my haunches, letting my arms play over the table of my knees.

CHAPTER 25

IT SEEMED MY ABDUCTORS were pissed at me that they couldn't find the cursed objects in my room. That had to be the reason they'd abducted me instead of just leaving me for dead. They wanted me to cave and tell them where I put them. But that didn't explain Jasmine's presence. The only link between us was that blasted token.

Someone would come for me, she'd said. But why hold her as well? She had no link to me except the token.

"Why are you here?" I asked, thinking that maybe she had some insights into the men and their motives. I doubted she'd been knocked out. I probably would have stayed conscious too if I hadn't fought.

Her voice was clear when she answered, suggesting, as I thought, that she wasn't hurt. Just afraid.

"Seamus requested that I keep some fae company," she replied, veiling her activities behind a euphemism. "But it turned out they were more interested in prying into details about you. Your identity, your companions, your tenure in the Fae realm. They even asked which room was yours."

And she'd willingly provided them with that information, of course. Trained to give men what they wanted, accustomed to being compliant and helpful. It was hard to summon any anger toward her, considering I hadn't been able to resist them for long either.

She edged closer to her cell's entrance, brown eyes peeking out from behind a curtain of leaves. "I told them I didn't know the answer to anything except your room, and the leader—someone called him Flint—well, he said if I was lying, he'd take great pleasure in punishing me." She sank back into the darkness again, and her voice grew quiet. "Once he saw I wasn't lying, he decided he would take me along anyway. For fun, he said."

Flint. The name struck a chord in my memory. His face, his piercing gaze. Hard as flint yet sharp as a blade. The feel of his fists on my jaw.

"I'm sorry," I said and meant it. Because it was my fault she was here. Now, it wasn't just my sister's life tangled in this mess. This stranger, who had extended kindness to me amidst a whirlwind of chaos, was now entangled as well.

I sighed to myself. I wasn't exactly in a position to help her, either. Stuck in a cell God knew where and for whatever reason, I was totally helpless.

My mind raced through several possibilities and explanations for why Flint had taken me hostage, but each time, they caught on one fact. If the Shadow Court expected me to kill the King, that certainly wasn't going to happen. Trapped behind these bars, it was just a matter of time before they decided I'd escaped.

That meant Kit's life would be forfeit.

I had to fight back images of her innocently strolling with her cat, a sleek car pulling up, to dispatch an assassin to end her life—all because they thought I'd reneged on a sacred vow.

Jasmine's voice broke my mental spiral of doom and gloom, drawing me back to reality, and I realized she'd been speaking for some time. I just caught the last of her words. Things I hadn't even considered before she mentioned it.

"They mentioned something about a dark enforcer. Do you think they intend to torture us?"

That she even asked gave me a shiver. She knew more about Fae than I did. The fear in her voice made my stomach churn. I hadn't even considered that the sole motivation for Flint might be to take that pleasure he'd mentioned when I first met him: that he liked his women running and bloody.

It took all the will I had to inflect a note of calm into my voice. "No," I said. "I don't think they'll resort to torture. Flint probably thinks you have some information."

She seemed to accept that explanation even though she couldn't possibly understand that the information she'd have was gone, swept away by magic. I wasn't sure if even torture could retrieve it. And I worried they'd try. Years of experience taught me that there were creatures out there who reveled in causing pain. Usually, they reveled in prolonging the agony. Emotional torment could be as rewarding to them as physical suffering.

But when they appeared in a group, like Flint and his companions, there was typically more to it than sadism.

Leaning my head back against the cold stone wall, I mulled over the thought. An intuition prickled along my spine.

The dark artifacts were safely in Stone's possession, and had been long before Flint and his cronies attacked me, so even if I told them where they were, I couldn't do anything about retrieving them. I wondered how long they'd torture me or Jasmine before they gave up.

Of course, they could have seen her pass me the token, and maybe that was what they wanted, but if they'd found my karambit and my Bloodmist, they'd have found the golden token too. Imprisonment made no sense on that score.

I was beginning to believe we were victims of pure trafficking and no more, but some part of me insisted a connection existed. The fae who'd broken into my room were the same ones who ambushed me at the witch's lair. There had to be a reason they'd tracked me to the tavern, and just how they'd done that was a matter all in itself.

But first things first. If their motivation was greed, the token should have been plenty to satisfy them. They wouldn't need to sell a couple of human women. If they were after the dark objects, however, then Stone's presence in the Rot Gut and then again at Gideon's was no coincidence. And his disappearance from the tavern under the threat of the guard and Flint's appearance later when Jasmine insisted someone would come for me wasn't happenstance, either.

I ran the question through the sandpaper of my mind, smoothing it down to its essence. Stone had vanished with the artifacts, but abducting me didn't align with his aim of getting me to assassinate the King. Plus, he'd entrusted me with the token via Jasmine. There was no reason for him to steal it back. And that had to mean he wasn't to blame for my incarceration.

That left one other possibility. A thin thread of chance, but the only one I could conceive to be closest to the truth.

I'd tried to warn the Captain of the Guard about the King. Although he wouldn't know about the artifacts or the token, he might have shared the information with the monarch after all. It was entirely plausible that he'd been sent to fetch me for interrogation.

Odd as it sounded, that was the most feasible connection. Maybe they were detaining us until they could question me. The thought of that gave me hope. My luck might be improving.

"What exactly did they say, Jasmine?" I prodded. "The men who took you... Were any of them bearing the royal emblem? Are we within the royal dungeons?"

She clicked her tongue. "I've been in Fae long enough to know castle dungeons are much bigger and more populated than this. This is a big enough house, but it's no castle. And I did get to see where they brought us. It's situated at the heart of the city. Whoever they are, this isn't the work of the Iron Court."

Sinking onto my heels, I ruminated over the possibilities. If it wasn't the King or the mafia, then who could it be?

"The man who abducted us," I mused aloud. "Have you met them before? Worked for them?"

"No," she said. "But Seamus seemed to know him."

I gave that some thought. Seamus had lost a son because of a token. Jasmine had shown him the object. Maybe it was as simple as Seamus wanting revenge and finding collateral damage in me and Jasmine.

Whatever the reason, we were here, and I knew we had to get out. A glance around my cell proved only two modes of escape. The door and the window. Of both, the window seemed the most logical. Faster to the outside, without having to sneak my way through a layout I didn't know, past any number of guards.

"Jasmine," I said, eying the window once more. "Do you have a window in your cell?"

"Yes, but I'm not tall enough to climb out."

Measuring the width of mine visually, I nodded silently, agreeing that she couldn't have managed an escape from hers. Jasmine was a shorter woman than me, average height for a human.

The thought of going out that window made every inch of my skin crawl with dread, but it had to be tried.

"I'm going to try to get out through the window," I said, keeping the knowledge of the shock it might hold to me. I didn't want to worry her unnecessarily. And if I could get out and needed her to crawl out on her end, she couldn't know it would hurt until I had her completely onboard and was hauling her through.

"If I can hoist myself up and out, I'll find a way to your window and drop in a rope or something to haul you out."

One thing at a time, I always said. Right now, that one thing was getting free. The rest, finding a rope, freeing Jasmine, getting to safety where ever that was, all that could come later.

I pivoted to put my back to the vines and my front to the open window. Beyond its frame, twilight was settling its cloak over the city. The boots and shoes passing by had a hurried pace, the way workaday people did at the end of a long day.

I measured the paces mentally. Five big paces to give me thrust. One cat leap straight up from a foot away. I wasn't sure I had the strength for such a vertical parkour technique, but a body wedge and crawl was not going to be possible. The walls were too far apart.

The hope was that the run up and pull up onto the window frame would lend me enough thrust to push through quickly, hopefully minimizing the pain as the magic snapped and sizzled along my body.

Shaking out my arms and legs, I considered the last time I'd done a pull-up. I'd had Gideon riding my ass and telling me my training had gotten sloppy. He'd made me do a hundred pull ups, telling me if I could manage it and still lift a shot of mezcal, he'd pay my rent for the month.

He'd paid for two when I went twenty-five extra, and the lactic acid soaking the next day that put me out of commission for a week was entirely worth it. But that had been two years ago. Hunting lately had been of the round kick, punch, and slice flavor. No real running or parkour techniques needed. Not to mention those times did not have the added punishment of magic stinging my ass if I got stuck.

I blew out a bracing breath and did several run ups to get the feel for the distance. I was barefoot, which made it worse. The floors were slick with condensation. I'd be lucky if I managed the cat leap, really.

Still, I had to try.

Turning on the tap of energy, I bolted for the wall and took the leap too soon. My fingers caught the lip of the window and, for a second, I thought I might be able to pull myself up.

I fell onto my backside, biting my tongue in the process.

"Are you alright?" Jasmine asked when I let loose a series of unladylike phrases.

"The tunic is too long," I said, realizing that was indeed the issue. I hiked the fabric up over my hips and tied it in a knot around my waist. More naked than I would have wanted for a great escape, but who cared about nudity when their life was on the line? It couldn't be helped.

So, I leaned over enough to load the energy in my thighs, then with one explosive movement, I raced for the wall.

My toes struck out, reaching like fingers for purchase. Hands flew up over my head as I contacted. Fingers grappled for the ledge.

They caught. I gave the pull-up my all.

I was hefting myself with the kind of glee that comes from knowing you've just accomplished the impossible when someone slammed into me from behind.

I let go as sudden and unexpected pain lanced across my bare thighs and backside.

With a shriek of surprised pain, I fell awkwardly as I tried to twist out of reach of the searing agony, rolling as best I could to land with the least harm possible. All while instinctively trying to cradle the bits of my thighs and ass getting lashed. Hornet bites stinging trails across my skin. I cried out involuntarily, the wails coming unbidden.

When I hit the floor, it was with a loud thud. My ribs connected with the flagstone hard enough that I could almost hear the crunch of broken bone.

A roll, a painful, determined twist filled with a groan, and boots and faces came into view. My breath came out in panting gusts. I couldn't cover all the parts that hurt. I didn't have enough hands.

Three burly looking men with hairy cheeks stood around me. One held a whip made of broad leather instead of the tightly rolled cat gut of the typical thong. The effect was more bruising than cutting, but my legs didn't appreciate the difference. They just knew it hurt and pain was pain.

I tried to get up, but meaty hands grabbed me and held me down by my head. I was no more than a bug being pinned to a corkboard. Furious, I snarled at them, called them every sort of awful name. That just made them angrier.

Part of me wanted to stare them down, but that quickly dissolved to the greater part of me that dearly wanted to avoid pain. I flinched as the strikes came again, and quailed into the wall. I kicked. I screamed. I sobbed like a toddler. Begging did no good. Neither did trying to roll out of the way. The cell was too small. They were too greedy for my pain.

One second I was thinking I could kick out and take my attacker in the stomach, and the next, I was curled into a ball, screaming for them to stop. Hating myself for being so weak.

Someone sobbed from beyond my cell doors, and I guessed it was Jasmine. It was the sound of her weeping and wailing that finally signaled to them that it might be time to stop.

I panted up at them. My skin felt like it was on fire. The one holding my head as I thrashed growled down into my face.

"You bitch," he said. "Are you trying to get us killed?"

"No," I said through gritted teeth, doing my best not to say that when their deaths came for them, they'd see my face clearly and know exactly when and how they would die.

I covered my face out of instinct, and when nothing happened, I peered out between my elbows to see them breathing heavily. Beyond them, the vines had been peeled aside and hooked on something out of sight.

I licked my lips. If I could get up. I could run and get some space and find a weapon and play tick tack toe on their bodies until they bled news of my victory. But all that depended on me being able to get up, and I couldn't. Just trying to lift my head made me nauseous.

But I couldn't just lie there either. If I couldn't stand, I would crawl. Awkward as an army crawl was, as painful as it felt to dig my elbows into the stone and leverage my weight, I did it. Inch by inch. Ache by ache. The tunic dragged at my neck and then down my chest. It tore as I moved. My knees fetched up into it and made progress even more difficult. But I kept on.

And they watched me struggle, damn them. They watched me fight to move, and I kept thinking: just stand there, then. Stand there till I get close enough to tear into your throats with my teeth.

Each inch I progressed pushed the nausea down further. It put the pain into a compartment that I closed the lid on with more commitment than a nun taking her vows. Oh, how delicious would be my revenge.

Ahead of me, through the door and across the cellar, Jasmine had lain on the floor on her belly, facing me. Her eyes peered through the vine barrier of her cell. They held my gaze with laser focus. She waggled her fingers at me. Come, they said. Keep coming.

So, I did. It didn't matter that the guards could stop me at any time. They didn't. Several inches moved beneath my arms, gritty now with pebbles and sand. My nostrils filled with the stink of old feces and urine. Twice my chin dropped to the floor out of pure exhaustion, and I tasted earth. The savor renewed me. It ground my resolve into a fine powder that packed itself into my nose, my ears, my fingernails and kept me going.

With every bit of stone floor my progress devoured, I grew more determined. I watched Jasmine's eyes, and I ignored the stinging of my thighs where bruises no doubt married the wounds. I ignored it all but her gaze, and I kept going.

One thought pounded through my mind with each heart beat I felt against the flagstones. Kit. Kit's life. Kit's future. Mine didn't matter. It hadn't mattered since the day I'd gotten high and passed out and missed my parents' funeral. I was nothing. A worm. A worm dragging its way across the dirt, searching for a hole to crawl into and whet my soul for at least one more pass of the sun.

But Kit. Kit's life mattered. She'd given up too much for me already.

If I didn't get out of the cellar and find my way to the Iron Court and kill the King, the Shadow Court would take its revenge. Stone was gone. Jasmine was here with me. There was no one to inform the Fae Mafia that I couldn't perform my task. No one to know the reason I couldn't, and that would mean Kit's life.

It was when Jasmine jerked back from the doorway that I noticed the light coming from the torches had shifted, shimmering to a bright blue before fading again. The cell seemed a little darker.

At first, I thought it was the guards behind me, realizing I was within an inch of freedom and had decided to peel back with their whips. I was concentrating so hard, working so fiercely to push down the pain that I didn't realize someone else had come into the cellar until his shoes scuffed into my vision.

The guards behind me rustled about. I imagined they were clustering together. Fear prowled into the room on frigid currents of air.

I knew the sound of terrified movement as well as my own breath, and when I heard a new voice break the icy tension into shards, I knew someone was going to die.

"Who did this to her?" he demanded.

CHAPTER 26

The voice that cut a path to my ears was cold, hard as a diamond, and just as sharp. I knew I should recognize the voice, but it was so bloated with rage that it took far too long for me to nail it down, and by the time I did, a hot rush of anger flooded me. I couldn't speak for the tightness in my throat.

Someone stepped into my line of vision, and I swiped at the legs in front of me, annoyed that whoever stood there would come between Jasmine's gaze and mine. Soft material met my fingers, then the hardness of bone beneath trousers of a suit. I used the material to gain leverage enough to angle myself to roll my head back, to peer up into Stone's face.

I shot him an equally hard glare with as much hatred and hurt as I could muster from my trembling core. "You," I said to him. "You did this to me."

It took such an effort to hold his gaze that I dropped back to the cold floor, my palms planted beneath me. I couldn't get up. Even breathing sent razors of pain through me. Instead, I stared at the flagstones, the beads of condensation from my breath, the droplets of blood. *My blood*. Dear God. I was going to die here. Useless, weak. I wasn't even dying in service to anything. Just a god-damned waste of skin sinking into black oblivion.

There was a long, tension filled silence before Stone crouched down to my level. His knees rustled against his pants. The tips of his shoes were pristine. I gathered what spit I could to change that, but it only dribbled onto his toes. A weak laugh escaped me. I sighed. Dropped my forehead to the floor. I was a failure even in that.

"I would never hurt you, Ava," he said, and my hair moved, he was that close. Close enough to choke, to punch, if I had the energy to lift a fist. I didn't. What I had was enough energy to snort.

Another long, agonizing moment of electricity and Stone pushed himself to his feet again. I felt his eyes on my back, roaming to my occipital bone and grazing my hair. He was waiting, I think, for me to turn over, to acknowledge his declaration. I could only tremble and fight to keep the subtle movement from his scrutiny. I couldn't bear his pity.

But at his movement, the guards shuffled about again, this time faster, as though they were fighting each other to get out of range. The soft, threatening sound of footfalls as they dogged the guards' movements whispered along the walls. Death gathering his cloak.

"What happened?" Stone asked in a voice that was crypt-soft. Even I shivered at the tone.

"She was trying to escape," someone said. I didn't bother to look. Whoever it was, it didn't matter. I was hurt. They weren't. It was the way of things.

Stone's next movement was so swift, I didn't hear it until one of the guards was gargling around what could only be an obstruction blocking off his breath. A long sigh of relief fled my lungs. My eyes closed. No matter how ashamed I was to be lying there, with Stone raging above me, my entire body shook with the release of adrenaline. It was over. I could sort out how to repair my body, my ego, my sense of purpose later.

"So you thought it was a good idea to harm one of the boss's assets," he said, his voice holding onto that same, even tone. No high note at the end to indicate a question. Because it wasn't a question. It was an accusation. A judgment.

I realized then, where I was. The Shadow Court. What my world would call the Fae Mafia.

Another shuffle. Several voices raised at once, begging. Explaining. I was just another prisoner. An asset wouldn't be in the dungeons. An asset wouldn't be dressed in a shift, barefoot.

A dull, sickening tearing sound muffled the growl that vibrated through Stone, and a heartbeat later, the guard fell beside me. The flat thwack of the whip handle echoed twice through the chamber, nearly drowning out the tell tale sound of choking, but I recognized that noise all too well. I turned to see the guard bleeding from a gash in his throat. No. Not a gash. The wound was too ragged. A bite, then.

Stone had torn into his throat and tossed him aside like a lamb chop half-eaten. My gorge rose, and on the hind legs of it, a swell of victory, of hatred. Good. I was glad the bastard was dead. I blinked around the tears that threatened to spill. No matter how mad I was at Stone, I savored the victory of that guard's death as if I'd cut his throat myself.

At the sight of their comrade on the floor, the rest of the guards hustled into the corner. I could see their feet clustered together. One of them spilled liquid from the bottoms of his breeks. Ammonia stung my nostrils.

"She tried to get out the window." Someone said, and I could imagine this someone jerking his chin toward the opening of the wall I'd been trying to scale.

Another deep-chested sound thrummed in the air. Non-committal. Mysterious. Thoughtful.

"The boss told us she wasn't to get out of the cell."

"Did he?" Stone asked quietly. Too quiet. He wasn't done yet. I wondered if the others knew it. "I would think the *vinyalia* would prevent escape," he said in a tight voice. "Without your intervention."

He paused for a long moment. Considering. Weighing choices. I knew the feel of calculation as it rode currents of air. Entire cultures cold ride on the thin line of a heartbeat. Then:

"It might be smart to leave now," Stone said, and a purr of anticipation crept into his voice. He didn't want them to leave at all. I got the feeling he very much hoped they'd stay.

They didn't. Their rush to the door was all the evidence I needed to realize just how terrifying Stone must have looked. Before they could exit, Stone barked at them to take the body with them and prop him in the hall so they could see exactly what might happen to those who decided indi-vidual thought in the Shadow Court might be encouraged.

By the time Stone sat on the floor next to me, I wasn't surprised to see his hand tremble as it cradled my chin away from the floor. Adrenaline had a way of doing that to even the most seasoned warriors.

"Ava," he whispered as he sought my gaze. "I'm sorry. I had no idea." He tried to slide his hands beneath me, to scoop me from the floor or roll me over, I wasn't sure. I just knew he planned to touch me and I wasn't ready for that.

"Fuck you," I said and managed to turn my face away from him. My cheek bit into a tiny pebble, but I wasn't going to move out from its pressure. Not yet. Not till he was gone.

He didn't leave. Instead, he ran his hands over the back of my hair. My eyes squeezed close of their own accord. I did not want to feel the tightness in my throat, the welling of tears at the gentleness of that touch. He was a bastard. Just like the rest of them.

Silent. The whole time. The cell was as silent as a dead man's lungs until I breathed, and the wheezing that came from my nose was too loud in the room.

We stayed like that for far too long. My cheek stung. My eyes stung. I hated the relief in my body that revealed to my stubborn brain that I was relieved he was there. I didn't want to feel glad about his presence. Not when Jasmine still waited on the other side of the jail. Her quiet presence reminded me that she had no one to save her. Just me. And I'd failed.

It took an effort to speak because someone had to. If any good could come from this, then I hoped it would be Jasmine's release. An ally. I needed an ally. I'd have to tell Stone I understood. Mistakes happened all the time. All that mattered was that he was there, and it was over.

But what lashed out of me was acid in the form of words, not the gentle, considered statement that could broach Jasmine's release.

"You left me there," I said, and the cold flagstones scraped against my lips as I spit the words out. It hurt. Damn, it hurt. And it wasn't just the wounds that stung. "And you stole the bag. You took the cursed objects, and you left me there."

A low, thoughtful murmur that might have been words, but I was already shutting him out, and couldn't make out what he was saying. I didn't want to hear his explanations. He'd betrayed me. I'd let my guard down, and he'd repaid me by abandoning me and stealing from me. Him. The one who was supposed to be my guide into this world. The one who'd brought me here in the first damn place.

Whether I wanted his touch or his words or not, I couldn't fight him off when he gathered me into his arms, rolling me onto his lap. He was cross-legged, I realized. I sagged in his embrace, neither accepting nor fighting. I only realized I was crying when his thumb swept over the curve of my cheek and smeared the liquid into my hair. A shudder wracked through me. The realization that I was crying made the tears come harder, until my face felt twisted with emotion, and I hated myself for the weakness.

"Shh," he crooned. "It's alright. You're alright."

"Fuck you," I said again, but it was through sobs that I didn't recognize as my own voice. I closed my eyes, squeezing the tears back in, holding them at bay the way Moses must have held back the Red Sea. A dam. Made of will and the flimsy buttress of righteousness.

"Blade," he said. "Blade told the guards where I was. It's his fault. I wouldn't have left you alone in Fae. Not when I know what can happen to a mortal woman."

I wouldn't open my eyes. Wouldn't seek his gaze to see if there was truth in his face. How could they even get to him out on that balcony?

His fingers ran over my eyebrows one after the other and I twisted away from each touch, only to feel the soothing whisper of it again as he spoke.

"The Shadow Court wants those objects," he said as he drew another line of liquid into my hairline. "They belong to us. Flint was sent to gather them from the witch, but you got in the way."

My lips pressed together at the words. Another happenstance. He didn't really think I believed that, did he?

"Ava?" he murmured. "It's the truth."

"And I suppose it was just a lucky break that you were at Gideon's?"

He made a noise behind his sinuses. "Not a lucky break for you, I take it. But yes. This hit has been a long time in the planning. That the raiment was in Gideon's possession is no coincidence—I paid a princely sum to get the goblin to sell it to him, so we would have no trail back to us should the assassination fail. When you mentioned you hid the objects, I knew Flint had failed. And when you agreed to take me along to collect them, I decided it was a good chance to succeed where he hadn't. There really is no more to it than that."

I snorted. "Some extensive planning if you could swap assassins at the drop of a hat."

His voice went flat. "That's your fault," he said. "Lilah is no lightweight. It's why we sent a full contingent to collect those relics. Gideon was too afraid to go alone. But you..." His voice softened, a sort of longing or pride or both swelling his voice as he sighed. "You are a force. A hurricane with cyclone winds." He adjusted me in his embrace, tightening his hold against my rigid arms. "You've blown me over, Ava, and I wasn't ready for you. Had I known, I'd have battened down my hatches, but no matter how I feel about you, I took a vow. A blood vow."

I opened my eyes at that, because no matter how hurt I was, I knew the sound of regret. I'd heard it plenty in my day. Felt it plenty. It wasn't the comment about how he felt about me that touched me. It couldn't have been. We meant nothing to each other.

When I held his gaze, unflinching and demanding, he took that to be an invitation to continue. Maybe he was nervous and was filling the silence. Maybe he wasn't sure what I'd do.

"You're the better killer," he said. "Because you aren't afraid of dying. And I had to deliver the best. A blood vow to the Shadow Court—to any fae court—is binding in a way you mortals can't understand," he said.

I wanted very badly to look down at the tattoo on my arm at his comment, but I resisted.

Bitterness laced my words when I said, "Oh, I understand how the mafia works."

He shook his head and adjusted his grip, moving his palm down my back to gather me closer. I didn't resist. I didn't have the energy to.

"I know you think you understand, but what applies in your world means nothing here."

He rocked back, leaning into the wall, taking all my weight. "A blood vow to the likes of the Shadow Court doesn't just put my life on the line, but the lives and magic of everyone I hold dear. My sons, my daughters, my lovers, friends...all of them are forfeit to the boss's pleasure. For generations, Ava. I've seen men languish in dungeons for a hundred years, held together by magic alone just so they could be tortured endlessly. I couldn't put any family I might have some day in that sort of danger."

"You're asking forgiveness," I said in a flat tone.

He laid his head back against the wall and I lost sight of his eyes for a time. The caramel fragrance that was him swept around me, almost as though he was pumping it into the air to soothe me. Or him.

"Forgiveness isn't something I ever expect," he finally said. "I knew what the Shadow Court was when I got my stripes. Maybe more than those poor sods who thought they were doing Don Sidhe a favor by beating you. I just want you to understand why I left. Why I betrayed you. Why I had to." His voice caught on the last words and it was such a strange sound that I peered up at him, watching his face.

He adjusted me in his embrace and made to stand. "What I want is understanding."

"Because, of course, some things are out of your control."

I twisted in his embrace as he gained his feet, hefting me along with him as though I weighed no more than a waft of smoke. Holding me as though I was a cat wrangling to get away from a hot bath as his eyebrow climbed upward. "Because once we knew you had those cursed objects, we had to get them out of your hands. The guards were never supposed to be there at the tavern, but they were a good distraction. I just planned to take them from you while you were busy with Blade, but when he got himself arrested and told them where I was, they had no choice but to arrest me, too. We're both made-fae, after all."

A useful happenstance, then. Something even Gideon would understand. Something he would exploit. Would I expect no less from my enemy? And he was my enemy. I couldn't forget that.

"And Flint was sent to retrieve me,'" I guessed. "Lest I find my way back to the mortal realm and ruin the cartel's plans to commit regicide."

"Flint is a literal male," Stone said. "He follows his orders to the letter." A strange tone infiltrated Stone's voice as he regarded me. "I will have to speak to him to find out why he would bring you here to the cellars instead of to one of our guest suites." His features grew hard. "But mark me, Ava, I will find out, and he will pay."

He eased me onto my feet, and waited until I could stand with minimal support while I toed the floor with my naked feet, feeling nothing and trying to find my balance on soles that had gone completely numb. He held me just long enough for the prickles of blood to fire, and then I leaned on him shamelessly, sucking in the air I hadn't been able to before. His confession seemed to have done that much, at least.

Weaving on legs too full of adrenaline and too mangled by exhaustion, I fought the urge to puke and decided that leaning against the wall might be the best option, relieving my core without having to rely on Stone. Because I didn't want to let myself rely on him. I understood why he'd done it. I just wasn't ready to trust again. Not right then. Maybe never. But at least the anvil had lifted from my shoulders. We might not be lovers ever again, but at least we understood each other. I wasn't sure why I felt so damn sad at the thought.

"Just get me out of here," I said, and jerked my chin in the direction of Jasmine's cell beyond the vine-covered doorway. "Jasmine too. I don't care what you do to Flint. Just don't leave her in there."

He shot me a tentative smile. In my mind, I saw Gideon's face, mouth tight, eyebrows lifted as he pinched a shot glass in his fingers. His slouch hat puddled too much beside his ears as he kicked at the duffle bag that had sent me running from the Rot Got tavern into the dark of night with a spelled garment in my saddlebags. See the opportunity, he seemed to say. Exploit the happenstance until it becomes opportunity. Then seize it the way the mortals glommed onto the tavern's signature drink.

Well, I was seizing it. I'd failed with the witch. I'd thought it was all about me, and I'd gone in to her lair all whole hog and loaded for bear because I was hurt and angry. I'd felt replaced. I was a dinosaur trying to hold back the asteroid.

"Jasmine has nothing to do with any of this," I said to him, returning the smile like an olive branch because a good hunter knew the crutches of her enemies even as she knew her own.

But this was about so much more than my ego. It was about Jasmine not becoming a victim of my pride. About Kit being safe from the life I led. Because everyone had their own signature. The Rot Gut had a drink that lured mortals to their death. Gideon had a way of turning the slimmest of odds to his advantage. Jasmine had a penchant for seeing the good in horrible things.

My signature might not make me a good human being or a good sister, but it did make me a very good hunter.

I knew how to stuff horrors into the back of my mind, into the marrow of my bones, out of sight and out of the way. Buried where they couldn't be exhumed but where they'd create a safe space, a hallowed sort of ground to sacrifice my enemies upon. And that sort of ground found betrayal just as sacred as hope.

"Send her home," I said. "Do the right thing."

His gaze flicked to the side, toward her cell. For a heartbeat, I saw something in his face—an ember of righteousness, a glimpse of the man I thought he was. My breath hitched, lungs burning as I held it, rigid as stone, waiting, *pleading* for him to act on whatever instinct was tugging at him.

But his jaw clenched, his expression twisting as he struggled to swallow whatever words he couldn't bring himself to say. "This is the only way, Ava," he murmured, his voice dark and unyielding, edged with a strange pain that was no comfort at all. "If I could change it, I would."

The betrayal clawed up my throat, burning with each breath I fought to keep steady. I knew I was about to beg, knew I'd hate myself for it—but for Jasmine, I would do it a thousand times. Because I had to. Because it was what I did.

"Stone... *please*," I whispered, barely able to force the words out, feeling the last pieces of myself breaking apart, shattering against his silence. For one fragile, fleeting second, his face softened, and in his eyes, I saw it—the regret, the torment, the *weakness* that might make him give in. I felt no victory in it. Just sadness.

His jaw ticked to the side, and he glanced down at me. For a second, he caught my eye, then averted his gaze with a flick of movement, as though he was ashamed or afraid, and neither of those could be possible.

"I care about you, Ava," he said in a gruff voice. "I didn't think I would. I just wanted to do my duty. I never expected you to be so..."

I slumped against the wall. "Ornery?" I asked, hating the weight that lifted from my chest at his words. Gods, I was pathetic. A stupid little beaten puppy looking for a gentle hand.

He smiled, a wan thing that echoed the way I felt. "Addicting."

The word made my breath hitch. Not because of the word, but because of the truth in it. The way her whole body felt at the way it wrapped tendrils of ironwood roots around every fiber of muscle. Because of the way he looked at her like sin was embodied in her flesh and marrow.

"You're... addicting, Ava."

She laughed, but it cracked. "Right. Addicting. Like poison."

He flinched. Good. She wanted to wound him. Because every part of her ached.

"I don't know what it is," he said in a hushed voice that suggested he could barely believe his own words. "I've never felt like this before. You're like a hit of sugar, a dram of warm whiskey after a night of hard magic or hard violence. There's never enough to quell that need inside that drives a desire for more. When I see you, I forget I'm dangerous. I forget what I am."

He roamed my face with a lingering gaze, not inquisitive or expectant. Just contemplative. "I never meant to hurt you," he says, softer still. "I was trying to save you."

"And yet you betrayed me," I said, lifting my chin.

"Yes," he said in a rasp. "Yes, I did. I wish to the gods I could have spared you that."

He made a move toward me, fast, the way he moved when he knew I'd resist. I held my hand up, desperate to hold him off. Knowing if he touched me I would shatter.

"I trusted you," I said.

"I know."

Shivers began to tremor though my core. This was too much. On top of everything else, I did not want to break down. Not in front of him. Not like this.

His throat moved like he was trying to swallow down shards of glass. The silence was a sharp, glinting razor's edge. If I didn't say something, do something, it would cut me to the bone.

It took ages for the words to gather on my tongue and they tasted bitter. I spit them out like chunks of sour lemon. "Leave me alone," I said.

Hard as it was, I locked my eyes to his and did my best not to blink. I just hoped my heart wasn't giving me away as it pulsed in my throat.

When he stepped back, arms dropping to his sides, he looked defeated. I couldn't take any pleasure in it. It was all I could do to hold the mask. My throat felt like it was on fire. It ached like it was tightening beneath an invisible rope.

He gave me a shuddering sigh as his jaw ticked to the side, then he swallowed and turned. With a sweeping movement, he shoved aside the vines and pushed through the door and into the darkened space between cells. Before he disappeared, he looked back at me, eyes shadowed.

"Forgive me, Ava," he said, his voice fraying at the edges.

The vines slithered back into place, quivering as they sealed the threshold, weaving a lacy prison between us. Shadows carved his face into something unreadable. His broad shoulders sagged, his throat working as he swallowed—once, twice.

I held my breath, bracing myself for whatever he might say to me, that might make me forgo my righteous rage when I needed to hold it tight to my chest.

His gaze dropped to his boots. Then, without another look, he stepped back into the dark. Silence swallowed him whole. His footsteps faded, hollow as an echo in an ancient cave.

And then I was alone. The only sound in the cell was the ragged slip of air that broke from my lips—half a sob, half a whisper. I bit it back as the darkness drew itself around me, swallowing light from the corners and drawing a shutter over the night-carved cobbled street beyond the window.

Long moments, I spent staring at the seams of light trying to reach in from the outside, rage coiled inside my chest, an impotent, righteous fury that tightened with each breath like a fist around my heart. Then the darkness shifted. The air pressurized the way it does before a fight, they way a deer might sense an unseen predator getting closer or the encroachment of a vast, all-consuming fire. Like the moment it catches the briefest whiff of something other than itself tickling the back of its neck.

I breathed in and there it was. The faint note of smoke. Of spices. Of something I'd worn before, back at the witch's lair, maybe. Something that felt like a warning even before a group of fae had ambushed me and drove me into the basement with a hellhound on my heels.

That same thing lurked out there beyond the limits of my cell, its rage not impotent, but restrained. Waiting. Seething.

My skin prickled as I glared back. Challenging that thing. Come at me. Come for me. Don't just lurk in there in the damned dark. Make a move.

A low growl answered my unspoken dare. And I knew in right then that if it came, I wouldn't be ready. It would break me in ways I couldn't even imagine.

Author Thanks

I have many people to thank for their help and support on this one. People who helped me write more romance into my tales as well as finding my grammar, spelling, and consistency issues as I forged through at high speed to finish a book that excited me in ways I hadn't enjoyed for a while.

Debra L. Martin: a stellar romance author you should check out.

Caroline Jenkins, Evelyn Dotson, Denise Sherman, and Julie Pederick, who beta read early copies for me and helped immeasurably with things like fae culture and consistency.

A list of betas who found me for the first time and gave me their unbridled thoughts

-thea-